what *if*

A NOVEL

Rita Szollos

Cover photo © Rita Szollos

A BusyBella publication

Acknowledgements

Thank you: Molly Schulman for your insight and belief, and Shannon Shields Szymborski and Caroline Booth for pushing me forward. Thank you Frieda, Piggy, Bill, Sam, and Diego for the memories. But most of all, my eternal gratitude and love to Kevin, Busybella, and Sky for the gift of time.

1

Among the sheep.

The pilot in the small, yellow craft squinted to better see the controls, but his vision was blurry and his hands felt heavy. He had trouble connecting his thoughts. He thought he heard the wheels of the plane hit something, bounce off of something. He wasn't sure. He tried to reach for the controls, but his hands would not move toward the instruments.

In a distant field a farmer tended his sheep. He heard the whir of an airplane engine, a routine noise in the surrounding hills; he ignored it. The sound was especially familiar on days like this, with endless blue skies.

The sheep began to nervously trot. Several started to run away from the herd, and the others followed quickly behind in a massive panic. The farmer turned his head in the direction of the airplane as the noise grew louder. It flew extremely low, over the pasture in front of him, touching the highest part of the slope and ascending again, as if bouncing off the grass. It continued past him, low and unstable over the hilly fields, its wheels occasionally brushing through trees.

The man reached for his cell phone, mumbling expletives. He turned to look for his sheep, when behind him the sound of a terrific crash caused him to turn back toward the plane.

He couldn't make out the actual aircraft, but large plumes of smoke rose from the crash site. The farmer glanced down at his cell phone again, but couldn't see any bars. He halted for a second trying to calculate if it would be faster for him to run to the house or to the airplane—trying to decide which option would be more helpful, which option would be more dangerous. He started to run toward the accident, over the hills, as fast as his muddy boots and heavy gut would allow. Before he made it to the next hill an intense boom echoed through the small valley.

2

It's real. It's raw.

Ailie sat in her chair and stared out the window of her office. The sun had just set. It was nearly 8pm. The days were lengthening with the promise of summer. She surveyed the bright lights across the city, the stoplights changing, the steady glow of taillights as more cars filled the roadways and people emptied from buildings onto the streets below. She scanned the cityscape until her eyes met with her own reflection in the glass. She looked at herself and contemplated, trying to figure out why she felt deeply aggravated about work. She'd felt this in the past, on occasion, but tonight it was especially intense. Perhaps it was a need to escape, but to where she wasn't sure.

A loud knock interrupted her reverie; she nearly jumped out of her seat. *"Ayylee!"* boomed a lively voice from the other side of the door, before it flew open. It was one of her closest friends, Ruby, clutching her coat and purse. "What are you still doing here, Ailie? You were supposed to meet Olivia at the restaurant twenty minutes ago. I was just about to join you two, but I saw your light was still on."

"I texted Olivia. She's fine," replied Ailie. "I just had to... I don't know...it's these stupid emails." She slammed her laptop shut as though it had betrayed her.

"What happened? Have I seen the emails?" Ruby retrieved a cell phone from her purse and proceeded to scroll. "Did someone send an update? Did they request a change? Did I get copied? I hate it when they forget to copy me. Which email is it?"

"It's all of them." Ailie opened her laptop again. "Every time I'm done with one email, a new one shows up."

"That's what assistants are for," Ruby replied, waving her hand toward the hallway. "I know yours is new, but give her time."

"It's not that." Ailie paused for a second and then pointed at the screen. "Look, there's another one. Watch this, every time I delete an email— Boop!—a new one pops up."

"What are you deleting? You didn't even read that one."

"I'm not reading any of them."

"But it looked important." Ruby looked at the screen of her phone again. "Was it the one about the Reynolds account?"

"Deleted that one." Ailie closed her eyes, rubbing her temples.

"What about the one from Brian, asking if we're ready to finalize?"

"Deleted."

"Okay...how about the one from the boss about tomorrow's meeting?"

"Double deleted. Permanently gone. You'll have to tell me what we're meeting about."

Ruby's eyes widen. "What? Please tell me you're joking."

"I am. Kind of." Ailie giggled. "Relax, Ruby, I'll transfer them all from the trash back into my inbox tonight. Or maybe I'll wait till morning."

"You could just shut down your email," Ruby suggested.

"No…this just somehow feels better. Every time I hit delete I feel like I'm squishing their tiny, little voices."

Ruby responded with a short, nervous giggle. "Seriously—this is so unlike you—what the hell is going on with you? Are you burned out? Again?"

Ailie sighed and leaned back in her chair. "I don't know. It's something like that…but I'm not just worn out, it's…I can't put my finger on it. This is different."

Ruby shook her head. "I knew it. I should've seen this one coming. You do this to yourself every year. You work too many hours, on too many days, and then, when it looks like you're ready to explode, you disappear somewhere. Is this your way of telling us you've got your bags packed…and you won't be joining us for dinner?"

"No, I really don't want to go anywhere. There's no big vacation planned. This time I'm considering a real change."

"Are you quitting?"

"I'm not quitting."

"Good." Ruby seemed relieved. "Because we've been at this for nearly twenty years, you and I. We clawed our way to the top of this ad agency together. I would miss my best friend."

Ailie smiled, affectionately. "You know what it is? I have been looking at Instagram quite a bit lately. Here, let me show you." She pulled out her own phone and titled the screen toward Ruby. "I follow a lot of firefighters and rock climbers."

"Oh? And who's that?" Ruby asked, slowly scrolling through photos.

"Well, I also follow some lumberjacks and a rancher named Doug."

"Doug's cute."

"They're all cute."

"Yeah, but Doug's got something good goin' on. If I had to make a calendar, Doug would be my December, with a fireplace and a soft rug. Or…forget the rug, I'd just curl up on top of Doug."

"Okay, forget Doug. He's just eye-candy; he's married. The point is," Ailie returned to the images of firefighters and rock climbers, "look at those forests and blue skies. Well, this one's a bit smoky, but the rest of the pictures are clearer. And look at those guys, scaling that cliff wall…with their bare hands. They're out in the elements. It's real. It's raw."

"I'm sure it's raw—all that heat and chafing."

"Think about it, Ruby. They're living in the moment. They're not boxed in by this routine. Lately, I've started to wonder what it's like…I don't know…to feel unencumbered by all of *this*." She gestured wildly, indicating her office. "And look at this guy," Ailie added, eagerly pushing a magazine toward Ruby. "He looks so content…in the countryside. It's so…so simple."

"What is that, a new *Gap* ad?" Ruby picked up the magazine and stared at a photo of a handsome, well-dressed man tending hundreds of sheep on a lush green hillside. "He looks like a young Antonio Banderas."

"Don't you get jealous sometimes when you're on Facebook or Instagram and you look at pictures like this?"

"No. I think, 'Thank God someone else is fighting the fires for me. Why the fuck would anyone want to climb without a rope? And what is Antonio doing in Ireland? With sheep.'"

"Well I've started to admire them." Ailie stared at the photo with something akin to maternal pride. "I mean, these people, they're out there doing it."

"Doing what?"

"It. Stuff. They're getting their hands dirty. They're not restrained by emails and deadlines and phone calls."

"That's not true. Firefighters have a very special deadline; they have to put the fire out before they die." Ruby set the magazine back on the table and took a long look at her friend. "I thought you stepped back from the executive position so the stress wouldn't get to you as much. Now here you are again, a regular ol' creative director, and it sounds like you're dangerously close to throwing your laptop out the window or running off with the first rock climber or window washer who looks at you from the other side of that glass."

"Window washers." Ailie said in a low voice, turning her head toward the windows.

"It sounds to me like you *do* need a vacation," Ruby continued, "but you just don't realize it yet. As your best friend, as someone who has known you since you were young enough and drunk enough to think that a stick and poke tattoo was a marvelous idea…"

"Ouch, don't remind me," Ailie interjected. "I'm so glad you talked me out of it."

"Exactly. Which is why I'm now recommending that you go somewhere. The sooner the better. But this time take a real vacation, Ailie. You always go to these cold places where you have to pitch a tent and shoot your food."

Ailie playfully rolled her eyes. "I keep telling you, I've never hunted for food on any of those trips. They're participatory, which means we help with cooking."

"Whatever," responded Ruby, "the point is, even last summer you went south, to Patagonia. It was their winter. You deliberately went from hot to cold. I mean, most of us like to go on vacation somewhere warm, Ailie, to relax...not to do more work. I'll hook you up with my travel agent. She can easily find you a place with cabana boys and umbrella drinks."

"No. I am definitely not going anywhere this year." Ailie's tone was steadfast.

"Or better yet, fly to Ireland and you can help Antonio here." Ruby glanced at the magazine again. "He looks like he could use some help." She shook her head. "That's a lot of sheep. How does he see them when it snows? You should ask Doug, the rancher."

Their phones buzzed simultaneously. It was a text from Olivia.

"Go ahead, without me," offered Ailie. "I'll catch up."

"Okay." Ruby appeared uncertain. "But should I be concerned about leaving you alone here right now?"

"I'm fine. Seriously." Ailie smiled again at her best friend. "I'll be better in the morning, I promise. But start dinner without me. I'd like to walk there instead."

After a hug, Ruby departed. Ailie returned to her inbox momentarily, but then swiveled her chair to view the city again.

Outside, it was an unusually beautiful, warm spring evening. Ailie would be late to the restaurant, but walking often helped her think.

***

The restaurant was still humming with activity when Ailie arrived, forty-five minutes later. She found her friends easily. Ruby and Olivia were just finishing their entrees when she sat down.

Ailie had a lot of friends in the city. It was difficult to be successful in advertising if you didn't make friends—or at least "friends"—everywhere you went. But these two women were definitely her closest. Ailie was the oldest, at 39, and Olivia and Ruby were both 37. Ailie was an only child, and she considered Olivia and Ruby like sisters. The three of them were acquaintances at university, where they attended some of the same classes and social events. After graduation, she began working with Ruby, and Olivia was her roommate for several years. They weren't instantly best friends, but over time their mutual interests kept bringing them together. At first they'd bump into each other at friends' houses or special events or popular bars and restaurants, and at some point, perhaps four or five years into their working lives, the three began to increasingly rely on one another.

Ailie and Ruby embraced their careers and grew with them, but Olivia became increasingly distressed and unhappy trying to follow in her father's footsteps in investment banking. She hated the long hours and the emotional ups and downs accompanied by the fluctuation of the markets. Then, one evening, she walked past a yoga studio, looked inside the windows, and instantly fell in love with the handsome teacher, whose name she'd learn was Mathéo. The next morning she went to the nearest sporting goods store and bought every stretchy yoga-themed outfit they sold, all of which flaunted her slim figure, and signed up for Mathéo's beginner yoga class. Six months later, Olivia and Mathéo moved in together. One year later, Olivia quit her job and invested her money in a wellness and fitness center. Mathéo directed the center and taught classes, while Olivia tended to some arbitrary *business matters* (still vaguely following in her father's footsteps, she'd convinced herself), but mostly she enjoyed the benefits of weekly massage and spa treatments.

Ailie, Ruby, and Olivia met nearly every Friday for dinner, and often during the weekends, to celebrate triumphs, talk about their relationships, share gossip, or just relax in one another's company.

"There she is!" Olivia stood up to hug Ailie. "Feeling any better?"

"Kind of. A little. It'll pass." Ailie was relieved to sit down. The waiter walked over, and she ordered a glass of wine. She sat quietly and listened while Olivia, four months pregnant with her first child, finished telling them about a birthing class she'd recently attended. When her glass of wine arrived, Ailie took several large gulps, nearly finishing the glass before setting it down.

"Oh boy." Olivia shook her head at Ailie. "It could be your Qi. It's probably restricted." She had the occasional habit of dipping into her cursory knowledge of holistic medicine, carried over from her endless spa treatments. "I recommend you take time for yourself, Ailie. Maybe this year, do something bigger, something more significant...like a sabbatical. Step away from work or go visit your mom. Maybe then you can figure out why you get like this at least once a year."

Ailie squinted suspiciously at Olivia, "Did my mom call you?"

"No."

"Did she text you?"

"No."

"Did she email?"

"Nope. Nothing. No communication with your mom, what-so-ever," Olivia confirmed.

Ailie sighed. "Well, I am putting a plan together. I don't want to explain it now. Not until I'm ready. I'm...I'm thinking of a major shift. Maybe that's what's stressing me out—the idea of executing it."

"Well then...how long has it been since you've gone out with someone?"

"What? With a man?" Ailie responded, incredulously, as though Olivia had inquired about fish bait or the life cycle of a diseased cantaloupe.

"Yes. A man," confirmed Olivia. "Ruby and I were talking about it earlier, and we couldn't remember the last time you'd been on a date. You know as well as I do—sex, the human touch, releasing those hormones—it's *good* for you."

Ailie stared at her wine glass. It had, in fact, been more than a year since her last date. Dating had become a very strange affair in the last couple of years as the pool of available men, in her age range, dwindled.

In the very beginning she wanted a man who was ambitious, but not controlling; articulate, but not gossipy; relaxed, but not lazy; active, but not addicted to the gym; daring, but not impulsive; in touch with his emotions, but not sad; organized, but not obsessed; cared about his looks, but didn't compete for the mirror; enjoyed the outdoors and the city; wanted a cat and a dog; loved to read, loved to laugh, loved to play; knew himself and understood her. It wasn't a long list. Really, it wasn't.

However, as the years flew by, these prerequisites fell to the wayside like leaves off a tree gone dormant. At this point her only expectation on a date was someone who showed up on time, didn't brag about himself the entire night, and didn't rate his burps throughout the conversation.

Ailie smiled at her friends. "Look, I know that I'm anxious. I know that I've been acting weird, but when I'm ready to take action, then I'll be ready to talk about it. And you guys will be the first to know."

Ruby and Olivia returned to swapping stories about their weeks, while Ailie sat quietly, picking at her plate. They asked if she wanted join them for dessert at a café a couple of blocks away, but Ailie declined, telling them that she preferred to go home.

Normally she'd walk to the nearest subway station, but tonight she hailed a cab and sat in silence during the long ride home to Park Slope. The cab drove through downtown, past endless blocks of high-rise buildings, towering over the Hudson, and into a more residential enclave outside of the city. Soon the stimulations and distractions of urban life gave way to more tranquil streets. Elegant townhomes, clad with varied colors of brick or brownstone, decorated the sidewalks. Cafes, boutiques, and restaurants mingled with the houses.

Ailie fell in love with this area many years ago. She still recalled her first visit to Park Slope, while on a date with a man named Ryker Young. He called himself an entrepreneur. Ryker introduced her to the community with a visit to his favorite bar, and she sat next to him while he watched football with some of the locals. After the game had finally ended, they went to a nearby café and he talked ad nauseam about his past, his plans for the future, and investing in real estate and small businesses. As he spoke, her attention drifted toward the sights and sounds of the neighborhood: kids playing hopscotch, toddlers digging in the sand and mothers with strollers, chatting on the benches. Somewhere far off a barbeque was taking place, and from a nearby open window she could smell onions and garlic sizzling in a skillet. She felt at once relaxed and invigorated. It felt miles away from the buzz of the city.

Before, when Ailie had her apartment in the city, she never stayed at home much. She barely knew her neighbors. She was always on the go, and always at *work*—work, work, work—striving to put her name in the spotlight with influential projects at the office. She knew she had to be exceedingly social and constantly present at work so she made herself available for any role in any campaign, no matter how minor. She was always at her computer or fastidiously taking notes in a conference room, and she introduced herself to countless people coming and going from the office and at meetings around the city. After business hours, too, she had to keep up appearances—frequenting social events, opening nights at galleries and theaters, operas, dinner parties, wine tastings, fundraisers, and large company annual event celebrations. It felt exhilarating to attend all these grand spectacles. She had, in fact, been dreaming of this lifestyle, planning for it really, for as long as she could remember.

After her thirtieth birthday, though, Ailie began to feel uneasy and a bit faltering—like all this hard work and all this *activity* wasn't necessarily *going anywhere*. So, she focused on figuring out *exactly* where she wanted to be in ten years. Planning ahead would help, she thought. It always did. Ailie wanted more than a job in an industry traditionally dominated by males— she wanted more than note-taking in a conference room, she wanted full and total success. She wanted to be at the top. So she forged a plan, and she was on track.

For a time her routine worked, and she only allowed herself to unwind on the weekends and holidays. But at some point, her 10-year plan began to splinter and dilute, too. She wasn't sure if she wanted more or less of what had come before—juggling campaigns, remembering names, the latest trends and innovations, and staying on top of social media and ahead of the curve. In her pursuit to reach the top, her assignments multiplied and became a great distraction during her most creative moments. But the time between the end of one project and the start of a new one felt more and more like a patchwork of tiresome emails, updates, and meetings. She was exhausted. Then one day, while avoiding high priority emails, she clicked on a real-estate advertisement that appeared on the sidebar of one of the multiple tabs open on her laptop. Within a week she hired a realtor, touring small flats at the outskirts of the city, and she found this place—her home away from the city.

The cab's squeaky brakes brought her back to the present as they pulled up to her house. Well, it wasn't exactly *her* house. She owned part of a house. One floor to be exact. But she found her small home very calming and restorative after long hours at work. As soon as she moved in she'd painted every wall of the house, leaving only the trim a bright white. Plants abounded, large and small, giving the home a tropical feel. A couple of skylights accentuated the loft ceiling. All around the home, dotting the walls and shelves, were framed photos from her travels—jagged peaks in the Rockies, icebergs in Antarctica, outposts in Tibet, the Ice Hotel in Sweden.

Ailie walked in and, as per routine, immediately dropped her keys into a small hand-woven, grass basket at a table in the front room. An arched doorway led to a large open-spaced living room and kitchen, with a view to a balcony behind the house. Her bedroom lay to the side of the living room.

She went straight to her bedroom and pulled a letterbox out from a small shelf in the back of her closet. Then she poured herself a glass of wine, grabbed the letterbox and a blanket from the sofa, and went out on the deck. A minute later she came back again, grabbed the entire bottle of wine and returned to the deck.

The night was still warm. A string of small lanterns ran along the rail, illuminating the balcony, creating dark shadows in the patch of grass below. She sat back in a chaise lounge with large cushions and placed the glass of wine and letterbox on the low table in front of her. She sipped her wine and stared at the box for several minutes. The box stared back. Then she poured herself another glass of wine.

Finally she opened the box. Ailie pulled out three sets of documents and placed them next to one another on the table. The dim light of the tiny lanterns didn't hide the folded corners and the frayed edges of the paperwork. She had pulled them out of the box, stared at them, and put them back in the box, and into storage many, many times. Each form had the same logo at the top and a faded photo of a man. The photo on the oldest form was black and white. Below the pictures were bullet points listing their subject's physical characteristics, and a bit about their background and education. On the pages' margins, Ailie had scribbled dates and jotted down notes.

One by one she picked up the papers, examined the photos, and read them carefully, as though it were the first time. It was the 100th. She poured more wine into the glass. Finally she picked up the oldest document. The pages were stiff and probably appeared yellow in full light. The black and white photo, which was more like several shades of grey, was of a young man in his twenties. Only one name was given under the photo, "Levi."

Ailie peered at the photo in the faint light. She'd taken an immediate liking to his face when she first looked at his profile ten years ago. He had handsome eyes. She noticed that he didn't exactly look at the camera. Perhaps he was looking at something beyond the camera, maybe the photographer. He had a playful smile that created small wrinkles at the corners of his eyes, which were intent, giving him an ambitious look. Every time she stared at his photo she was sure he was flirting with the photographer. An entire decade had gone by since the paper was printed, and she wondered where he might be today, what his life must be like.

Ailie lay back in her chair, holding her glass in one hand and hugging the paper with the other. She looked up at night sky and detected a few stars beyond the city light. "Who are you, Levi?" she said to herself out loud. "Where can I find you?"

3

What's in the freezer section?

Ailie sat in her office, staring at the screen of her laptop. Her assistant, Emily, peeked in the door. "Hey. I'm going out to lunch now. Do you need anything? I'm stopping for coffee too if you want any."

Ailie smiled back. "No thanks. I brought something to eat here."

Emily closed the door and Ailie tapped her fingers on the table. One long minute later she got up and walked to the closest bathroom. She hastily checked under the stalls, to be sure she was alone, and then stood in front of the sink, looking at herself in the mirror. "We are doing this," Ailie whispered to herself. "Today *is* the day. We are making the call." She considered her thick, long, chestnut hair—it fell below her shoulders, with a few blonde highlights, sometimes bronze in the right light. *I wonder how my hair will change?* she thought. *Is it supposed to get thicker or thinner?* Ailie maintained herself very well and was often told that she looked younger than her 39 years, with only a few faint wrinkles to show. High cheekbones and a strong jaw gave her a classic square face, softened by large, brown eyes, rosy cheeks and white skin—skin that looked more pale than usual after a long winter. Ailie examined her reflection more closely, pressing her fingers into her cheeks. *I hope my face and neck don't swell. I need to spend more time outside. Olivia mentioned vitamin D.*

Ailie took a few steps back from the mirror. Her breasts were small, but she didn't mind; it worked well with her slim figure. She'd worn a skirt today that ended just above the knee. People had always told her she had nice legs. *I hope I get to keep them,* she said to herself, admiring them uneasily as though someone was about to walk through the door and force her to exchange them for another pair. Ailie turned to view her profile, specifically her flat stomach, retained through years of yoga and Pilates. She ran one hand across her smooth belly and shook her head. *I just need to do this. I've been thinking about it for way too long.* Ailie hurried back to her office, her head held high, her stride long.

From behind her desk, Ailie looked through the windows and surveyed the activity in the hallway. Ruby walked by, smiled, waved, and continued down the hall. Ailie flashed her a quick smile.

When she thought no one was looking in her direction, Ailie snuck a thin box out of her purse. It was the letterbox from home. She opened the box slowly and pulled out the print-out with the profile of Levi. She surveyed the office again and then gently picked up her cell phone and dialed a number from her stored contacts.

A voice on the other end answered immediately. "Bacon Gynecological and Reproductive Services, this is Barbie speaking, how can I help you?"

"Barbie?"

"Yes, Barbie. How can I help you today?" the girl on the other end chirped.

Ailie hesitated, and then responded quietly, almost in a whisper. "Yes. Well. My name is Ailie Faulkner… and I'd like to set up an appointment with Dr. Bacon…with Frieda. Please."

"And your date of birth, Ally?" Barbie asked loudly on the other end.

"It's Ailie… um, August 4th, 1975," she whispered again.

"There you are! Ailie Faulkner!" Barbie answered boisterously. "Okay…Hang on, let me put you on hold for just a second."

Without waiting for a response, Barbie put Ailie on hold. Ailie stared at the photo of Levi. Lionel Richie's "Hello" played as she waited and waited.

Ailie remembered her introduction to Dr. Frieda Bacon over a decade ago. So much had changed since then. Frieda told her that she came to the United States at a very young age and her parents, both doctors, pushed her into the field of medicine, and at some point she decided on gynecology. It was in that department that she met the love of her life, Bob. After graduation they married and opened a practice together.

Bob was the 'nice one' while Frieda was the brains of the operation. Frieda consistently received 'fair' reviews because she was said to be too clinical or too candid with her patients. But Ailie didn't mind her straightforward approach.

Bob had retired a few years ago, and Frieda was always at the cusp of retirement, in the same way Barbara Streisand and Cher were *always* on their Goodbye tour, year after year. Every time they met, Frieda told Ailie it's 'gonna happen next year, I svear it!' Therefore, at this point Frieda had a very small list of clientele that she maintained, the 'old timers,' as she liked to call them. Ailie was considered one of those old timers.

With retirement on the horizon, Ailie noticed that Frieda's temperament had softened; she became more laid back and more personable. In the beginning every appointment was like a strict physical exam—lots of questions, note-taking and fast facts. But in the last few years Frieda joked around more often.

Lionel Richie suddenly quieted and someone picked up; "Yoo-hoo! Ailie!" She immediately recognized Frieda's low, raspy voice, complete with the German accent. Frieda gushed, "How is ze girl who keeps me in business? I haven't seen you in a vile. Please, tell me that you are ready! Those eggs can't hatch vidout you, you know. If you don't come and get them soon I gonna hand them out at Halloveen!"

Ailie peered around the room again as though Frieda's voice was blasting through the telephone. She turned her chair so that her back was to the office. Her quiet voice waivered, "Yes…yes. Yes, I am ready…this time. This time will be it."

Frieda sounded delighted. "Zat's vonderful!! I gonna hand it back to Barbie so she can set it up. I look forward to seeing you! Bye-bye!"

Barbie picked up the phone. "How's tomorrow sound? We have a cancellation at 2 p.m., and I could slot you right in."

"Tomorrow? 2 p.m.? Well…um, let me check my calendar." Ailie cupped the phone in her hand and looked around the room. She knew that the office was often very quiet by Fridays after 1 p.m., and her schedule was more open now that their latest campaign was in the final phases of approval.

She closed her eyes for a moment, took a deep breath, picked up the phone again and said, "Yes, okay. Let's do 2 p.m."

Out in the hallway Ruby walked passed Ailie's window again; she waved and smiled.

***

The next day Ailie was early for her appointment. She sat in her chair, trying to read a magazine, but she couldn't concentrate. She scanned the enormous, plush waiting room. A few couples sat together, one of them held hands. Others read on their phones. A flat screen TV situated on the far wall played a video of goldfish swimming, accompanied by relaxing music. Frieda's office had grown tremendously throughout the years.

Ailie recalled her first visit ten years ago. She was twenty-nine, and several of her colleagues and most ambitious friends mentioned that they were thinking about having their eggs frozen. They wanted to focus on their careers first and plan for families later. At that age Ailie had barely considered what she wanted to do about marriage and family, and she was just coming out of a string of bad relationships that never seemed to go anywhere. It's not that the men were bad people, but her sense of affection toward them never deepened into anything close to love. Every time she met someone whose personality or appearance she found remotely attractive, she would date them on and off for a few weeks or months, but ultimately her sense of caring and commitment always wavered, leading to an official break-up or a fizzle without any further phone calls. So, when she looked into freezing her eggs, she decided to take it one step further and pick a sperm donor for some of the eggs too. She thought it was a fantastic idea since it guaranteed her more options in her future.

As she sat in the waiting room she thought about a few of those friends, acquaintances really, who mentioned that they might freeze their eggs. She wondered what happened to them. Were they married? Did some of them already have children? Were they happy?

A voice jolted Ailie out of her daydreams. "Ailie Faulkner! She's ready to see you now!" Barbie was tall and lanky and wore a huge smile. She led Ailie through another door and back to one of the patient offices.

Ailie was familiar with all the rooms at Frieda's office. This one was decorated with flowered wallpaper of a Japanese print. Serene black and white stills of adorable, naked, sleeping babies hung on the walls. Another assistant came in to take Ailie's vitals. "So…let's see," she said, scrolling on a laptop. "Are you still five foot seven…and one hundred and thirty pounds?"

"Yes," Ailie confirmed. Although, she was anxious whenever she came to the fertility center, the pressure of making sudden decisions about her future, too much, so she spoke again, "I'm sure I haven't shrunk…but my weight's always slightly different. Sometimes I go to the gym a lot, but sometimes when I'm busy at work I just go running, but then I might get *really* busy, you know, and then I might top out at 145 at the holidays and go back down to 130 at bikini season, but…"

Before Ailie could finish, the assistant opened the door and indicated that they go back in the hallway; there she was weighed and measured, and then they returned to the exam room. "Please take everything off and put this gown on. Frieda will be in in just a few minutes."

Ailie changed into the paper gown, sat down on the exam table and waited for Frieda. This time would be it, she decided. She would not back out or change her mind as she'd done in the past. She was ready.

Or maybe not. As she contemplated her readiness she decided that the exam table was too uncomfortable without back support, so she opted for a chair in the corner of the room. As soon as her she sat down she remembered that she wasn't wearing any underwear so she went back to the exam table. This time she lay down, but her knees hung over the end of the table, so she sat back up again.

"Hello!" Frieda burst into the room and gave Ailie a tight hug. "How *are* you?" Before Ailie could answer, Frieda motioned her to lie down, while she pulled out the stirrups. "Now lay back, sveetie, we gotta take a qvick peek. I am sure you are fine, but you know... vee godda do this."

Frieda was short, perhaps just over five feet tall. Ailie guessed she was in her sixties at this point. Her hair was always styled in a bob, and these days she dyed it jet-black.

Laying on the exam bed, Ailie stared at the ceiling. A strategically placed colored poster of an adorable, naked, sleeping baby was plastered to the ceiling tiles. The baby was cupped in a giant flower. Naturally.

"Okay, things are looking goot!" Frieda exclaimed as she performed the exam. "I am so happy you vant to do this. Finally! I keep telling my husband, 'zat Ailie, she is too alone.'"

"Well..." Ailie responded pensively. "I'm not doing this so I automatically have someone...or, I mean, I'm not doing it because I'm lonely..."

"Ja, ja, no, don't vorry, don't vorry my dear," Frieda responded. "I have known you for many years. I know zis is a big decision for you. I know you vould not be here if you veren't ready. And I also know some very handsome young doctors," she said, winking.

***

After the exam Ailie dressed and met Frieda in another office. Frieda was on her computer looking at Ailie's files. She tilted her head back as she peered through her glasses. "Na…who do vee have vaiting for you in the freezer. Do we have eggs, do we have sperm? Vat's in ze freezer section?"

"I'm interested in using the embryos," Ailie said.

"Ha! No kidding. Zat works. Who are ze candidates?" Frieda clicked and scrolled, adjusted her glasses, and clicked and scrolled again to get to the right screens.

Ailie reached into her bag and pulled out her letterbox. She set the papers on her lap and leafed through them for the profile of the man named Levi. "Well, I've settled on this one. I know that it sometimes takes a few trials, and sometimes many trials. So I thought we'd start with him."

Frieda walked around the desk, grabbed the thin stack of papers from Ailie, and sat down in the chair across from her. "Ooh, let's have a lookie. Now zis one, zis one is handsome! You like him?" The name at the top of the paper was 'Mark Green.'

"No. That's not the one. I mean, I like him too. I like all of them, but he's the second runner-up. I really want the one named Levi."

Frieda shuffled the papers until Levi's was on top. "Ah, ja, ja. I like him." She thought for a moment and walked back to her computer, papers in hand. "Now, how old are those embryos? Zat is my old address on ze logo, and that is a black and vite photo. Shit…that vas long ago."

Frieda scrolled and clicked as she spoke. Finally she found the right page. Then she exclaimed, "Ten years?"

Frieda looked at Ailie, Ailie looked back at Frieda.

Ailie spoke. "Well, yes, everything I've read says that embryos stay good indefinitely…and you said that too…every time I've visited…and…"

Frieda said gently, "Ja, but you've got ze other two. Ze embryos haven't been frozen as long. Maybe vee have more success vid them."

"I know," Ailie replied. "But I've thought about it for a long time. Years. A decade actually. This is the one I want. This is the guy that speaks to me. I mean his picture. We connect. I do. With him. With his photograph."

Frieda smiled. "Okay, okay my dear." She looked down and studied the calendar on her desk. "If you feel a connection, zen you feel a connection. I am not a psychologist. I look at vaginas all day. Let's do zis. Mr. Levi it is."

Frieda picked up the phone and called the front desk. "Can you get Helen in here, please? Vee need to schedule ze procedure for Miss Ailie. Ja! She's going for it! Ja, ja, finally!" Frieda winked at Ailie and spoke into the phone again. "Vee need to do ze blood tests, make a calendar for her, all of it."

***

"You're going to do *what*?" Olivia and Ruby stared at Ailie in disbelief. It was mid-morning on Sunday, and they were sitting at a café. Ailie and Ruby were drinking mimosas and Olivia a creamy avocado smoothie. The waiter had just taken their order.

"I am going to be impregnated. If the embryo takes, then I will become a mother," Ailie explained in a very clinical manner, before reaching for her mimosa.

Her friends looked stunned. They sipped from their drinks, as if synchronized.

Ruby spoke first. "Are you sure you've thought this through? Can't you just take some time off and call it a day? I'm not trying to talk you out of this, but to me you've always been 'Independent Ailie.' And I don't think I've ever seen you near a baby, let alone holding one. Don't forget, once those eggs turn into a child, it'll be like a barnacle. It latches on and just goes with you. Everywhere."

"Even when you pee," Olivia chimed in.

"I know that my life is good right now. As a matter of fact it's great," Ailie responded. "I'm at the top of my game." She stirred her mimosa. "But the game's become so predictable at times, so dull. I've been contemplating this change for years. I'll have to pierce myself with needles. We're talking possible headaches, swollen stomachs, miscarriages, irritability, acne, mood altering hormones, vaginal bleeding, and thrombosed hemorrhoids that protrude from your anus like grape clusters."

"I should get hash browns, instead of fruit," Olivia mumbled, picking up her menu again.

Ailie continued, "It's not like I woke this morning, read these risks for the first time and said to myself, 'Gee, that all sounds neat.' And besides," she added, "these aren't eggs. They're embryos."

Olivia and Ruby spoke at the same time, a cacophony of questions and exclamations.
"Wait, what? There's a dad?"
"Who is it? Don't tell me it's that guy from the investment firm!"
"Is it the painter? I loved him."
"Please don't let it be the painter. He was an ass."

Ailie waited for them to stop and then said, slowly, "No. It was not any of them. You guys don't know him. At least I don't think you'd know him. Hell, *I* don't know him. Not, personally, anyway. And besides, he didn't leave a last name, so it's kind of like an anonymous donor."

Again, her friends spoke over one another.
"How do you pick donors?"
"I'm sure they do background checks, but what if he's a very stressful person?"
"How do you know he's not in prison?"

Ailie looked at both of them. "Seriously? *Neither* of you have ever even looked into this before?"

Ruby shook her head. Olivia pointed to her stomach. "Nope." Then she added, reassuringly, "But, you know, a friend of mine did."

Ailie sighed. "What have we been talking about all these years? We've talked about guys, kids, futures…am I the only one who saved my eggs?"

"Embryos," Olivia corrected her.

"I've always said that I'm pretty happy being single," Ruby replied. "So it's a wonder that I even let Barry move in with me. But it's been good…and I got you guys. I've got a lot of family nearby. You've met my family, Ailie; they're everywhere. You can't go across town without bumpin' into one of them. Even with Barry living with me, sometimes I like to wake up and just figure it out as I go on the weekends. No plans, no commitments, no embryos."

Olivia chimed in, "I kind of thought about freezing my eggs once. I remember you and I talked about it. But I figured if I wasn't crazy about the idea, then I probably shouldn't. I knew if I met someone then I'd still have time to change my mind."

The waiter came by with their brunch.

"Do you know how much your egg quality goes down after the age of thirty-five?" Ailie asked, looking at Olivia. "Look at your eggs," she said. "LOOK at those eggs."

Olivia looked down at the eggs in front of her as Ailie continued, "They're ripe, they're tight, they're firm. They're ready to burst open when you touch them."

Olivia held her fork and considered the eggs for a moment.

"Have you ever seen a bad egg? The white and the yellow, they're all mixed together, slimy and gooey and…just…old," said Ailie. "And you're 37 now Olivia. How many tries did it take before you and Mathéo got pregnant?"

"Ah, well…just one," replied Olivia. "First try."

"Well, have you heard of secondary infertility?" Ailie countered.

Olivia shook her head. "But that's okay, it won't happen," she said, confidently. "We've already decided this'll be it for us. Anna helped with that decision."

"Your accountant?" Ruby asked, puzzled.

"Oh yeah," confirmed Olivia, "You remember her—the tall Asian, gorgeous, with long, black hair? It turns out she's got five kids. *Five*," she gasped, almost in a whisper. "I know that's not that uncommon, but I don't know how they do it. She and her husband work all the time, poor woman. She's always saying their marriage is about to fall apart because they've never got any time for each other, but they've got to see each other at least every other year because they keep having babies." She took a bite of her eggs and continued, "So I went to her house just before Christmas, this past year, and outside the door I can already hear the kids running around, inside, screaming, and one of the smaller ones answers the door."

"One of the smaller ones?"

"Look, I know I'm about to become a mom, but I've never done this before, so I can't tell the difference between a two year-old and a three year-old, and sometimes those fours and fives. The point is, it was one of the shorter kids. Anyway, Anna's standing behind him in the hallway, waving me in, talking on her phone to someone. So I stood there in the entryway for about a minute, with this two or three-year old staring at me. I had no idea what to say. Finally I knelt down and asked him if he was ready for Santa to come. He claps his hands excitedly and points to the living room and says, 'Santa works at Amazon.' I look over at their tree and sure enough there are stacks and stacks of Amazon boxes all around the tree. They didn't even take them out of the boxes, Ailie. And that's just odd, because we all know that Amazon can wrap the gifts for you."

"I'm sure the gifts were for other people." Ailie spoke as she sliced her toast into small squares, arranging tiny portions of food on each, like finger sandwiches.

"I asked her about it. Anna said that originally they were just too tired to unbox the gifts, and the kids were too little to know the difference. But then at some point their new tradition just replaced the old tradition because that's all the older kids knew, so that's what the older ones were telling the younger ones. Now when I order online I imagine these poor little elves schlepping away in these massive distribution centers." Olivia dabbed her mouth with a napkin. "Anyway, the point is we're sticking with one kid. Mathéo was born with a laid-back personality, but it takes work for me to feel stress-free."

"Well…" said Ruby, who had been quietly listening. "I'm sure that story made *everyone* more excited about having babies… But I do want to hear more about this plan of yours Ailie. Please…tell us about the lucky guy."

"The first set of embryos," Ailie spoke cautiously, trying to decide which facts to share, "was fertilized by someone named Levi."

Again her friends asked in unison –
"What? The first one?"
"There's more than one? How many times have you done this?"

"Three times. I went to the clinic three times over the years."

"Then tell us about Levi," Ruby said.

Ailie thought for a moment, at this point she knew his stats by heart. "He's twenty-five years old…"

Olivia's eyes widened. "Twenty-five? You picked a twenty-five year old? When can we meet him? They're so cute at that age."

Everyone laughed. "Well, now don't forget," Ailie said. "I started all this when I was near thirty. So this was almost ten years ago by now."

Ruby and Olivia were silent for a moment.

Olivia was the first to speak. "So Levi's like…thirty five by now?" Ailie nodded.

"Maybe he has his own family," Ruby said. "Or," she added, taking a bite from her toast, "he could be dead."

"I wonder why men donate sperm," Olivia wondered out loud. "Do you think he needed the money? Maybe he had two, three jobs just to make ends meet?"

The waiter walked over to refill their water glasses. The women considered him, quietly.

As soon as the waiter walked away, Ruby asked, "So what does he look like? Is he your traditional type—tall, dark and handsome?"

"Well, I probably shouldn't give away any more details about him. It's never a guarantee that the implantation will be successful, which is why I'm glad that I have so many in reserve. But I picked him because I really felt like I had a connection with him. You know, with his photo. You know how you can sometimes look at a photo, and you just kind of…feel something?"

"Totally," agreed Olivia. "I've looked at photos of old people and if you look for a while, then it's like they… they want to tell you something. But not photos of *old* people, I mean old photos of people."

"And it's not just that," said Ailie, "but it's like our paths once crossed, just for an instant. Well, we didn't physically cross, but it was over the Internet. I was scrolling through photos of donors, and none of them appealed to me. But then I hit the refresh button, and suddenly there he was. I knew we weren't in the same building, but I remember I actually looked over my shoulder, thinking he might be there, in the room with me, the moment felt so…so real."

"That is so sweet." Olivia placed her hand on Ailie's. "It's like he reached through the screen to you."

"You should've gotten there earlier," Ruby responded. "You could've introduced yourself to him, gone on a date, and done this the old fashioned way."

Ailie went on to explain to her friends how the next few weeks or couple of months would go, what drugs were involved, the chances of success, and how the implantation procedure worked. "Just bear with me. Some women are sensitive when it comes to the drugs and the hormones; others are not. My doctor said most likely I won't be because I'm not usually the emotional type."

"I'm excited for you." Ruby donned a wide smile. "*We* are excited for you. So what's next? When do you start?"

"It starts with a visit to my mom's house," Ailie replied. "I need to break it to the ladies on the west coast..." she trailed off momentarily. "Because they'll probably have something to say about it."

4

I paid them with money and Playboys.

Two weeks later, Ailie stepped off a plane in southern California. She rented a car and drove north towards her mother's house in the next valley. From the congested highways of Los Angeles her route meandered through hills soft and steep, some covered with enormous trees and others with scrub. It was close to 10 a.m., and the air was still a little moist, smelling of dry grass laden with dew. Her mother's home was situated in the hills, between the small town of Fillmore and the smaller town of Piru. Their house was just close enough to the valley floor so that chilly mornings were offset by hot afternoons and warm evenings.

Ailie parked her car in front of a large house. Her mother always used words like "eclectic" and "exceptional" to describe the composition of the house. The original building, in the center, was an adobe, Spanish Mission style structure, which was flanked by additional rooms that were built of wood. The first owners added a room here and there as the family's needs grew. This resulted in semi-enclosed courtyard at the back of the house, where Ailie's mother, Gloria, planted her vegetable and flower gardens.

Nearly every room of the house had French doors that opened to the courtyard and backyard.

Inside the house, aged wide-plank wood floors, slightly uneven or lightened by the sun in certain sections, gave way to a weathered and worn stone floor in the kitchen. Plants, pottery, and baskets were in every available corner. Vintage photos of people and cars hung on the walls. Skylights added just the right amount of light to the darker corners of the interior.

Gloria bought and sold old furniture, as well as ceramic and woven accessories. She usually managed to hold on to the pieces just long enough so that the look of her home was cozy but not cluttered. Ailie was never sure what to expect when she entered the house. She'd never actually lived there, so she was also always unsure which room was hers when she arrived.

"Ailie!" her mother came running into the house from the garden, enveloping Ailie in a tight embrace that seemed to last nearly a minute.

She hugged her mother back, the scent of her clothing and shampoo brought Ailie directly home. "Hi, mom."

They stood back and looked at each other, and then hugged again. Her mother wore her usual, a peasant blouse and a long, flowing skirt. "I was so excited when you called! A surprise visit. I can't wait to hear more about…everything!" Gloria threw her arms up in the air with delight and hugged Ailie again.

By now several dogs were at their feet, squirming, barking, tails wagging. "Did we adopt more dogs since my last visit?" Ailie asked as she knelt down to pet one of them.

"Of course!" Gloria confirmed, proudly. "This one's Otis," she indicated a small bulldog, missing one eye. "And that's Fester, over there." Gloria nodded in the direction of a Chihuahua, missing two legs.

"And I know you guys," Ailie said softly as she scratched behind the ears of two small poodles. Beside them sat Genghis, and enormous

Newfoundlander, who towered above the other canines, like a quiet sentinel. His large tail wagged, betraying a hint of happiness, sweeping the floor behind him.

"Quiet! Quiet!" Gloria yelled at the dogs, before turning to Ailie. "We're so glad you could come! You look radiant. Come, come inside." She pulled Ailie further into the house.

"Where is she? Where is she?" Ailie's grandmother, Vivien, entered the kitchen, quickly crossed the room, and embraced Ailie with another minute-long hug.

While Gloria typically wore her hair down, or in a ponytail at the base of her neck, Vivien's hair was always well-coiffed. And her perfumes…although they were never the same, Ailie always thought they were the most captivating scents. They reminded her of luxurious linens—expensive and delightful to behold.

"You look gorgeous!" Vivien exclaimed, as she stepped back to fully look at Ailie. "Let's get you to your room so you can unpack and…don't forget there's the bathroom," she said pointing to one side of the room.

Gloria added, "And we have brunch all set up at the table outside."

Ailie hastily unpacked her things and refreshed herself, after which she quickly peeked into each room to become reacquainted with the house. Her mother had a habit of switching the furniture around every few months, in addition to the items that she regularly swapped out from thrift shops and yard sales.

The three women sat down at a farmhouse table in the backyard, a few steps away from the kitchen's French doors. Ailie looked at the enormous spread before her—stacks of buttered bread, both soft and toasted, crispy bacon, steaming scrambled eggs, oozing small bits of cheese, pitchers of water, cold milk, and orange juice, sweating in the early morning sun, and lattes for all three of them, topped with heaps of froth, and a single jar of pickled herring. The sweet smell of fresh strawberries wafted over from a large bowl at the center of the table.

"Wow! Are we expecting more people?" she asked, surveying all the food.

"No," replied Vivien, rolling her eyes. "Once your mother found out you were coming, she used up every drop of gas in her car to buy things that were local...and in season."

"Mother," Gloria replied. "Let's enjoy this food with smiles on our faces."

"Well all I'm saying, Gloria, is that you could've gone to the grocery store, bought all the same crap, and been back in an hour."

"It's not the *same*," Gloria countered. "I *like* to support our neighbors. And it's even better when I can find organic."

"She drove two hours to find that bacon, Ailie. You *really* shouldn't leave the table until you eat it," Vivien said quietly, motioning to the stack of meat. Some of the bacon looked burned.

Ailie forced a smile. "Mm...looks good, mom. Aren't you guys vegetarian?"

"Only six months out of the year," Vivien replied. "It's good for the colon."

Ailie picked up the jar of fish, tipping it to better view the contents, "Well this doesn't look local..."

"Oh." Gloria giggled, her face flushing as Ailie handed her the jar. "That is the most delicious pickled herring. I do eat a little fish now and then, by the way," Gloria said, admiring the label, and then trying to pry the lid off. "It can only be found off the coast of Norway. Only one import store, two towns over, carries it, and only in winter."

Vivien rolled her eyes. "It takes just a little jet fuel to get it here."

"Don't worry," Vivien said, winking at Ailie. "You remember where to find the good stuff in this house. Just come to my room when you're hungry for a snack. The tasty kind that everyone else eats, with wood chips, corn syrup and food coloring. They can process the hell out of anything today and it tastes like heaven."

***

After breakfast the three of them brought the dishes inside. With the table cleared, Vivien tied a painted silk scarf around her hair and said to Ailie, "Charlie and I are going to the shops. I can introduce you to him later. This way you and your mother have time to catch up. I know you haven't said anything yet, but I know you've got some news. I can tell. You seem happier than usual, more relaxed. I can't wait to hear about it." And with that, Vivien stepped out the front door and drove off in her convertible.

"Who's Charlie?" Ailie asked her mom as they watched Vivien speed down the road. Dry grass and debris tumbled in the wake.

"He's a carpenter. I think she met him on a dating site, or maybe at the bar…I can't keep track," Gloria shook her head. "But he's great. He's replaced all the floors in the bedrooms, a couple of those steps that would always creak if you stepped in the wrong spot. I hated that at night. It scared the crap out of me, and then the dogs would bark…"

"Well the house really looks great, mom. I mean, it's come such a long way…and what you've done with the garden. Just beautiful."

"Yep, and now the shower won't go cold, when you flush the toilet, or when you run the garbage disposal…oh, and there *is* a garbage disposal now, that's new too."

"Wow! The antiquing and pottery must be going well for you."

"Well, honey, mostly I refurbish things. It does bring in some money. But you know, me and your grandma, we've always done well looking after ourselves. You know, lately I've kind of been seeing this guy, too, Paul. He's a plumber. He does great work."

"Paul, the Plumber?" Ailie looked at her mom, wryly.

"Yes…" Gloria rolled her eyes. "Paul, the Plumber. And Charlie, the Carpenter. Kind of cute, huh? Anyway, you really should respect his work. Not everyone knows how to handle old pipes."

"I'm sure," Ailie teased.

Gloria blushed. "Oh hush. You know, the house needs lookin' after too."

"So no more corpses, right?" Ailie asked, smirking.

"No. No. Although every once in a while your grandma swears she hears someone at night. It still gives me the heebeegeebees sometimes to think of Old Arthur walking around here." Gloria and Ailie looked out the window at the backyard, as though Arthur was standing just outside.

Old Arthur was Arthur Filbert, the house's previous owner. "That man hated small talk," recounted Gloria, shaking her head. "As a matter of fact, I think he hated talking to anyone. And I still remember the day that Sheriff Baylor found his body. He said the dry air did a great job preserving his body. It was the first time anyone had seen Arthur with a smile on his face."

Ailie recalled her mother phoning when the house went up for auction. Gloria and Vivien pooled all of their savings, and borrowed money from Ailie. Ailie was more than happy to give them money because it was the first time that she could remember Gloria and Vivien agreeing on a house in which to invest, a place in which they promised to settle.

Old Arthur's house was a nightmare at first. He had been an avid collector of reading material. Books and magazines were stuffed into every room, leaving only thin strips of walkway to access the doors. At first the women hired a few teens from the local high school, looking for summer work, to help them load the books and magazines into a dumpster.

But shortly after hiring them, Vivien discovered several twenty-dollar bills tucked into a novel that had accidentally fallen from her hands. Always the opportunist Vivien filtered through the pages of a dozen more books, locating money in each of them, in addition to signatures on the inside flap. Her eyes widened, overjoyed by the possibility that every book text in the house might be hiding some kind of treasure. Propelled by greed, Vivien promptly fired the teenagers.

"You fired those sweet boys?" Gloria exclaimed, shocked at her mother's rash decision.

"I didn't fire them in as much as I let them go. Plus I gave them all a ride home," said Vivien, matter-of-factly. "Don't worry. They got two weeks' severance. They were ecstatic!"

"Okay…but maybe I should bake them cookies or something and explain to their moms what happened."

"No, no, no," insisted Vivien. "Not necessary. I found lots of Playboys in Arthur's old bedroom. I've got to hand it to Arthur—they were in pristine condition. I gave each boy a stack. It's a win-win. We got rid of them all."

"You *paid* them with Playboys?" Gloria's eyes widened with disbelief. "What are their moms going to say?"

Vivien sighed. "No, I paid them with money *and* Playboys. And they're nearly eighteen! I doubt they're going to tell their moms. Plus I told them to stick 'em under their beds or in their closets, and they *all* agreed that was a good idea. You know, for decades men have said they read those magazines for the articles. I'm just giving those boys an option to continue that tradition. Some of those magazines looked vintage…or retro or whatever they're calling things from the 70s these days." Vivien chuckled. "I'm not sure any of them had seen a centerfold before, and a couple of them were amazed by the body hair."

Gloria shook her head and giggled. "I don't suppose you remembered to check if any of those Playboys were signed copies?"

For two years Gloria and Vivien labored through the leaves of every text, uncovering money, rare editions and signed copies. The more money they accumulated, the more jubilant, but paranoid Vivien became. She began to worry about break-ins, so they adopted a couple of pitbulls from the local shelter. The dogs were very old and didn't do much but bark, which was enough for Gloria. But not for Vivien, a hunter's daughter, who took it a step further by purchasing two large shotguns. Adept at shooting, Vivien could often be found outside during breaks, a clove cigarette hanging out from her mouth, target practicing on the surrounding trees, just to scare any would-be thieves who might linger behind the bushes.

"So how much money was it in the end?" Ailie inquired, curiously.

"Enough to keep us going," responded Gloria with a wink. "There's plenty left…and that's what safe deposit boxes are for. Besides, we don't spend a lot, not at one time."

Suddenly Gloria turned to Ailie and squealed with delight, "So? You're here! Out of the blue!" They looked at one another and then hugged again. "You must have some news! You've got to tell me what your news is."

***

Ailie, Gloria, and Vivien sat opposite one another in the backyard. It was late in the evening. They all wore sweaters to fend off the chilly air that set in just after the sun went down. Three varieties of wine congregated at the table's center. The bottles were half-empty.

They had been enjoying a light dinner when Ailie finally decided to tell them her big news, the reason for her surprise visit; within minutes the conversation disintegrated and the women were at odds. Ailie was shocked at how much her mother and grandmother opposed her plan, telling her it was not ideal to pursue motherhood on her own.

"But you've seen how difficult it was for us, Ailie," protested Gloria. "I just don't understand why someone would deliberately put themselves in that situation."

"Because hardly anything about what I'm doing is the same as what you and I experienced, mom. And you don't seem to get that."

Ailie found herself fiercely defending her decision to become a single mom. She thought that of all the women in the world, these two would rush to her side to support her. "Just look at how happy we...usually...are these days!" Ailie shouted, and then lowered her voice. "And we got here without the help of a dad...or a man...or anyone else."

Ailie stopped talking because she knew she might yell again, which made her feel disappointed in herself. Every time she was in the company of her mother and grandmother she discovered a part of her psyche that retreated to her younger self, perhaps her teenage self—still craving their understanding and approval. So when they disagreed, she sometimes, unsuccessfully, fought the desire to start shouting in order to get her point across. A period of silence descended upon them.

Finally, Gloria spoke. "It's not that we don't think you'd be a good mom, Ailie. As a matter of fact, I think you'd be a fantastic mother, and I'd be thrilled to be a grandmother. Finally! And, well, who knows, maybe Vivien could handle being a great-grandma." Vivien shrugged. "But what we're trying to tell you is that it's not a good idea to do this completely by yourself. It's best to have a partner, someone, anyone, so that you have help when you need it."

"I've already looked into all that, mother." Gloria knew that Ailie used the word 'mother' only when she grew impatient or angry. "I've been doing all my research so that I'm prepared for this next step. If I get pregnant this summer, I'll have the baby some time in the spring. I'll breastfeed exclusively for the first six months, as recommended by the World Health Organization, for optimal health and growth. After that I'd start her on formula, secure a nanny and be back at work."

Gloria and Vivien didn't say a word, so Ailie continued, "I'll probably pursue a free-range style of parenting, with just a hint of helicoptering, but not enough to make the baby risk averse. Because I've read about that too. In the first few months of a baby's life there are many developmental milestones to keep track of, and it's all about phases, but eventually they become like little people. I've read a lot of blogs and books. Oh, and don't forget, Olivia's having her baby in a few months, so she and I can compare notes as the kids grow."

Gloria and Vivien remained silent, both of them staring at Ailie. Finally, Vivien suggested, "Why don't you come here and have the baby. We can help you. We've got a world of knowledge between the two of us."

"I am *not* moving out here..." Ailie's tone was steadfast.

"Nannies and tutors are not a substitute for family and a home," Vivien insisted.

"But you guys are never in the same place for more than a few years. I think this is the longest you've stayed in one place in ages."

Since Ailie was little they'd been moving from town to town or apartment to apartment. Moving was almost an annual affair, and it was always for different reasons, and sometimes only on a whim—boyfriends, jobs, opportunities, more money, lack of money, and on occasion it was just because they'd heard good things about a place they'd never been to before. Life with her mother had been erratic, and, as a result, Ailie found substantial comfort, as an adult, sticking to one city and the same career. The move from Manhattan into Brooklyn, punctuated by vacations, had been more than enough movement for her.

"Well, this is it, Ailie," replied Gloria, calmly. "This is where we're staying. This is our home."

Frustrated by the direction of the conversation, Ailie protested, "Well, it's not *my* home. New York is where I've built my home, my life."

"That's okay, that's okay," Gloria said gently. Then she spoke in a more earnest tone, "Aren't you dating anyone right now in New York who might be interested in being...a father? You don't tell us much about the men you date. So...is there...maybe...there's a woman?"

"It's all the rage right now," Vivien chimed in. "We've read about it, we listen to the news. It's okay, you can tell us. You can tell us."

"Seriously?" Ailie asked, incredulously, looking back and forth at both of them. "Okay, I've had enough of this for tonight. I don't know if I'm more pissed because you think I'm leading a secret life, or because you think I'd be an idiot at this parenting thing… I'm tired. I'm jet-lagged. I need to go to bed." She defiantly stood from her patio chair and marched to the house, opening a set of French doors. Discovering it wasn't the right bedroom she went to the next set of French doors. Once inside, she tried to slam the doors behind her, but became furious when she discovered they were equipped with a soft-close system that closed quietly no matter how hard you threw them.

Vivien glared at Gloria. "I hate those doors. I've always hated those doors. Why did you have to put them in? Now she's probably even more pissed…because of those doors."

Ailie flopped down on the foreign bed. She wasn't tired, but she wasn't in the mood to defend herself any longer. A few minutes later her mother knocked on the door. Ailie spoke sternly, trying to keep her teenage self at bay. "Leave me alone. Please."

Gloria shuffled her feet for a moment right outside the bedroom door. "Okay. I support your desire to have time to yourself," she said loudly. "I just wanted to say that we're here for you…no matter what. However, we feel very strongly that you would benefit from help…like us…like family. We want to help. But over here. In California. Pregnancy and babies, it's hard. Life takes on a completely new meaning. You can't plan for…every scenario in the book. Just think about it." Gloria finished in a cheery voice, "Okay…good night! Love you!"

Ailie stared at the ceiling. She remembered that at a very early age she often asked her mother where her father was, and who he was. Her mother would always respond that he ran off with another woman, and then she would walk away, with tears in her eyes. After a while Ailie stopped asking, knowing how much it upset her mother. Even without a father around, Ailie and her mother had managed to get by. It wasn't always easy, and sometimes it was overwhelming, but they'd done it, without a man.

The real issue, thought Ailie, *hasn't been the lack of a man in my life, but that there have been too many men and too much uncertainty.* She felt that her mother had spent too much time chasing men, moving around, and changing her aspirations. Ailie firmly believed that if her mom had simply stayed put, stuck to one town and pursued one goal, then everyone's life might've been more balanced.

***

For the remainder of Ailie's visit the three generations agreed not to discuss the topic of motherhood. Ailie was there for only a few days, and they wanted to enjoy their time together and not get bogged down by 'what ifs.' What if the implantation wasn't successful, what if none of them are, what if the first one is successful, what if the baby came early, what if it was a miscarriage—it was all an unknown. But when *wasn't* it.

With the discussion of *what ifs* off-limits, they focused on distractions and entertainment instead. They visited the shops in the nearby towns, and Gloria was always excited to introduce her "successful daughter" to everyone she knew. At home Gloria taught Ailie more about pottery and working with furniture, while Vivien taught her how to use a shotgun. At one point, Vivien tried to show her how to skin a rabbit, too, but Ailie could barely hold down her lunch during the demonstration. In the evenings they watched movies or sat outside, under the stars, talking about everything but babies, and drinking wine until the early hours of the morning.

After a rocky start, Ailie was glad they salvaged the weekend, but as she packed her bags she felt more than ready to head back home. Their big discussion was not a success, but the more she thought about their conflicting views, the more she dismissed it as yet another mother-daughter-daughter disagreement that coincided with their differing approaches to life. This baby would have everything in a family that Ailie never had: a mother with a career and a secure income, and one place she loved to call home. Her baby would have a stable life.

5

Aliens. Zombies. Cavemen.

Once she was back in New York, Ailie began preparing herself for the next few weeks. She was a visual learner, so she created diagrams with If/Then statements and arrows, plotted around her projected implantation date. She hoped the procedure would happen on a Friday, in which case she'd have the whole weekend to rest and relax—but not too much rest, because she'd want good blood flow to the uterus, according to everything she'd read.

If it turned out she was pregnant, which was a long shot (perhaps less than 22% according to an online calculator she kept as a minimized tab for easy revisiting) because these things are not always successful on the first run, or the second run or the third… *If* any of the trials actually worked, then she would work until her due date, have the baby, and return to work after the suggested six months of nursing.

Everything was set.

***

Ailie was on the phone in her office when Ruby walked in and quietly closed the door behind her. Ailie motioned for Ruby to sit and continued talking on the phone with one of her clients. After a few minutes, Ruby pointed to her wrist to indicate the time. Ailie looked over at her and waved her hand signaling that everything was ok. Finally, after another ten minutes Ailie hung up. Ruby immediately stood up and grabbed Ailie's purse, "It's time. It's time. I can't believe you're not jumping out of your seat to get to the elevator. We need to go."

By the time Ailie stood up Ruby was at the door, holding it open for her.

"It'll be fine, Ruby," Ailie whispered as they walked down the office hall. "It's so early, it'll take us fifteen minutes to get there, and then it's another two blocks. We're not in a rush."

"What?" Ruby exclaimed. Then she whispered as they waited for the elevator. "You've been reading and researching the crap outta this. It's all we've been hearing about for weeks. Now I'm excited, so you better be excited!"

"I am excited," Ailie responded, in a business-like manner. "But you know these things don't work out the first time, and may not the second time…so this is more like practice."

"What?" Ruby said again, waiting for the elevator doors to close. "You paid like ten, twenty, thirty—however many thousand—to practice? You told us you might have to go back a second time, but I didn't realize this was practice. For that much money they'd better equip those eggs with flashlights and a map."

"Embryos," Ailie corrected her. "Yes, for many patients the first time is like a run-through, a dress rehearsal, if you will. You're telling your body, 'this is the plan, let's make it happen.'"

"Okay, well, it's your money, your dream. I just want to be the auntie who spoils her. Or him, I guess!"

They walked to the curb and Ruby hailed a cab.

A taxi pulled up immediately, and Ruby held the door open for Ailie. Ailie sighed and smiled. "Thanks Ruby, but I'm not pregnant yet."

At the fertility clinic, Ailie registered with the front desk and sat down next to Ruby.

Within a few minutes she heard a familiar voice across the room. "Yoo-hoo! Ailie!" Frieda walked over with one of her assistants; both were dressed in hospital garb. "I von't give you a big hug, except vid my smile. Vee are on track. Everyting has been going smoothly. What was his name again? And vere are my glasses?" she asked, patting her pockets. "Who is ze sperm donor? Is it Jake?"

"Um…Levi," Ailie responded.

"Oh jaa! Levi! Well, we gonna have a date vid Levi today! July 31st—today is ze day! I can feel it!"

Frieda found her glasses, grabbed a chart from her assistant and tilted her head back to see. She flipped through the paperwork. "And how many embryos did vee say vee vere gonna do?"

"One."

"One?" Frieda blinked. "Just one? But you know you gonna have better luck vid more. These ain't the youngest apples on the trees, you know?"

"I know. That's okay," said Ailie, confidently. "One is a good start. It's a good way to get into it."

"We're not just gonna get into it, my dear. We gonna DO it! Okay. I got to go, but vee see you soon, on ze other side!" Frieda turned back down the hallway, arms and hands gesturing as she excitedly spoke to the assistant that shadowed her.

"Hmmm," Ruby uttered as she read through one of the pamphlets in the waiting room.

"What? What do you mean by 'hmmm?'" Ailie asked her.

"Well, I know this stuff works, cause you've explained how it works. But I'm just reading this, and they're talking about egg and sperm, and this couple looks like they had their photo taken just yesterday," Ruby said, pointing to the photo of the smiling couple on the pamphlet.

"Yeah, people do it all the time," Ailie said, confused, staring at the photo.

"Well, your embryo is like ten years old. That's a long time. I've changed, you've changed...fashion's changed," Ruby said, indicating the photo again. "And, your embryo hasn't."

Ailie thought of this for a moment. Ruby continued, "It's like your egg and his sperm were alive way back in the day, and then they froze, locked in time, for a long long time. It's like in the movies, when go into stasis, traveling from one galaxy to another. Or they fall asleep at one planet, and wake up when they've reached another. Which is also when the aliens sneak onboard."

Ailie didn't respond. Ruby picked up another pamphlet and spoke again. "It's kind of like your embryo was dead, because right now it's not alive. And now...*you're* bringing *it* back to life, because it would feed off you, with the placenta and all. It kinda makes you think of zombies, you know?"

"Ruby, you have been thinking about this way too long," Ailie replied. "The science is there. There are no aliens involved. I am not having a zombie baby. It's just an embryo that has been waiting for me... for a long time."

"But," Ruby insisted. "It's not like you can bring *people* back to life after they freeze. Look at that caveman they found in the Alps. He was frozen solid. But he's not walking around, going to Starbucks for a latte...jumping online to update his status after five thousand years: '*I'm back!*' No. This is different. This has just a hint of the metaphysical, the dark and the mysterious. It's a lot of wow-factors."

Ailie sat back in her chair, quietly considering Ruby's statements. *Aliens. Zombies. Cavemen. Starbucks. Babies.* Just then a nurse came by to take her to her room.

***

Ailie waited in the bright-lit room, in her sterile gown, surrounded by sterile equipment. She'd been instructed to come in with a full bladder, to improve the visibility of the ultrasound, and now all she could think about was peeing.

Medical staff shuffled in and out, to examine her, and the instruments, and her paperwork.

A tall, plump nurse approached, her white hair planted in a bun on the top of her head. The bun bobbed as the nurse spoke with a hint of a Scottish accent. "Sit up, my dear. Here's yer Valium."

Ailie declined, "No thank you. I want to experience everything. I need to be present at this moment. I did yoga last night. I've thought about other people meditating. I'm perfectly relaxed right now."

"Ahh, but yer cervix may not feel the same way, dear. She's a wee fickle beast. Go on. Best to tame her with a small dose." The nurse winked and handed Ailie a mini paper cup.

Ailie smiled politely, titled the tiny cup into her mouth, swallowing the pill. It had been nearly six weeks since the visit to her mom's, when she'd last consumed alcohol, and she felt the affects of the drug rather quickly.

A few minutes later Ailie looked over at Ruby and asked her if she wanted a Valium too, because she looked anxious. Ruby chuckled, looking down at her own feet and patting the sides of her outfit. "These uniforms don't come with pockets. I have no idea what to do with myself when I'm not carrying my phone." She shifted nervously. "Wow…look at those instruments. Ouch. You sure this isn't going to hurt? Scratch that question. I am here to support you…"

"Don't worry," Ailie reassured her. "It's quick. With this Valium it'll be like happy Pap smear." Ailie giggled.

Ruby looked around the room and then grabbed Ailie's hand in eager anticipation. "Okay, I know it might not happen today, but, then again, it might. Just think about it—you are about to try to conceive. That's crazy." She laughed. "When we became best friends, I knew we'd be holding hands through a lot of events, but conception was *not* one of them."

Frieda entered the room, followed by two others in similar uniforms. "Hallo, hallo! You remember my assistant, Sherry, and zis young fellow is my doctor in training, Dr. Jones."

Han Solo, thought Ailie, smiling at him through the Valium. *His name should be Han Solo.*

"I'm going to lift off this off now," Dr. Jones said, pulling the gown that covered her abdomen and legs. "Let's just make sure it all looks good…"

Ailie laid her head back. "Well, I'm sure it looks great, I just had it waxed."

"He's talking about the ultrasound," whispered Ruby, gently squeezing Ailie's hand. Dr. Jones' face turned slightly red looking at the screen.

"Let's get to vork!" Frieda announced, in a celebratory tone.

***

The procedure was quick and painless, and so was the brief Valium induced post-op nap. After Ailie regained her faculties, she and Ruby said their goodbyes to Frieda and her team, and headed out to catch a cab for the long ride home. Ailie felt a surge of adrenaline as she reviewed the events of the morning. The thrill felt similar to the start of one of her exotic vacations. But this was more—this would be a whole new destination. *One, hopefully, without too many surprises,* she thought, reflecting on the visual diagrams she'd created for various If/Then scenarios. But what if the implantation actually worked? As if on cue, Olivia sent Ailie a few texts—

reminders of the power of positive thinking: *Pleasant feelings create more energy. Energy creates life. Broadcast good will. Call out and your embryo will listen.*

All the way home, Ailie and Ruby hugged and talked excitedly about what had just happened and their plans for the evening. Tonight Ruby would stay over at Ailie's and they'd watch movies like *What to Expect When You're Expecting, Baby Mama, Baby Boom,* and *Knocked Up.* Laughter, Ailie decided, was the best way to start communicating with her reproductive organ.

Saturday morning went fairly well. After Ruby left, Ailie tried to relax by thinking happy, positive thoughts, picturing her adorable little embryo, thawing after a decade, delighting at the warmth of her cozy uterus, snuggling in its new home. But after a short time she ran out of ideas for her happy embryo, so she took to the Internet for upbeat posts, watching videos of kittens playing and babies dancing. That didn't last long either because her mind began to wander, which led to strategizing and planning for the future. What if she became pregnant? What if she didn't? Where would the baby sleep? Would the baby be a good sleeper or a bad sleeper? What if the baby just never slept? Is that a possibility? Could she have a nursery in this corner of the house? Maybe that wall would be better for sound insulation? Do contractors work weekends? Ailie looked online to find names and read reviews for a handyman in the area. Perhaps she could find one that worked weekends and perhaps she could get a quote. After a couple of phone calls she decided she needed a change of scenery and some fresh air. She walked to the park. A game of chess would serve as a good distraction.

Sunday morning followed the same pattern. Anxieties about pregnancy and motherhood and things to come rushed into Ailie's head as quickly as she could dismiss them. She was thankful when her friends arrived and whisked her off to brunch.

"Have you gotten any sleep?" Ruby asked after the waiter took their order. "Your eyes look a little red."

"Sleep has been…okay," Ailie answered. "But in the daytime…I am such a doer, I have a hard time sitting still. And running is what I do to clear my mind, but I can't do that right now, doctor's orders, so I've been walking.

But the minute I sit back down…" she shook her head. "I know that I'm still waiting to find out if this procedure worked, but…in the last 24 hours I've been thinking so much about kids and the fact that this might become a reality for me—there's no turning around now—I could actually be a mother at this time next year."

"I'm excited too!" Olivia exclaimed. "Our kids could play together!"

Ailie smiled fondly at Olivia, then continued, "I don't know if I'm excited at this point or panicking. Just the thought of motherhood, raising a child…it's brought back so many memories of my own childhood…things I haven't thought about in years, good things, bad things…things I'd forgotten…things I've tried to forget or would rather forget…" She shook her head, reflecting on another memory. "Anyway, yesterday I tried *everything* to relax. Finally, last night I ended up at one of those meditation classes you've always recommended, Olivia."

Olivia's eyes brightened. "Oh? It's *so* good for you! And? How did it go?"

"I don't know." Ailie rubbed her eyes. "I don't get it. I'm not sure I liked it."

"It's meditation, Ailie, nobody gets it the first time," said Olivia, cheerfully. "Just keep practicing. Listen to the teacher. And eventually you'll get into a zone."

Ailie sighed. "I did listen to the teacher. She talked about freeing ourselves by opening our minds. But that's so…so vast. It felt more like work."

Olivia spoke encouragingly. "It is work at first, and you love challenges, so I know you can do this. And what about…did you focus on your breath?"

"Yes, I tried…but I have a hard time trying to free myself when I'm focusing. Aren't you supposed to let go, in order to feel free? And how can you focus on something when you're not actively…acting on it?"

Olivia leaned back in her chair. "Ooh…your forehead crinkled a bit when you said that… I hope you weren't annoyed the whole time."

54

Ailie sighed. "No, it wasn't like that. I mean, you're right, I was frustrated when I first started the class, but then it got better. The girl said to focus on my breathing. That was supposed to free me. So I was breathing…heavily, because I was working very hard to achieve focus. But that reminded me of Lamaze. And babies. So I felt distracted. So I looked at the little Buddha in the room, and his face reminded me of a baby…and then I started thinking about baby names. So then I thought maybe I should give *in* to whatever I was feeling, and that would free me… Because you've got to give *in* to let *go*, right? So I began to make a mental list of baby names. It worked for a while, but then I got lost in the alphabet. So I quickly revamped the list by shortening it to names I would *never* give to a baby. Names I dislike. And that worked better. After I thought about those…somehow I focused."

"I…I think that's a good start," said Olivia.

"Was Brenda's name on that list? You know, the witch from the third floor?" asked Ruby.

"No, her name was not on the list. Although it would've been if it included girl names, but this was just a list of boy names," replied Ailie.

Ruby laughed. "Is it all ex-boyfriends? Cause I'd have been there for hours."

Ailie took a sip from her water. "Kind of. You remember how my mom dated a lot when I was young? I mean, she wasn't like a revolving door, but she had a very open door policy. Some of the guys were boyfriends…others, she said, were just her friends. She always told me she liked the company…Some of the guys were okay and some of them were assholes. And, after this last visit with my mom, when she said I should 'find a man'…well, I've been thinking about *her* exes a lot more. So that was the list I put together: my mom's ex-boyfriends."

"Ahhh…" said Ruby, her eyes widening. "Your *mom's* ex-boyfriends."

Ailie continued, "In the end I think in the end it was a good exercise. I mean, in an odd way it felt like I was reconnecting with part of myself. I couldn't think of all her ex-boyfriends at first, but then I slowly remembered most of them…and then…I put them in various orders…like which ones I disliked the most versus those that were just annoying, and then I tried it alphabetically…"

"Oh, wow, you took the two hour class…" Olivia said, listening intently.

"Yes. It took a while… But…it was kind of useful… I remembered that I was a very strong-willed child, and I was also very angry at times. I hated my mom's boyfriends—they stole her attention, and half of them didn't want to bother with me—so I was mean to them, and, naturally, it made my mom's life hell. My grandmother empathized; she hated a lot of them too."

"I never knew any of my mom's ex-boyfriends," said Olivia, pensively. "That is, until I found her diary one day. It was by accident, of course. And at the back of it was this list—a list of names—and I think it's the guys she went out with because she wrote dates right next to them. And one of them, he's my dentist." Olivia whispered the last word. "I've been going to him my whole life, and now…I just can't relax as much when I go there. Because now I think about him and my mom…looking into each other's mouths and licking each other's teeth." Olivia shuddered, closing her eyes, as though trying to wipe the image from her mind.

"They lick each other's teeth?" Ailie asked, puzzled.

"Exactly," Olivia nodded. "I'm not sure what it means. It's a very strange nightmare."

Ruby sighed. "I love my momma. And, you know, I think the only person my mom ever dated was my dad. But sometimes I wonder if my mom ever gets curious…you know, about other men. I mean, she must, right? Just a little bit? But then that shatters that whole maternal, nurturing picture that I have of her, so I try to squash those thoughts quickly."

Ailie nodded her head in agreement. "Well, you guys know that I never knew my dad, so all I've got is my mom's *stream* of ex-boyfriends. I'm all about forgetting about the past, Ruby, but…my mom hated to cook, and that affected my relationship with her boyfriends. I think that really followed me into adulthood. At least for a while."

"That might answer some questions." Ruby joked.

"My mom called herself a feminist," Ailie continued. "And said that didn't involve cooking, or cleaning, or…anyway we often ate canned or boxed foods, unless we were living with my grandmother, but that's another story. So…my grandma—always the opportunist, and a bit of a survivalist—advised me to be nicer to the guys who could cook. I mean, she also gave me lots of other recommendations, but the cooking one really stuck with me—my grandma told that me I'd have better control of the situation if I offered to be…civil…to the guys who could cook. Sometimes it was a win-win: I'd get a fresh meal and my mother thought she had a happy house…" Ailie then looked at Olivia and said confidently, "I probably won't meditate again for a long time, but it really was freeing once I put that whole picture in focus."

"I still can't picture any of that," replied Olivia. "Your mom is so nice when we talk. And you've never mentioned the cooking thing before. So how did that carry over to today—I mean, is it something you look for in a guy then?"

"I don't…think so," Ailie replied. "But it's nice, right? When he can cook too."

Ruby agreed. "Oh yeah. Barry does all the cooking at our house. I don't mind."

"That's true," responded Olivia. "Now that I think about it, Mathéo does most of the cooking at our house too." She smiled, coyly. "So would this be a bad time to segue and tell you guys that we're having a boy?" She looked back and forth at Ailie and Ruby, who broke into huge smiles. "I know we said we were going to wait till he was born, but the waiting was killing me, so I called the doctor this week…and…like I said, it's going to be a boy!"

The women shrieked with joy, hugging and congratulating Olivia.
"That's awesome!"
"Yay! Now we can start planning!"

"Wait, wait…" replied Olivia, gently, still smiling. "I should tell you that Mathéo and I want to be sure he is raised with gender neutral toys and clothes, so we don't want everything to be just blues and browns. So far I've avoided shopping in stores where everything is either pink or blue. Ailie, you'll see it's all the talk on the mommy blogs…"

"I've looked at many of those mommy blogs too," Ruby chimed in. "I've got cousins."

"And Mathéo is very sensitive about plastics," continued Olivia. "So we're sticking with organics—cotton, wood, metal, glass—that type of stuff. I'll send you some links."

"Can we at least plan your baby shower?" asked Ailie. "It could be earthy, like in a park…with lots of wooden trees…" she teased.

"Yes, but it'll be cold by then. Mathéo's family believes it's bad luck to have a shower before the baby arrives, so it'll have to be after. So…that brings me back to your list, Ailie. We've been thinking about names for the baby, and, we're still at the very early stages, but now I'm curious what's on your list of most hated names. Is it really a short list? Or is it a longer kind of a short list? Can you just rattle off some of the highlights so I have an idea?"

"Really? Hmm…Okay…well…there was Oak, from Idaho… and Pablo, he was the brooding, silent type…and Brad, who cooked a wonderful steak…" Ailie continued with the list as Olivia mentally checked the names off one by one.

***

In the short term, Ailie discovered that her work at the office was probably the best diversion for what seemed like an endless wait before she was supposed to take a pregnancy test. Even though she had not planned on doing so, she stayed late to assist others with new leads and current assignments, and she was mildly tempted to tell her boss that she was ready to take on something new. Ailie also noticed that Ruby found an excuse to drop by her office every morning, to borrow tape, scissors, a stapler, and ask how Ailie was feeling.

Nine days after her procedure, Ailie woke up feeling horrible. Though she had eight hours of sleep, she felt absolutely exhausted.

Ailie walked to the corner coffee shop and ordered a large latte. She'd been weaning herself off caffeine with decaf lattes, but she wasn't sure how she'd make it through the day feeling this groggy.

By the time she arrived at the office her latte still hadn't kicked in. She wondered if she was coming down with the flu, so she decided she'd stop by the pharmacy for some medicine, after her morning meeting.

The meeting seemed to drag on forever. She could barely keep her eyes open. At one point her head jerked back as she realized she was falling asleep. Ruby kicked her under the table a couple of times.

As soon as the meeting ended, Ailie marched to the door with Ruby trailing behind her. "Are you okay?"

"Yes," replied Ailie, wiping her brow. "I think I have the flu. I'm going to the pharmacy and then home."

"Are you sure it's not...you know..." said Ruby, pointing to Ailie's stomach. "Maybe this is normal."

"No, this can't be normal. I don't think so."

"I thought you read about all this. Did you ask Olivia?"

"I *have* read! I read a lot. But there's still more to cover." She whispered as they approached her office. "There's stuff to know before the pregnancy, during the pregnancy, after the pregnancy, stuff about the baby, stuff about me. If you read too much you go crazy. There's also a lot of scary information out there, especially online. And what would Olivia know? She's having the perfect pregnancy. If she gets any bubblier she'll float away."

Ruby rolled her eyes as she trailed behind Ailie. They entered Ailie's office, where she grabbed her purse. "You know," continued Ailie, still whispering.

"I'm pretty sure this is the flu. Besides, I've still got a few more days till I'm supposed to take any pregnancy test. And...at this point I'm not even sure if it's still in there."

"What?" Ruby looked at Ailie, confused. They headed to the water cooler.

"Well, you know I've been super anxious and then I get annoyed because I'm so anxious. So when I go home at night I...I go jogging." Ailie saw the look of disapproval on Ruby's face. "I can't help it. I can't sit still. This waiting is killing me."

"Well...it's probably okay by now." Ruby tried to reassure her. "Doesn't everyone exercise during pregnancy these days?"

"Well, it's possible that I went jogging before the embryo had time to latch on, you know. I mean, they tell you to take it easy the first day and kind of easy the second day, and why else would they tell you that if they weren't worried that it might bounce around? But on day three you're suddenly on your own; no instructions except to wait and go back to your regular life. But the embryo still might not be attached. It might still be sitting there, hanging out, waiting for something or someone to come along, I don't know. In the meantime I had to go back to my routine before I went crazy, and my routine is to go running when I'm stressed. So I went running...and now part of me wonders what if... maybe it slipped out."

Ruby squinted at Ailie, as though considering the logic to her theory.

Ailie fanned her face with some paperwork while walking to the elevator. "Remember how I told you that my mom practiced as a healer at one point? You know, it was one of those things she tried out for a while? I was like twelve or thirteen, and one morning she took off to the desert with some guy."

Ruby nodded. "Yeah, and you stayed with your grandma." She snapped her fingers. "Her boyfriend's name was like Flying Falcon, or something. But you'd call him Flying Poo."

"Exactly. My mom was gone for months," continued Ailie. "But…I remember one of the things she taught me when she came back was that in order to get your ovulation cycle back on track you have to stand outside, and look for the moon, every night for a month. And you have to be barefoot…in the grass."

Ruby was about to say something, but Ailie spoke again. "So I should preface my next statement by saying that, I know I'm not ovulating, and you *know* I'm not the type to easily believe in…things my mom says. *But* I had horrible insomnia and I was feeling a bit desperate about this whole thing—is it going to happen, is it not going to happen, did it fall out? So…please don't judge me, but I figured that if the embryo got dislodged, well… you know we had a full moon the other night, it was warm out, and I was in the mood for a walk, so I figured I could try…getting things back in orbit. So I went to the park…found a patch of grass, took my shoes off and then I stood there …staring at the moon."

"And?"

"And, that's how I think I got the flu. The grass was wet and kind of cold, then someone asked me for money…"

"Well…how long did you stand there?" Ruby asked, holding the doors of the elevator open. "Here, why don't I walk you to the pharmacy. We can find you some flu meds together. And a pregnancy test."

"Ailie! Ruby!" Ailie's boss, Geoffrey, walked toward them, arms stretched out, just as they were about to step into the elevator. He was always perfectly attired in an expensive suit, his hands manicured, his hair styled, and his assistant, Timothy, was always following close behind. "It's in the bag! Another job well done!" Geoffrey exclaimed.

"I'm not feeling great." Ailie said, clasping her mouth.

"Oh," Geoffrey said, halting in mid-step. He pulled out the tiny pocket square that rested in his suit pocket and covered his mouth with it. Everyone in the office knew he was a germaphobe.

"You'd better get that taken care of," he said, his voice muffled by the pocket square. Then he retreated and turned the corner quickly, but not before Ailie saw him pull out some hand sanitizer. Timothy followed.

***

Ailie leaned against the wall outside the pharmacy while Ruby went inside to buy flu medication and a pregnancy test. An early morning chill hung in the air, and Ailie was grateful for it.

Ruby returned with a small paper bag in hand. She pulled out the box of pregnancy tests. "Now, where do you wanna do this? Here? Back at the office?"

"I can't take that," Ailie said.

"I knew you'd say that…" Ruby shook her head.

"No. I'm serious," Ailie protested. "I just remembered that if I take a pee test now then it might give me a false positive because of all the hormones I'm taking."

"Yes. But…" Ruby reached into the bag for the flu medicine. "This here says you can't take it if you're pregnant." She smiled at Ailie, gently shaking the container as though dangling a carrot in front of her. "See? I have cousins. They've all been pregnant. I know what I'm doing."

Ailie stared at the boxes in Ruby's hands.

"C'mon, let's eliminate some possibilities," Ruby said encouragingly. "If you wanna drink some of this, you've got to pee on one of these."

"Look, I feel like shit. I just want to go home and lie down. I'll take the test later." At this point Ailie felt like curling up on the cold sidewalk.

"First of all, when you go home, I'm going home with you, because I don't want you to pass out with your head in some pee-stained lap on the subway. If it says you're pregnant I'm taking you to Dr. Frieda to find out what we need to do next. Maybe she's got something that'll make you feel better. But if you're not pregnant then we need to get you to the hospital or something. Seriously, you look like shit. You look worse than shit. You look like you could have Ebola or something…and you never know what you're going to get with all these unvaccinated children roaming the streets these days."

"Fine," Ailie relented. "But I am not taking the test at the office."

"That's fine. Go inside. Take it here at the pharmacy. Hell, this is New York you could take it here on the corner if you want. Let's just get this over with. If you're not pregnant, then I want to know if I'm gonna die today."

Ruby paced outside the pharmacy, checking her messages, as Ailie sat on the restroom toilet, first staring at the pregnancy tests, and then reading and re-reading the instructions. Ten minutes later Ailie emerged through the doors.

"It's….I'm….it says I'm pregnant," she said in amazement.

"You *are*?" asked Ruby, sounding equally amazed. "Did you take both tests? There were two in that packet, you know."

"Yes…both…" replied Ailie, stunned. "And then I bought two more from a different brand. I mean, they could be wrong, but…for the first time in my life they all said… 'yes.'

"Perfect!" Ruby clapped, grinning from ear to ear. "This is what we hoped for!" Ailie didn't look convinced. "Now we have to get you to Dr. Frieda's and she can tell us what to do next." Ruby hailed a cab.

6

Remind me again why you never bought a fridge with a freezer.

Barbie greeted them at the front desk of Frieda's office. She told them it shouldn't be a problem to see Frieda "soon," they just had to wait for a short opening.

About an hour later, Ailie was ready to go home. She wasn't feeling any better and nausea was starting to set in. Finally one of the nurses called her name and took some blood.

Inside the medical office, Frieda came marching in the door, announcing proudly, "Vee did it! It's positive. You are pregnant, my dear. On the outside you are a veteran in your field, you are high flying in your career, and in zere," Frieda motioned to Ailie's stomach. "In zere vee are starting out and twenty-five again!"

"I was almost thirty when we retrieved the eggs," said Ailie.

"Ja, but *he...he* was twenty-five! He was just a young buck." Frieda winked at Ailie before opening her laptop. "Now...you are pregnant...I gonna tick ze box, 'yes.'" Then she turned to Ailie again. "Now you've got ze instructions and information vee gave you before, right? And you've got all ze medications, right? Helen can go over any qvestions you might have about those. Anyting else vee can do for you today?"

Frieda's assistant leaned in and whispered, "We'll schedule the next ultrasound."

By now Ailie was tired and upset, but tried not to sound too frustrated. "What? That's it? I came halfway across town just so you can tell me that I'm pregnant and send me home? Just so I can reconfirm the same thing that some pee stick just told me?....What do I do now? What's the next step?"

"Ailie, Ailie…" Frieda said, comfortingly. "You must calm yourself, my dear. Shtress iz no good for ze baby. Does someting ail you, my dear? How are you feeling?"

"I feel like shit!" Ailie exclaimed. "But it's not even a pregnancy thing. I mean, I don't think it is! It's like I have the flu or something. Everything hurts. My bones hurt. I'm hot. I'm cold. I'm dizzy. But it's not even one of those morning sickness things where you perk up later in the day. I mean…what time is it now? It's way past noon and I'm still feeling sick! And what is this?"

"Vat? Vat are you talking about?" asked Frieda, examining Ailie's face.

"This? Why am I crying?" Ailie angrily wiped the tears that formed in the corner of her eyes.

"Ailie," Frieda said calmly, and with one of her small hands she gave Ailie a quick slap on the face. "You must hold it together." Frieda clasped her hands behind her back and began pacing back and forth inside the tiny medical office. "You are a grown vooman. A vooman vid a notable career. You are no shpring Küken! You are a leader! You don't sit in my office and let a tiny thing like an embryo dominate your day. Vee von't make an elephant out of a mosquito, do you hear? You vill have an ultrasound. You vill take some blood tests. You vill go home and lie down. Vee vill be in touch with you about ze test results. In ze meantime, if you continue to feel very sick, zen ve gonna put you on some anti-nausea medication. Do you understand?"

"Okay," replied Ailie, in a small, raspy voice.

***

Ruby and Ailie sat silently during another long taxi ride to Ailie's house. Eventually she leaned on Ruby and fell asleep.

Ailie took some sick days, and was grateful once it became the weekend. She continued to feel sick, but hoped that it would taper off by Monday. Normally she would go for a run, stop by the grocers, and spend time at some of the cafes and restaurants on her street, talking with the owners and other residents. But today she could barely make it out the door without wanting to lie down or vomit or both. On Friday she had called Frieda's office for help, and the girl at the front desk, Barbie, sent a prescription to a pharmacy near Ailie's house. Barbie also cautioned that one of the possible side effects of the medication was fatigue, and Ailie couldn't imagine being more fatigued than she already was.

The bottle of anti-nausea medication now sat on Ailie's counter, next to several varieties of canned chicken stock, their lids pried open and still attached. Some of the cans were nearly full and others half finished. The stock was Ailie's attempt to consume something other than toast and water, but she found none of them appealing and felt like her body was wasting away. She imagined herself withering in her tiny home, only to be found by her friends after they made the long journey out to see her. And by then she'd be dead. She thought about death. She thought how good death might feel right now compared to the sickness that had taken over her body. Listening to Ailie's anguish over the phone, Ruby offered to come by and make her grandmother's chicken stock, and soup, from scratch.

Ruby arrived, three hours later, clutching two over-stuffed grocery bags, letting herself into Ailie's apartment. Ailie was lying facedown on the floor, in the entryway; her face, cushioned by her arms, was buried in a shaggy rug. Seeing Ailie on the floor, Ruby's eyebrows shot up, but she remained calm, "Please don't tell me that you're dead. I just walked up all those stairs carrying all these groceries."

"I'm not dead," was Ailie's muffled response. She turned her face to the side and looked up at Ruby, "But this cold tile feels so good on my stomach right now."

"Have you tried an ice pack?" Ruby asked, stepping over Ailie's body. She walked into the kitchen and looked around before setting the bags down. "Don't answer that. I always forget that you don't have a freezer."

"Oh yeah," replied Ailie, crawling toward the couch. "I keep meaning to remedy that. That fridge is old, and I'll definitely need a freezer once the baby comes along."

"And remind me again why you never bought a fridge with a freezer in the first place?"

"Because of my great-grandfather."

"Someone you've never met?" Ruby asked, unpacking the bags.

"Kind of," Ailie said, trying to find a comfortable position on the couch. "But it was more about his house than anything else. Remember? If he was alive today, I think he'd be called a prepper, like those people on TV who're always preparing for the zombie apocalypse. Or maybe he was a hoarder...or somewhere in between."

"Oh yeah, I remember part of the story now. He had a lot of guns, right?"

"Yes. His family lost just about everything in the Depression, and later in life he became obsessed with collecting food and guns. I guess that made him a prepper. But he wasn't very organized. Preppers always separate things with shelves, don't they?"

"So, why did you guys live in that house again?"

Ailie heard the clanking of pots and the opening and closing of drawers and cabinets. "We didn't live there that long," she responded. "We were only there for a couple of years when I was really little. We didn't have much money, I think, and my grandma inherited the house. It was basically falling apart though. My grandma actually liked it because it was at the edge of a forest that went on forever. We grew vegetables in the back, and she went hunting when...I guess when we needed it or when she felt like it. But I don't think we really needed it because we had so many freezers and some fridges filled with...all kinds of killed...things. I was always confused about them."

"Confused about the dead things or the fridges and the freezers?"

"Both, really. At first I was curious about the dead things, but then...I began to get nightmares. Like for Christmas my grandma got a baby pig from one of the neighbors. I thought he was so cute, so I named him Piggy. Thing is, my grandma told me not to get attached because we'd eat him at some point. But there weren't many other kids to play with, and...so Piggy and I bonded. Then one day, I remember it was so hot, and I ran out to the front yard, in my underwear, to ask my grandma to turn on the sprinkler. And there he was, Piggy...dead, hanging upside down from the tree, blood dripping. A big barrel under him. I was so upset. So my grandma set the sprinkler up in the back yard..."

"What?" Ruby popped her head around the corner. "She killed Piggy just like that?"

"Well, no, I think they *tried* to talk to me about it ahead of time...I don't think I talked to my grandma for at least a week after that. But, you know, it wasn't just Piggy. This other time I went to grab some milk, and opened up the fridge, and there's this giant deer wedged in there. I guess my grandma was too tired to prepare it, so she just...I don't know...stuffed it in there for a few hours. It might've been a small deer though...because *I* was small, so it just looked big. I had nightmares for a long time after that. Years. And there were so many stacks of things around this house. Everywhere—dirty things, used things, sharp things, bagged things, rusting things. That whole house gave me the creeps. But mostly it was the freezers that *really* give me the creeps."

"No wonder your mom took off at *every* opportunity," replied Ruby, chuckling. "Hell, I'd have latched on to any man that could take me away from that mess. You *know* I hate clutter. You know I like everything to be super clean."

"I'm not sure that was the reason my mom always tried to move away. My mom liked action. She liked towns and cities. My grandma always picked farms or remote places to live. She preferred to lived off the land."

"Really? Aren't you always complaining that your grandma eats way too may processed foods and junk?"

"Well, yeah. Because now she can afford it."

Ruby pulled a fat, uncooked chicken from one of the bags, stripped the wrapper off of it, and set it on the counter. "I was going to make a roast and then add some of the chicken to a big pot of soup..." Ruby said, drumming her fingers on the countertop, looking around the kitchen.

At the sight of the chicken Ailie turned pale, her eyes widened, and she ran for the bathroom, retching. Kneeling before the toilet all that dripped from her mouth were small amounts of water. *I definitely need that soup*, she thought, dabbing her lips with toilet paper.

"I'm just going to lie down on my bed for a little bit!" Ailie shouted from her room.

"Whatever you need to do!" Ruby shouted back, chopping vegetables.

Ailie lay down, her eyes scanning the room for a point on which to focus. She felt agitated; her hands shook slightly as she waited for her strength to return. Her discussion with Ruby, about the past, had generated an abundance of memories—many of which, at one time, had been extremely negative, but with the passing of time her visceral reactions had softened. However, the sight of the uncooked chicken immediately took Ailie back to her mother's ex-boyfriend, Bill. It had been years since Ailie had thought about him. She tried to dismiss any further recollections of Bill, but as she lay miserably sick in her bed, with nothing else to do, all she did was think about him.

Ailie was about sixteen when she and her mother moved to the tiny town of Dead End, South Carolina. Her mother said she'd always wanted to write a book "about something," and had decided that Dead End sounded like an intriguing, but no-nonsense kind of town that might inspire her writing. It was just off the highway, and she'd said it would be a great experience to wait tables and talk to travelers at the local diner. Four weeks into their relocation her mother invited Bill, a line cook, over for dinner. After that first evening, and to Ailie's great displeasure, he came over to their apartment nearly every night for the nine months that she and her mother lived in Dead End.

Bill never did much, except sit and watch TV, so Ailie was mystified as to how he stayed so skinny. He was like a beanpole except for a small, protruding belly. Bill didn't talk much, either, except about sports, so Ailie trained herself to treat him like background noise whenever he came over. Most annoying of all, to Ailie, was that she could not find any angle, any topic with which to try and connect with Bill—not even cooking, because Bill never cooked for anyone outside of work. It was also at about this time that Ailie began to teach herself how to cook. She could still remember the day she walked into the local library to find a basic cookbook with instructions on how to boil an egg.

Gloria didn't appear to love Bill, not the way Ailie had seen her mother fall for guys in the past, but, against Ailie's quiet protests, Gloria and Bill fell into a relationship—one that stuck to a regular routine. It didn't take long for Ailie to create a mental calendar of their habits: Wednesday nights were poker night, Thursday night to Saturday night Bill drank with his buddies, Sunday and Monday were often game nights, and Tuesday night was…sex night.

At sixteen Ailie was very aware that her mother's relationships might involve more than mere kissing. It had been a few years since Ailie had experienced that crushing blow, that extreme revulsion that every child feels the first time they realize that their parent is a sexual being. But this understanding of human nature never made it easier when, on Tuesday evenings, her mother and Bill would retire to their bedroom, giggling and whispering and shushing behind the thin walls of the apartment. Ailie loathed the image of Bill, with his yellow hair and pale skin, wriggling on top of her mother. Just the thought of Bill's naked body made Ailie shudder.

After many months Ailie decided that she'd had enough of Bill—he was a waste of space in their small home, and a waste of her mother's time. She felt that he contributed not one iota of meaning to the lives of her or her mother, and she was puzzled as to why her mother devoted so many evenings to him. Therefore, one night, one *Tuesday* night, Ailie decided to take matters into her own hands.

The idea came about as she was in the kitchen, attempting for the first time to prepare a whole chicken to roast. As she rubbed butter onto the bird, she heard her mother and Bill laughing in the bedroom. It was in that moment—when Ailie's slick hands slid across the ribs of the cold, lifeless chicken, with its pimply, spongy, yellow flesh, and short, abrasive hairs— that it occurred to Ailie that perhaps that's what it felt like to make love to Bill, like slapping a wet, bony chicken. At first Ailie gagged, quickly pulling her hands away from the bird as she thought about Bill. But as she washed her hands, repeatedly, she decided she was too hungry to throw away a potential, home cooked meal. Determined to eat, she placed it in the oven to roast.

Two hours later Ailie was crestfallen as she pulled out a very dry, overcooked bird. Angry and bitter, Ailie sat in the dark at their small breakfast table, quietly crying. She wept because her mother had taken up with a loser like Bill. She wept because her mother brought them to this shithole, Dead End, with the intention of writing a book that she'd never started. She wept because she missed her mother incredibly, but her mother didn't seem to notice. Between tears, Ailie pulled every last piece of meat off the dry roast, and she ate them while ruminating over the quickest way to get rid of Bill.

The next morning, Ailie told her mother two lies—that she'd seen Bill kissing another woman, and that she'd heard that he had another girlfriend across town. As an added measure, Ailie also borrowed a thong and condom from a neighboring girl, whose mother "dated a lot." She then dug through the garbage and found the original packaging for the chicken, and squeezed any remaining fluids from the package into the condom. She nearly vomited from the scent as tiny chunks of dissolving flesh dripped into the condom along with the liquids. Next, she ran downstairs and tucked the underwear into the passenger side of Bill's car, just to be sure her mother would see it, and placed the condom on Bill's side, slightly under the floor mat.

Later that day the relationship between Gloria and Bill ended, just as quickly as it had begun, on the ride to work. A month later Gloria and Ailie moved back with her grandmother, who was living in Michigan.

As the years went by, Ailie's perspective of Bill had greatly mellowed. She'd never talked to her mother about Bill, but she was no longer revolted by the thought of his relationship with her mother—long ago concluding that it might've been loneliness that brought Gloria to him, rather than any form of passion. Regardless of the true meaning of the relationship, Ailie stayed away from raw chicken for more than a decade after Bill.

Maybe it's all these hormones that are making me so sensitive. Ailie thought again about the bottle of medication now sitting on the counter in her kitchen. She had to take them at some point if this awful, nauseated, feeling continued.

After a bowl of Ruby's soup Ailie opened the medicine and swallowed a pill. She slept blissfully all night and into the next morning.

7

If I pass out, please call Ruby De la Vega for assistance.

Tuesday rolled around and Ailie was determined to go back to work. She yearned for all of the diversions of a typical work day—emails, phone calls, meetings, more emails, more phone calls, more meetings, and after 5pm there was finally time to get some work done.

Ailie took an anti-nausea pill from the bottle and stared at it for a moment. She decided to cut it in half, figuring this would give her all the benefits of the medication, but only half the fatigue. She was hungry. She tossed around the idea of eating some bread, but then reached for a carton of crackers instead. The ride to work went smoothly enough. She was tired. The nausea still lingered a little, but her eagerness to get back into the office sustained her. Best of all, the weather was unseasonably cool for August, so the fresh air delighted and energized her.

Once she stepped off the elevator she avoided any small talk about the weekend and slipped into her office. She responded to lots of emails, but skipped over any that required critical thinking. She flagged those for later…for when she felt back to normal…which she hoped would be tomorrow. Or, in the worst case, some time later this week. But the email that kept grabbing her attention was Geoffrey's meeting request that asked several of the employees to join him in one of the conference rooms, in an hour. Ailie opened her purse and took the other half of the anti-nausea pill.

Several people had already gathered when Ruby saw Ailie enter the meeting room. "What are you doing here?" Ruby whispered loudly. "You should be at home! In bed! Taking care of yourself."

"I'm fine, I'm fine," said Ailie, trying to reassure Ruby and herself. "I am taking care of myself, and this is what I need. I need to get out, get a change of scenery. I need to do something other than laying at home, waiting for this torture to end."

"But if you need a change of scenery then go to the park or the movies," Ruby insisted. "You still look pale."

Geoffrey, entered, followed—of course—by his personal assistant, Timothy, and one of Ailie's colleagues, Brandon. Brandon chose the seat right next to Ailie; he brought a coffee and a donut. As soon as Brandon sat down Ailie caught scent of his cologne. Usually she found his cologne, with natural notes and a hint of citrus, refreshing. But today she found it overbearing and overwhelming. She wondered if he'd put it on two minutes ago because he smelled like he'd bathed in it. And it didn't mix well with the aroma of the coffee and donut; the combination made Ailie feel very queasy. She stood up and tried to leave the room as quietly as possible. Geoffrey looked in her direction but continued talking. It was four short steps to the glass door of the conference room, but Ailie had taken only three when she suddenly began to retch. Her feet had escaped the vomit's trajectory, but some of it splattered on the glass walls, the floor, and the door.

Geoffrey immediately brought his arm up to cover his face and turned his back to the room. "I can't look. I can't look. Somebody tell me what just happened." Timothy ran over to check if Geoffrey was okay and, in a few whispers, explained what happened.

By now everyone in the room was holding their nose, and a couple of them were brave enough to leap over the vomit and into the hallway for some air. Ailie held the door open for them. The door swept some of the liquid and chunkier bits to the side.

"Well," began Ailie, her face flush with embarrassment. "I think I should go now."

"Yes, yes. Out you go," replied Geoffrey, without turning around, his arm still shielding his face. "Tim! Timothy! Where are you? Tell me how I'm going to get out of here."

Ruby kept up with Ailie's quick pace as she walked briskly to the bathroom to rinse her mouth. "You okay?"

"Yes," replied Ailie, feeling better now that the nausea had passed. "I just need to get outta here," she said, grabbing her purse.

"Just tell me where you're going, Ailie," insisted Ruby.

"I have no idea…" Ailie responded, flustered. "I'm actually feeling better. But I *really* don't want to go home and I really hope it doesn't come back."

"Maybe…go shopping…or the library…or try a museum?" Ruby asked, skeptically. And then more confidently she added, "Look, you may or may not throw up, but if you do, at least it should be in front of strangers, right? Because if you don't want to go home, who'd you rather puke in front of—strangers, co-workers, the people you wave to everyday when you go to lunch?"

Ailie considered the question.

"Okay, hang on a minute," said Ruby. She ran over to the lobby desk and wrote something down on a piece of paper and folded it. She walked back to Ailie and tucked the piece of paper into the pocket of Ailie's cardigan.

"What's that?" Ailie asked, slightly amused.

"It says, 'My name is Ailie Faulkner. If I pass out please call Ruby De la Vega for assistance.' And I wrote my number on there. You know, just in case."

Ailie gave Ruby a hug and walked back to the bathroom to freshen up before going outside. She still had no idea where to go. She didn't want to go home where she'd sulk about what happened, and end up feeling trapped again. She certainly wanted to avoid all-things-food, so going to a restaurant or café was out of the question. Ailie also dismissed the idea of clothes shopping because she knew her sour mood would result in poor choices (like strapless dresses that squeezed her breasts into flapjacks). Therefore, she decided to follow Ruby's advice and go to The Met, the Metropolitan Museum of Art. With its vast holdings and climate control she looked forward to great airflow and halls full of strangers. The walk up to The Met, many blocks away, would hopefully help, too.

The long walk and cool air indeed did wonders for Ailie's mood. Halfway to the museum she began to feel like her old self again. Her mind no longer clouded by nausea and malaise, she thought about the new life that was growing inside of her, the fact that she would be a mother in just a matter of months, holding this tiny being in her arms. She would be its teacher, its caretaker, its protector. Once again she felt the elation of embarking on a journey that would be unlike any other. Soon she realized that her step was light and that she was smiling, radiant with joy. This change in disposition was sudden, drastic, and totally welcome.

Ailie had also worked up an appetite by the time she arrived at the museum, so she nibbled on some crackers, stored in her purse, before entering. As soon as she was finished she walked into the Great Hall, the colossal and impressive entrance of The Met, where massive limestone arches support immense domes above a mosaic of marble; the size and grandeur of the entry was on par with many of the cathedrals that Ailie remembered touring when she backpacked through Europe in her twenties. Visitors lined up in long queues before emptying their pockets, walking through metal detectors, and paying the confusing "recommended but not required, although highly encouraged" price of admission. A multitude of languages greeted her ears, voices echoed in one direction and muffled in the other, the play of sound bounced off the tall and short walls of the museum.

Once inside, Ailie's plan was to view the newer exhibits before revisiting some of those she treasured. She knew she could easily spend the whole day here. If she found a space on a bench, she would sometimes lose herself in a painting or a sculpture, trying to imagine the artists at work and how they achieved what they did with the materials they used. But, looking at her watch, she decided she should limit her time and leave the city before rush hour, when trains would be packed. The thought of a crowded train, jostling along the tracks, made her uneasy.

Ailie blissfully meandered the museum, devoting nearly an hour to gazing at various ancient fertility statues. *What reproductive issues did they struggle with?* She wondered, studying their impressive physique. *Should I get pregnant before the annual hunt or after the fall harvest? If I get pregnant we'd need to move into a larger hut and buy an extra cow.*

Soon Ailie stood in a more crowded room of The Met, viewing a painting by Johannes Vermeer. She looked for a place to sit, but nothing was available. Feeling a little faint, she pulled the water bottle out from her purse, only to discover it was empty.

Following the signs to the closest drinking fountain, Ailie finally found the right room. But the fountain was not out in the open as she'd expected, and many people were coming and going to the nearby bathrooms, so she peered around the various hidden corners of the room until she located it behind a trash can. There, she found a man hunched over the fountain, drinking.

Ailie waited impatiently as he sipped. The man turned his head and looked at her. Her first impression was that he was very attractive, but as soon as they made eye contact he began coughing as though water was caught in his throat. He recovered quickly and then walked away looking slightly embarrassed.

As the man walked off, Ailie stood still, convinced that she knew him from somewhere. She flipped through images in her head wondering where they'd met before. *But he didn't say anything to me*, she thought. *Was he a client? Did we date? Was it a bad date? I always remember the bad ones.*

That brief moment of recognition provided Ailie with just enough adrenaline and curiosity to overcome the lingering bits of morning sickness, which at this point she was ready to re-coin the term as *sickness*. She took a quick sip from the fountain and then pulled out her water bottle. "C'mon, c'mon," she muttered, as the water slowly filled the bottle. She kept looking over her shoulders to watch where the man was going, but to her relief he didn't seem to be in a hurry as he casually made his way out of the room.

This is going to nag me until I figure out how I know him. She filled her bottle about half way, screwed the cap back on and started to follow him.

His pace was leisurely but he stopped several times, turning his head. She was certain that he was glancing at the paintings that he passed, but a couple of times she suspected that he saw her, so she hung back further. As she trailed him she began to take note of his other attributes, wondering if they might jog her memory.

He had broad shoulders, but she couldn't get a good look because he wore a light jacket. She moved her eyes down to his legs for a couple of seconds but then fixed her attention on his butt. *Very nice*, she thought, tilting her head slightly as she continued to stare at his behind, shuffling through memories to see if any of them matched. But then he came to a complete stop. Ailie nearly tripped over her own feet, halting in mid-step.

The man turned his entire body and stared at an oil painting in a gilded frame. The picture, in various hues of pastels, was of a beautiful woman standing in a garden. Her long hair and simple dress flowing, as she stood in lush grasses, and surrounded by flowers. He studied the painting for several minutes.

There were only two other people in the large room and Ailie didn't want to look conspicuous. But her stomach felt funny again so she made a beeline for the soft bench at the center of the room. The man's back was to her. Small waves of nausea came and went. Her water would not last long, she thought, with the desperation of someone stranded in the desert.

The man shifted on his feet, and then took a couple of steps toward the next doorway. Ailie thought he might leave, so she stood up during a moment when her stomach seemed settled. She walked toward the painting, but didn't want to stand too close to him because that might look odd with so few people in the area. She chose a spot where she could view his profile with just a slight turn of her head. At first she was nervous so she took a few quick glances in his direction and then looked back at the painting each time. But with every glimpse it dawned on her that perhaps she didn't know him at all, perhaps she'd seen him in a news story, or maybe he was a celebrity. *In which case it might look like I'm stalking him.* Her cheeks burned with mild panic. This would be her second embarrassment for the day.

Suddenly, though, in her periphery, she noticed the man noticing her. Ailie turned her face slowly, her eyes wide with wonder, her mouth slightly open. Their eyes met, and he smiled at her. Ailie was lost for words; she remained stiff, almost stunned, staring at him. His phone buzzed, breaking their gaze. He checked the message, and then turned back to her. Ailie thought for just a second that he might come over and say something, but then he looked at his watch, and then back at her. They stood there for a moment longer, staring at one another, but not saying a word, and then he turned and walked out of the room.

Ailie gasped, but cupped her hand over her mouth as though she was afraid that she might scream out loud. *Where do I know him from?*

It dawned on her. She remembered his eyes. She reached up and gently touched her lips as she remembered his. This wasn't someone she'd dated. This wasn't a man she knew. Not really, anyway. This was the man whose picture she'd been staring at for the last ten years. It was Levi. It was her sperm donor. "Oh my god!" she squealed quietly but loud enough for the others in the room to look in her direction. "It's him…It must be him…I know it's him."

8

It was just air. A little bit of air.

Ailie rummaged through her purse to find her cell phone, while walking in the direction Levi had taken. Her shoes echoed loudly as she stepped across the marble museum floor. With Levi's fast moving feet still in sight, she tried to keep her distance but still keep up. Once her shaky hands finally located her phone, she nearly stumbled a couple of times, slowing and quickening her gait, and looking down at her phone, for Ruby's number. She considered referencing Ruby's little In Case of Emergency paper, as her fingers frustratingly kept hitting the wrong buttons; she stared at her phone like it was a foreign object.

Ruby picked up after one ring. Ailie almost felt like a schoolgirl again. She knew she shouldn't be on her phone at the museum, let alone to talk about boys, but this discovery was monumental. She whispered hurriedly to Ruby, "I found him! I found him!"

"I can barely hear you. You found who? And where are you?" Ruby asked.

A security guard approached Ailie, so she cupped her hand around the phone and held it down, next to her side. Ailie noticed that Levi was heading toward the lobby. She flashed the guard a smile and dumped her phone into her purse and walked briskly after Levi, who exited through the front doors, strode down the steps and hailed a cab. Ailie made it to the large pillars at the entryway, but the excitement of the last several minutes coupled with very little food sent her insides reeling. She ducked behind a pillar and coughed up some clear fluid and bits of crackers. A few tourists looked her way. One might've taken a photo with his phone. As soon as the last wet lump hit the pavement, she carefully descended the steps, wiping her mouth with her sleeve at the same time.

Ailie watched as Levi climbed into a taxi and momentarily considered that this *should* be the end of the line. *I should NOT follow him any further,* Ailie scolded herself. *This is ludicrous. I'm a grown woman. He's got a life. I've got a life. But…this is also an opportunity—an opportunity to know more. I could follow him for just a little bit. And it would be like research. Is this the pregnancy hormones or the baby talking?*

In the next instant she jumped in a waiting cab. "Go!" She yelled and pointed. "After that one!"

The cabbie turned around, grinning. "You want me to 'follow that cab?'"

"Yes! Now! Please." As the cab pulled forward she felt dizzying liquids build up in her stomach again. Her phone buzzed with an incoming call, but Ailie ignored it.
She pushed her knees forward to try and recline in her seat as much as possible without taking her eyes off the road.

"Oh, this is so exciting," said the old cab driver. He continued to talk, calmly, telling her about similar episodes when someone asked him to pursue another car or another taxi. Ailie had to tune out the driver. She held her nose against the smell of the old upholstery, the perfume of whoever sat in the taxi before. The taxi rocked gently with each start and stop, bumping its way across intersections and through traffic. Ailie stared at the horizon; it was all she could do for the churning that she felt inside. Without warning the air within the cab felt very hot. Ailie fanned herself with some paper and focused on her breath, breathing in and out through her mouth, rapidly, in a Lamaze fashion.

"Lady, are you okay?" the driver asked. "You ain't lookin' so good. I think I should pull over."

"No! No." Ailie tried not to raise her voice at him. "Please, please keep going. I'm fine."

Without looking Ailie reached inside her purse for another cracker or her bottle of pills. She figured whichever her hand found first would do the trick.

"Can I get you somethin'?" the driver asked. She noticed his eyes in the mirror, looking at her with concern or sympathy, she wasn't sure. Ailie took a liking to him. She really didn't want to throw up in his taxi.

Ailie popped another pill.

"Do you have some crackers maybe? Or just some bread? Bread would help. I'm just hungry, and I get a little faint when I'm hungry."

"All I got is a sandwich my wife made me. She makes the best sandwiches. But you don't look so good. I'll go halves with ya. But you gotta promise to leave me the other half," he said, opening the little door in the clear barrier between them. He handed her a paper bag with a sandwich in it. As Ailie opened the bag, the cab hit another bump. The urge to vomit overcame her; she frantically covered her mouth with the bag. The driver heard gagging sounds. "Lady! That was my lunch!"

"It's okay!" Ailie was relieved. "It was just air. A little bit of air."

"My wife told me I gotta eat my lunch. I was at home. She makes the best sandwiches. I shoulda listened..."

Ailie tuned out again as her driver continued to follow Levi's cab. They stopped at Penn Station where she handed her driver his fare and an additional twenty for a new lunch. She took the paper bag with her when she slid out of the taxi.

She staggered a little on the sidewalk, and then stood up to inhale the outside air, looking in Levi's direction. She spotted him in the crowd. He was hugging someone. Her back was turned to Ailie. She had long, beautiful hair and Levi hugged her close. Ailie combed through her own hair with her fingers as she continued to watch them hug. Her hair felt knotty and disheveled after slouching and bouncing around, and nearly vomiting, in the taxi.

Ailie was startled when, in the middle of his embrace, Levi looked in her direction and the two of them made eye contact again. He stepped back from the woman he was hugging and squinted, seemingly trying to get a better look at Ailie. She panicked. *Shit! He's seen me! Do I walk over to him? In front of his wife? Or is it his girlfriend? That's definitely not his sister. What the hell would I say? Who the hell is she?* But all that entered her mouth was a flood of saliva as she began to heave again. Ailie scanned for the nearest bush, but instead spotted a nearby trashcan. She ran over to it, spiting several times before she belched up a yellowish liquid. Her hands trembled. *Bile,* she thought, looking into the trash bin. *I really need water. I have to eat something.* Ailie glanced back to where Levi and the woman had been standing. They were gone.

***

Exhausted and embarrassed, Ailie lethargically walked along the sidewalk. Her pace was slow. The adrenaline rush was gone. Although she had no idea what she would've said to Levi, she was utterly disheartened after her failed pursuit, and in desperate need of sustenance and a place to rest. But food would certainly make her sick again, she thought. But wouldn't it be foolish to take more medication without something in her stomach? She decided to call Frieda's office for advice.

Ailie was almost relieved to hear Barbie's chipper voice. "Frieda says that if you feel that bad you *can* take two pills at the same time. But not more. And don't do it on a regular basis. BUT you have to have something in your stomach, and you might get more sleepy."

After what felt like an eternal trek, Ailie arrived at the park by the city library. She followed the scent of food to a nearby deli. There she bought a large club soda and a simple sandwich with one slice of turkey and one slice of cheese. Returning to the park, she delighted at the sight of an empty bench. First she swallowed an anti-nausea pill, and then greedily consumed her sandwich. The flavors were all too inviting after so many days of crackers and soup. After she finished her meal Ailie took another pill. Her insides twisted and turned, churning up gas and liquids. Each minute brought sensations of digestive pleasure interrupted by stomach upset.

Ailie sat on the bench, waiting for her meal to settle or exit, whichever came first. She was too tired to hunt for a more discrete place to possibly vomit. The early afternoon sunlight filtered through the leaves, warming her skin and the bench. At last the nausea pills worked their magic, soothing her stomach and calming her nerves. All at once she was overcome with a wave of contentment, her belly full and the eyelids heavy. *I'll just close my eyes for a minute...* Ailie drifted off.

9

Go deep.

"Stop that, Caesar. Sit." A voice penetrated Ailie's sleep. Ailie wasn't ready to open her eyes, but she suddenly became aware of the outside world. A dog licked her leg. "Caesar! No! What are you doing? Down!" The voice commanded.

Ailie fought to open her eyes as the sunlight and soft breeze lulled her senses again. She raised her head in the direction of the nearby voice. A police officer smiled back at her. His beagle, Caesar, barked and eagerly wagged his tail. The officer spoke to her. "Hi. The kids over here tell me you've been out a while. They asked me to check on you." He nodded toward a group of youngsters who all stood close-by, in a line, shoulder-to-shoulder, gawking at her. Ailie instantly felt the drool that had pooled on the bench below her cheek and was still sliding down the side of her mouth. She sat up as quickly as she could, but then leaned back and closed her eyes again as she waited for her blood flow to adjust.

The officer spoke again. "I couldn't wake you, so I looked for some ID, and that's when I found your note. I called your friend. She promised me you weren't drunk." He chuckled and held his hand up to his cheek, cupping his mouth so that the group of youngsters might not hear. "She told me about your condition."

"My friend?" Ailie tried to think. She was groggy. Her head felt light, separated from the rest of her body.

Someone shrieked and Ailie and the officer both turned to see Ruby and Olivia approaching. Olivia picked up her pace, gasping, "Oh my God, they probably think she's homeless."

Olivia took off her cardigan and held it up in front of Ailie, as though she were naked, shielding her from view of the curious youngsters. "Okay kids, you can go play now. Go home! Go play!" She turned to the officer. "Don't they have parents?"

The officer asked the kids to leave, but none of them moved. By now Olivia sat on one side of Ailie and Ruby sat on the other.

Caesar jumped up and placed his front paws on Ailie's lap, licking crumbs that were still stuck to her clothes. "Down!" commanded the officer again. "Don't worry, he's harmless. He's training to be an airport dog, so he's always looking for food."

Ruby and Olivia helped Ailie to her feet and then walked her out of the park. They wouldn't let go of her, even as she protested and said she was fine. Ruby hailed a cab. "I think we should take you home. Do you want us to take you home?"

Ailie yawned. "I need something to drink. My throat is so dry."

***

Upon Ailie's insistence, the three of them went to a restaurant—one with outside seating, just in case her nausea returned. The sun hadn't set yet, and the early evening summer rays cast long shadows around the women.

A waiter greeted them. Ailie was famished but reviewed the menu with caution. Finally she turned to the waiter. "Can I just get some oyster crackers? But…do you have a box of them? I'd pay for a box. But if all you have is packets, then could I get, like, a whole bowl of packets?"

"Well, I think all we have is oyster crackers," he responded, fixing his glasses. "But they come in bulk. Like a *really* big box."

"Okay, well then, can you just reach in there and grab a huge handful, at least four times? How big are your hands? I know that sounds like an odd question, but can I see one of your hands?"

He held up one hand, timidly. "We're not allowed to use our hands though. I have to use a spoon…so we don't contaminate the rest of them." Then he quickly added, "But it's a soup spoon…not a coffee spoon."

"Okay, well then can you give me at least a dozen spoonfuls…or just make sure you fill the bowl. You've got to *fill* the bowl. Please," she said with a smile. "And some seltzer too, please. Or…better bring me both seltzer *and* regular water because I'm not sure what's gonna happen."

The waiter pivoted back toward the kitchen and all eyes turned to Ailie. Ruby spoke first. "Okay, what the *hell* happened to you today? Do you remember calling me? You said, 'I found him,' and then nothing else. Who did you find? Where were you?" Olivia said nothing, waiting eagerly for Ailie's response.

"I found *him*!" Ailie exclaimed. "Levi!" And then she added a little more quietly, "My sperm donor. The father of my baby."

Her friends leaned in closer, eyes wide with amazement.

"*What?*" shrieked Olivia.

Then Ruby and Olivia spoke at once.
"How? Where?"
"What did he look like?"

Ailie stared at her friends. "Well, he looked like his picture." Then she reached into her bag and pulled out Levi's paperwork with the black and white photo. "Like this."

"But that's ten years ago!" replied Olivia excitedly. "Has he aged? Did he look nice …or sinister? And where were did you see him?" Olivia picked up the picture. "He's hot. And what's it say down here…" She scanned the page. "Five foot eleven, blonde hair, blue eyes. I'll take one."

Ruby pulled the paper away from Olivia and examined the picture as well, giggling. "I could use one of these—a nice cabana boy. You need to hire more people like this at your spa, Olivia. I promise I'd go more often." She turned to Ailie. "Okay, what happened? Just tell us the whole story from start to finish, Ailie. Everything. Don't leave out any details."

Without too many interruptions from her friends Ailie retraced the events of the day, from the museum to her awkward cab ride, ending with Levi greeting a woman at the train station.

"So…he's married," said Olivia, as if summarizing the whole story.

"We don't know that." Ruby countered. "She could've been anyone. I mean…did he hug her really *really* closely? Or how long would you say it was?"

"I'd say it was very close…for a while. Like a girlfriend…or a wife…"

"Or maybe a sister or a mom," Ruby suggested.

Olivia lightly tapped her fingers on her water glass. "And you have no idea how old she might've been? You didn't see anything…like maybe her hands? Did she have veiny hands? You know, when people get old their veins start to stick out."

"I don't know," said Ruby. "There's a girl at my gym—she's young and her veins stick out when she exercises."

"Well, what would you have said to him?" asked Olivia.

Ailie shook her head. "I…I don't know. Maybe nothing? Maybe I'd point to my belly, flash him a smile and say, 'I brought you something.' Who knows. But it was such a strange thing, to see this guy that I've been staring at in a photograph for ten years, to see him in person. It was unreal. It was so intriguing. I just…I had to look at him. I just couldn't help it…and then I followed him. I mean…ten years…and suddenly I'm connected to him." Ailie indicated her belly. "It's like there he is…standing right in front of me. It was this weird opportunity. I just wanted to know *more*."

"That is so…weird," mumbled Olivia. "But so beautiful and awesome at the same time. It's like the universe is calling…"

"Please don't talk about the universe right now," Ailie replied. "Don't you think I need a reality check? It's strange enough that I followed him. But now I can't stop thinking about it. I keep replaying the whole incident in my head."

Everyone was silent. The waiter brought out a large bowl of crackers and placed it in front of Ailie. At first she scooped up a couple of fistfuls into her mouth, like popcorn, devouring them greedily, but then she realized she should pace herself if she didn't want get sick again.

"You know what I think you should do? I think you should call Frieda," Ruby proposed. "And slow down with those crackers."

"Why would I call Frieda?"

"It's been ten years since you printed this thing." Ruby pointed to the tattered piece of paper. "And maybe there's more she can tell you about Levi. Who knows? The laws change all the time, that's why we have so many lawyers in this country, nobody can keep up, so maybe the same is true about donors? Maybe now Frieda can tell you something extra, some piece of information stored in someone's computer that's not on your paperwork."

"And then what? I show up at his house and introduce myself to his wife and kids?"

"No...first I'd google the shit out of him. Go deep. Go hard. Do all kinds of searches, whatever you can think of."

"And then you can decide if you want to...stalk him," added Olivia. "You know, that reminds me of a story," she continued. "I had this friend once, and she used to date this guy with the biggest testicles. And this is about stalking, by the way. Anyway, she was fascinated with these testicles. It's all she'd talk about at the gym. So one day she decides she's done with him, and his testicles, and she doesn't want to see him anymore, but he's *so* into her at this point..." The waiter delivered everyone's plates. Olivia continued talking.

Ailie sat back in her chair, turning away from the savory but pungent dishes on the table. She stared in the direction of the street. By now the sun's evening rays danced across rooftops and illuminated only the taller buildings. Pedestrians littered the sidewalks. Streetlights bathed the pavement with soft halos. Hungry diners streamed into nearby restaurants. Ailie considered the enormity of this city that she called home. It was at once comforting and alive, with cozy nooks and familiar neighborhoods, but at the worst of times it could feel so obscure, disconnected, and overwhelming. She didn't believe in fate or some kind of cosmic balance, but now she questioned why she'd accidentally encountered someone who, up until this point, had been a mere image etched onto paperwork. *One in a million*, she thought. Why had she bumped into him of all people? And what if she hadn't? Now that the seed was planted, she didn't want to let go of the idea that maybe, just this once, she was meant to meet someone. Maybe even meant to be with someone. As with any of Ailie's projects at work, she wanted to dive in, headfirst, devoting herself completely to her newest enterprise.

10

You call me more often zan my son.

Ailie stayed at home, the next morning, answering emails and working from her laptop. She'd lay low as surges of nausea developed and then subsided every passing hour. At first she was in bed, then on the sofa, and for a short time outside on her chaise lounge, then she took a nausea pill and went back to bed, and then back onto her sofa, and then back outside for some fresh air…and so the day passed. It was not until the afternoon that she found the energy to call Frieda's office.

Frieda's voice practically shouted through the phone. "Hallo my little Ailie! Or should I say, mine growing Ailie! How are we feeling, my dear?"

"Awful. I really hate this phase. I know I shouldn't say that because I'm lucky to even be at this stage… and with just one try. But this nausea sucks."

"It'll get better, my dear. Don't vorry. I am sure. Only a small percentage of vomen are sick troo ze whole pregnancy."

Ailie sat up. "Ah…so there's a chance this won't go away?"

"Ah…vell…let's not put ze cart in front of ze cow, Ailie, not yet. Every voman, every pregnancy, is different. Some get dry skin, others get oily. Some develop baby bumps qvickly, and others slowly. And some people tink zey have indigestion till zey give birth in the toilet. It happens." Frieda changed topics. "So Barbie said you have some qvestions for me? How can I help you?"

"Yes, well. I have some questions about my sperm donor, Levi. Do you think it's pronounced Leevi? Or maybe it's pronounced Lehvi? Anyway, I was curious if you could provide me with more information about him. It's been ten years, and I was just wondering if there's anything that wasn't on this paperwork when we printed it out way back in the day. Some details that might've been…missed? Left off? Maybe a second page?"

Frieda was quiet at first, and then asked, "So vat exactly are you looking for, my dear? Let's get to the heart of the nut. Vat piece of information are you seeking?"

"Well…," said Ailie, choosing her words carefully. "Perhaps he left a last name…somewhere? The name of a hometown, maybe? Some…thing?"

"Ah, you chose someone who gave only his first name, zat's right…. Maybe it's not even his real name. You know I cannot give you his last name if he did not vant this information out zere."

"Yes, but the other two donors had a first name and last name written on their paperwork. One even listed a hometown…and I just figured that if the laws had changed over the years, maybe the laws for donors and what donors might share, maybe those changed too? Maybe it's… retro-active?" Ailie knew she was grasping at straws.

"Zis is very unconventional, Ailie. I don't have a lot of time." Frieda was quiet again for a moment. "Just for you. Just because you've been my client for a long time. You call me more often zan my son. I gonna go back to ze agency and see if zere is something I can find. If ze agency still exists. I have to see."

"YES!" Ailie squealed, and then calmed herself. "Thank you."

"Don't thank me yet, my dear. It may take days or maybe veeks. I gonna be in touch if I find someting. See yooo!" And with that Frieda hung up.

Ailie enjoyed a fleeting moment of content and then began to wonder what she should do with any new information. If she found his address online, would she phone him? What if there was no phone listed, would she send him a letter? Or drive down his street? Though she craved more information, she hadn't a clue what the next steps would be.

In the days following their conversation, Ailie checked her messages constantly to see if she'd missed a call from Frieda. But the rest of the week passed uneventfully. Even Ailie's morning sickness, as distressful as it was at times, began to feel like part of a routine. She learned to identify some of the triggers that caused her to sprint to the toilet, and she continued to be amazed by the newfound sensitivity of her olfactory senses. She could smell herbs and spices in just about any food, not that she could identify them by name, but every familiar dish seemed to take on a new smell. She also discovered she couldn't handle her own perfume on certain days, so she made a quick trip to the pharmacy to stock up on un-scented toiletries.

Ailie continued to work from home, relieved that she didn't need to physically be in the office to get work done. Clients barely knew the difference because she usually spoke with them on her cellphone, and for team meetings she could call in or log on or video, whichever. Technology made everything possible. When Geoffrey suspected that she was looking for work elsewhere, Ailie had to reassure him it was just temporary, and he nearly offered her a raise. This made her feel a little anxious but empowered.

11

Old people know things.

It was not until a few weeks later, very late on a Monday evening, that Ailie received the call.

"Hallo, my dear. I bring good news and bad news. You ready? Ze good news is that there was one vord in Levi's file that you might have missed. One vord I am legally allowed to share. Ze bad news is I have no idea if it's a last name or someting else. It's 'Sommerfeld.' Nothing further can be found online."

"Oh, summer field?"

"No, my dear, 'Sommer,' wid an 'o' and then 'feld,' wid just an 'e.'" Frieda spelled the name as Ailie clicked away on her keyboard. "You won't find anyting online, my dear," Frieda added, with a hint of disappointment.

"Well, maybe I could…"

"Yes, you could. But it's not zere."

"But if I just try…"

"Believe me I tried. You von't find a ting online."

"We all have different ways of searching, I'm just going to…" Ailie searched again. On the other end she heard the deep sound of Frieda exhaling. "Are you smoking a cigarette?" Ailie asked in disbelief.

"Yes, my dear. But it's late. And I'm old. It's okay."

Ailie mumbled some expletives under her breath as query after query yielded nothing.

"It's to no avail, my dear. I have been around for ze birth of more than 10,000 babies, including ze Internet. You could google ze boy's name all you vant and…it's just not zere."

"There's nothing." Perplexed, Ailie set her laptop down on the table in front of her. "How can someone *not* be on the internet these days?"

Ailie thanked Frieda and hung up. She stared at her computer screen, and then punched in combination after combination of names, towns, and addresses. The results were nothing but images of random women, books by authors with the last name Sommerfeld, and a video about geoducks, *The Love Muscle of the Pacific*.

"That's impressive," Ailie whispered to herself as she watched the video, tilting her head to the side, trying to gage the actual size of the giant, spurting mollusk.

Several minutes later she went to bed. In the middle of the night, she woke again and continued to search for the name Levi Sommerfeld in a few online newspapers. By 4 a.m. she fell asleep again. In the morning, and she opened her laptop for another search. Perhaps simple searches weren't enough; she also joined a couple of lineage databases and news archives. Still, she found nothing.

On Thursday evening Ruby came to visit. She brought pizza from a restaurant down the street, while Ailie dined on soup and mashed potatoes.

"Do you mind if I have some wine? It's been one of those days at the office," Ruby said as she pulled a bottle of wine out of a paper bag.

"That's okay," said Ailie, enviously eyeing the glass as Ruby poured.

"So you couldn't find anything about this guy? Not even a snippet?" Ruby sat down on the couch beside Ailie.

"No. I'm not sure if I'm disappointed or relieved," replied Ailie, looking at her laptop on the living room table and then back at Ruby. "I've been so excited about the idea of finding him that I tend to forget that he has a life already. To me he's always been this clean slate of possibility. He was this secret option in my life, an open door that I could just walk through if I wanted. Do I take the red pill or the blue pill? Do I pick these embryos or those embryos? For so many years, I'd look at his photo, his smile. He became a fixture in my brain. I made up all kinds of exciting details about his life. But in my mind he was always single, you know? In one dream he'd be like Indiana Jones, in another dream he was a high-powered attorney, but with a really interesting life, you know? Or sometimes he was an intelligent doctor, traveling the globe to find the cure…for some deadly disease. Or a firefighter, with lots of muscles. I could reinvent him every time, again and again."

"So…I need to ask you this question." Ruby looked directly at Ailie. "You know I love you…But…*three* donors? How many embryos is that? Isn't that like Costco size? I mean, how many eggs *was* that? And why donors? Why not just eggs? And why *now*? Sorry, I guess that's more than one question."

"I was young, Ruby."

"You're still young."

"Okay, well, the first time I was *younger*. I thought it was the smart thing to do because all the other women my age, the ones who really wanted to make it, they were all talking about it. You remember what it was like. I

96

don't know how many of them actually went through with it…but in the end…when I took out the business aspect of it, you know, 'banking my eggs'…when I took that out, it was all so *personal*. And you know me, I never had a steady boyfriend, not one that I was really into for too long. A part of me said that would never change…no matter how many guys I slept with. So every time I thought about the future I'd think about who I might pick as a partner. And that seemed to change every time. So when I got around to thinking about it again a few years later I was attracted to a different type of man, someone with more distinction in his photo, the look of success. And…then the last time I went to Frieda's, four years ago, I was actually thinking about doing the whole thing. I thought about actually *having* the baby."

"Is that when you were dating the writer? The one who cried easily?"

Ailie nodded. "But in the last minute I panicked. I just picked another donor and froze the embryos instead…again. And then I picked somewhere in the world that I'd never been to and traveled there. Again. It's not like any of this was cheap."

"So what's your mom got to say about all this? I'm sure she's been dying to give you advice." Ruby laughed.

"Well, we talked about it for all of five minutes and then I locked myself in a room. It went very well." Ailie forced a smiled.

"What? This was while you were out there in June? What about now? What does she say about the pregnancy?"

"I…haven't told her yet." She shrugged her shoulders.

"*What?*" Ruby stood up. "*When* are you going to tell them? You have *got* to tell your mom! And your grandma! You know *I'm* going to hear about it if you don't tell them. Just like I hear about it whenever you don't call them for a long time."

"Exactly how often does my mother call you?"

Ruby ignored the question, shaking her head. "Nope…you are *not* doing that to me. Did you know my cousin—they live somewhere north, somewhere outside of the city, I have no idea where—anyway, they didn't tell us they were pregnant until she was six months along. Six months! They just showed up at a family picnic. Bam! Just like that, pregnant! My grandma…My poor grandma…words were just coming outta her mouth that no grandma should say. Remember she's got that lisp and how the spit gathers in the corner of her mouth? It wasn't pretty."

"Calm down, Ruby," Ailie protested. "I will tell them. But it's only been… a couple of months. We don't even know yet if this pregnancy is viable. They keep using that term, 'viable.' It's so clinical."

"Viable?" Ruby sat down again. "It's a baby not a chair." Ruby paused briefly. "Just tell your mom. Tell your grandma. You should tell them no matter what happens. And besides, you're mom's old, and your grandma's older. You need to listen to them."

"Old? What does that have to do with anything?"

"Old people know things, Ailie. They give advice. It's what they *do*. You know all that stuff you find on the Internet today? All that information had to come from somewhere. Originally it came from old people."

12

Let's get y'all hooked up.

It was a surprisingly smooth landing, almost smooth enough for her to forget the bumpy flight and multiple trips to the bathroom. Ailie had planned to spend her flight time mulling over how she would tell her mother and grandmother that she was 10 weeks pregnant. Would she tell them during a quiet dinner at the house? Would she take them to a restaurant to create a sense of celebration? Would she tell them at the beginning of the week? Or would announcing it at the beginning of her trip spoil the good mood? What if they questioned her decisions again? Perhaps she would wait until the end of her trip and tell them just before leaving?

But instead of making any decisions, Ailie spent most of the flight with a waxy white bag over her mouth or slouched over the tiny tin toilet, expecting her breakfast to reappear. Fortunately, she vomited very little, and once she stepped off the plane her stomach recovered quickly. Within a couple of hours Ailie was climbing out of her rental car, and standing in front of her mother's house. She took a deep breath, preparing herself for whatever might follow—arguments, dogs jumping, heaps of locally-sourced, organically-grown foods. She was ready this time.

Gloria ran outside and embraced Ailie. "Oh, it's so good to see you again! I can't believe our luck. We get to see you twice in just a matter of months."

Ailie held her mother tightly; she was surprised at how happy she felt to be back again so soon. During a typical visit she usually stayed for just a few days, and was always keen to get back to New York. But as she stood there, hugging her mother, she felt overwhelmed with a sense of nostalgia for all the things that were directly in front of her: the aroma of rosemary and basil that lingered on her mother's hands after a morning in the garden, the perfume of her mother's shampoo still present in her damp hair, the scent of freshly baked bread that cut through the air as soon as her mother opened the front door. Ailie's eyes welled with tears. Gloria stepped back to look at her daughter. Ailie let out a gentle laugh as she wiped the corners of her eyes. "I'm pregnant mom. Can you believe it? It won't be just us girls anymore."

***

Ailie and Gloria sat at the heavy wooden table in the center of the kitchen. Vivien stirred an enormous pot on the stovetop. "You should have a little bit of this every day while you're here," she said. "This is so good for you. While I was pregnant, my mom cooked it for me. Her mother cooked it for her, I'm sure. I cooked it for your mother when she had you."

Gloria nodded her head in confirmation. "It's delicious, Ailie, really. When I was pregnant with you, I loved it. Just divine." Gloria smiled, watching her mother fussing about the kitchen, reaching for the salt and then the pepper, occasionally leaning over the pot to taste the soupy mixture, then dumping in a garlic or an onion or some other vegetable that she plucked out of the refrigerator, and finally tasting the soup again and adjusting the spices, again.

"And this is something you can eat after you've given birth, too. It'll help you get your energy back." Vivien turned around to taste the soup, looked satisfied, and then stepped back to let it simmer. "I ate this right after I gave birth to your uncle George. Now Georgi was not a big baby, mind you, but he was born with a full head of hair *and* a tooth. The nurses said he came out with everything but his schoolbooks. Oh, and he had a big head. Nearly split me in two. Good lord. When I got done it felt like I'd been pushing for a week."

"Ouch," said Ailie, almost to herself, then she turned to her mother. "Was I a big baby?"

"No, honey." Gloria shook her head and smiled. "You were perfect."

"Now Gloria, on the other hand, she was a big baby," Vivien continued. "But her head has always been freakishly small."

"Mom! My head is the same size as yours. We wear the same sized hats," Gloria insisted, rolling her eyes.

"Yeah, but you popped out in no time. It's like I sneezed, and there you were."

"How is Uncle George by the way?" Ailie asked. "I look at his photos online sometimes, but I think it's been at least three years since I've seen him."

"Well, if he'd just return my call now and again, maybe I'd know," Vivien responded with slight vexation.

Gloria spoke to Vivien reassuringly. "Mom, he's still hurt. Give him time." Then she turned to Ailie. "The two years that we were sifting through all those books, Mom wouldn't let him come out here. Not once. Every time he offered to come out and help, she told him he'd have to wait until we were done 'moving in.' I think it confused him."

"Why wouldn't you let him come out?" Ailie asked, perplexed. "I came all the way out here to help you a couple of times. Why couldn't he come? He's just in Colorado."

"Because your Uncle George loves money," Vivien calmly responded. "That's why he's a financial advisor. I'm sure he would've been full of advice for his poor old mother and sister. He'd have lots of opinions about what we should do with our tiny collection of bills. Lots of legal advice."

Vivien stopped to mix the soup for a second before continuing. "I love that boy, but, you know every part of him lives by the book. Even when he was a boy, he was a creature of habit. He still lives in that house in Colorado. They added on to it after the kids were born, but it's the same house. He works the same job. Thank God he's good at it." Vivien opened a drawer, pulling out a spoon. "You know, after your grandfather died, things weren't easy." Ailie knew Vivien's stories well, but always listened to them as though Vivien had something new to reveal. "Georgi took it hard. He was so young. Maybe we moved around too many times when he was little? Maybe I couldn't give him that secure upbringing that he desperately needed. It's a mystery. But…this much I know: he has a big head, and he loves money."

"So when will we know if it's a boy or a girl?" Gloria asked excitedly, changing the subject.

"Well, just a few more weeks and I can pay for one of those 3D ultrasounds. But I think I'll wait and see if we can get a peek at my next check-up."

"And, what about work? Are you working while you're out here or do we have you all to ourselves? Or will we be hearing from Geoffrey again?" Gloria was referring to Geoffrey's habit of calling their house when Ailie was visiting. It was impossible to get a cell phone signal at the house, so everything had to be done over landlines.

"I'll probably check email now and again, but I've taken a short leave. Just a couple of weeks."

"Two weeks!?" Gloria nearly jumped out of her seat with glee, but instead she reached over and lovingly cradled Ailie's face in her hands. "This is going to be fantastic."

"I'm waiting for this morning sickness to work its way out of my system. I haven't told anyone at the office that I'm pregnant. Well, Ruby and Olivia know, but Ruby's the only one at the office that has any idea… I think. Or maybe there are some rumors going around already. It's been a few weeks since I've been at the office…" Ailie trailed off. She shifted in her seat recalling the humiliation of vomiting in front of her colleagues, in a meeting room with glass walls. *Perhaps everyone saw that. They all probably know,* she thought.

After devouring a bowl of her grandmother's magic elixir soup, Ailie entered one of the spare bedrooms. This one was decorated with a few of her mother's oil paintings, featuring bowls of fruit and vases of flowers. One painting displayed two halves of an avocado, side by side—one half contained the flesh and the pit, and the other half was an empty rind. Gloria had painted it when Ailie was ten years old, while they were living in Florida. It was there that they'd befriended a man named Samuel; the painting always reminded Ailie of him.

Samuel was a soft man. That's how Ailie often thought of him. His voice was soft, his arms were soft, and his eyes were soft. Even his temper was best described as soft.

Ailie and Gloria met Samuel on the day they moved to Tallahassee, a move that Ailie vehemently protested. She recalled that she and her mother had been living in Maine, with Vivien, for a couple of years, when her mother announced, seemingly out of the blue, that it was time for her and Ailie to strike out on their own. Gloria was just shy of her thirtieth birthday and said she felt inspired by what she'd read in a guide book about Tallahassee, with its affordable housing, agreeable climate and promise of work.

Samuel introduced himself within an hour of their arrival, and said he lived just below them and worked at the local university. Ailie couldn't remember how old he was, except that his beard and greying hair made him appear many years older than her mother. He was a very kind and generous man, and Ailie and her mother quickly learned to rely heavily on him for answers to their questions about their new surroundings. Eventually they leaned on him for the emotional, and sometimes financial, support that they needed, separated from everything and everyone they'd known in Maine. But Samuel didn't seem to mind—he was a bachelor and loved to cook, often inviting them over for dinner. Ailie remembered delicious chili recipes, nights outside barbequing, and her first time enjoying a seafood dish.

As soon as they'd arrived, Gloria started her job as a full time receptionist, which meant that Ailie was a latchkey kid—she was left on her own before and after school—something she'd grown accustomed to whenever she and her mother lived on their own. As luck would have it, Samuel worked odd hours at the university and was often home, so once they got to know him well enough, Gloria allowed Ailie to visit with Samuel on her own. As a result, Ailie bonded quickly with Samuel— he was funny and talkative and she chatted to him every day after classes. Sometimes, he helped her with her homework and he had an answer for just about any question she threw at him. Samuel was great at making Ailie feel included, especially during their home-style dinners—after her mother and Samuel exchanged hugs and quick kisses, her mother would talk about her work at the office, Samuel about teaching at the university, and Ailie about her new school. As the weeks turned into months, and Samuel became more and more of a fixture in their lives, Ailie began to entertain the idea that she, Gloria and Samuel were becoming a unit, a family of three.

But just after the holidays that year, everything came to a halt. Ailie remembered that night—it was a very warm January evening, and they were sitting at Samuel's kitchen table, a bowl of his homemade guacamole dip in the center. Samuel had taught Ailie how to make the 'dip' using Florida avocados, which were not as common as their California cousins. He said that their thin skins made them more perishable, but once you cut them open, they'd last much longer than the California variety. He also said that Florida avocados didn't have as great a reputation because they were considered flavorless and boring, but the key to loving them was to understand what other ingredients made them shine. To make the dip he added livelier flavors, such as spicy onions and chunks of sweet tomato, paired with the bitterness of salt and the nuttiness of olive oil, and then he added lime juice and cilantro to give it a tangy, peppery finish. Once he tossed them all together, Ailie scooped the bits into her mouth with a chip, just like meaty salad. Samuel made the dish on special occasions, and it quickly became one of Ailie's favorites.

Ailie had a chip in her hand and was waiting for her mother to tell her that it was okay to start eating, when Samuel got down on one knee in front of Gloria, presenting her with a small box. Ailie was always confused about what happened next, but she recalled her mother protesting, insisting that she didn't feel the same way, while Samuel, in his soft voice, begged and pleaded, telling Gloria how much he loved and adored her—that he thought she wanted this as much as he did. This went on for many minutes, until Gloria, tears in her eyes, finally stood up, took Ailie by the arm, and they left. Ailie still held the chip in her hand as they walked back to their apartment.

Once they were home, Ailie and her mother argued back and forth. Ailie wept, she couldn't understand how her mother didn't care for such a kind, attentive man, the first person, and in retrospect the only person that Ailie had ever considered as something of a father figure. She remembered being furious at her mother for rejecting Samuel, for rejecting his love, and his desire to be a family. But Gloria didn't have the patience to explain to Ailie over and over again, day after day, why she felt nothing more than friendship for Samuel. Ailie wasn't allowed to see Samuel again after that fateful night at his house, and she couldn't remember seeing him anywhere at the apartment complex.

A couple of weeks later Gloria told Ailie that they were headed back to Maine—she claimed that the job in Florida was too stressful. Ailie was thrilled to move back to Maine and back to her old school. Reunited with her grandmother, she could forget about Florida and about the loss of Samuel.

Ailie remembered telling Olivia and Ruby about Samuel, one night over dinner and several glasses of wine. By the end of the evening, they'd concluded that perhaps Ailie's mother had also seen Samuel as somewhat of a father figure, someone who filled the void of Vivien and was an adult that Gloria could trust and rely on when she had no one else around. They discussed Samuel and Gloria for over an hour, and then the conversation turned to single moms, latchkey kids, and how much parenting had changed…and not changed.

Ailie traced her fingers along the tiny ridges of paint on the filled half of the avocado. She wondered where Samuel might be today, if he was still alive. She wondered if he'd found another family to adopt. Still looking at the painting, she sat down on the bed and laid her head on the pillow. It was late afternoon, but jetlag coupled with her grandmother's soup, and freshly ironed sheets smelling of jasmine, provided a euphoric cocktail that sent her into a deep sleep until morning.

***

Ailie looked out the window. Hints of dark pink and purple illuminated the farthest corner of the horizon. She made a brief search for her phone but then gave up when her craving for chamomile tea took over. She stepped out of her room, toward the kitchen, guessing it was nearing 7 a.m.. The courtyard was blanketed in shades of blue and green, muted by a delicate envelope of dew. Her mother had provided her with an enormous cardigan, perhaps a remnant of the '80s, hand knit out of a soft ivory-colored wool. Ailie wrapped it tightly around herself and knotted the front. She tiptoed across the courtyard to the kitchen door, fumbling in her pajama pockets to find the right key. Ailie didn't want to wake anyone, especially the dogs.

"It's okay, it's unlocked," someone announced from afar. Ailie jumped and turned to see her grandmother waving from a chaise lounge at the corner of the yard. As Ailie approached, she saw Vivien held a steaming cup of coffee in her left hand, and a shotgun rested between her right arm and her hip.

"What are you doing out here, grandma?" Ailie whispered.

"Don't worry." Vivien motioned for Ailie to sit down beside her. "Those dogs won't hear you, they won't bark. They sleep better than I do. And your mom always sleeps on her good ear these days, so she won't hear a thing."

"It's so early. Why are you up?"

"Sometimes I can't sleep. So I come out here. I like to watch the sun rise. It reminds me of your grandpa."

"Did grandpa like sunrises?" Ailie assumed everyone liked sunrises. But she'd never met her grandfather because he died long before she was born.

"No, no." Vivien gave a gentle laugh. "He hated them. But for all the wrong reasons. He was so annoyed in the mornings. The sunrise meant he had to get to work. Or sometimes he had to leave before the sun came up. No, he was better with sunsets…and a gin and tonic. But, you know…sometimes you remember a person for what they loved most, and your grandpa, well, he loved life, he loved us, he liked just about everything…except sunrise and going to work. So after all these years, that's what sticks in my mind. The sunrise is always a reminder. His fiery words, throwing his fist in the air at the sun…and then he'd calmly climb in the car…and then drive off to work."

"You must miss him a lot," Ailie said delicately.

"Well, of course I do. But, you know, looking back we were married such a short time… before he had that heart attack. It was enough time to fall in love, get married and start a family. When we met we knew right away…and we didn't even wait two weeks before we talked about living the rest of our lives together. Who knew 'the rest of our lives' meant two years. Just a blip. But it means I'll always remember him as a saint. Don't get me wrong." Vivien laughed again. "Sometimes he was such a pain in the ass! But time tends to blend his annoying traits with his good ones. In the end, it's the good memories that stay with you… Except the sunrise. Then I can feel his passion again." Vivien made a fist with one of her hands and waved it in the air.

For a few minutes, they watched the colors of the sunrise bleed across the horizon.

"You know, Ailie," said Vivien, in a soft tone. "We really owe you an apology."

"What for?"

"Because you never had anyone to call dad. You never had any male examples in your life. Well, except for your Uncle George, but he went away to college when you were still very little. I mean, it's a wonder you didn't grow up sleeping around with all the town riffraff, throwing your body at any old thing. It's amazing you weren't a slut."

"Oh…" replied Ailie, a bit shocked by her grandmother's choice of words. "That's an interesting way to think about it grandma. Thank you for your…apology, but I don't think it was a bad thing. If anything I think I had way too many 'male examples' in my life when I was living with mom. I think she had…a few too many things going on when we lived together— too many dreams and not enough focus, something like that…and I had the ill fortune to get dragged along for the ride. But, listen, I really feel like I have *you* to thank for keeping me on a straight path. You taught me how to be hardcore, not get emotional about bumps in the road or what other people have to say, and just focus on what's ahead. As a matter of fact, I think I was a little too hard on the outside for a while. I didn't invest much in male relationships…for a long time."

"Don't be too hard on your mom, Ailie. It wasn't always easy for her, growing up with me and Georgi."

"What do you mean, grandma?" Ailie smiled lovingly at her grandmother. "You've always been the rock in our family. A bit rough on the edges, but the one who holds up no matter what's going on."

Vivien returned the smile and looked down at her coffee cup for several minutes before saying anything. Ailie noticed her grandmother changed to a more serious demeanor. "Your mom was not always the flaky, irresponsible person that you seem to think. No…no…I see you shaking your head, but I remember the way you used to fight, the two of you. The things you guys said to each other. Even now, when you get along so much better, I've seen the way you sometimes dismiss her advice. And she calls you at least once a week, but you only return her calls about…once a month. Or maybe every other month."

"Well, I've been busy. I get home and I'm too drained for a long conversation. But don't worry I'll probably be calling more often once the baby arrives, especially while I'm away from work. And we'll come out here to visit you guys. I like coming out here now. This is a bigger space, and we have a great time together a few weekends each year."

"But there is a conversation, or maybe lots of conversations, that you and your mom need to have," Vivien insisted. "Without a dad around to help, your mom grew up quick. I wasn't easy on her because our life wasn't easy. She had you, when she was way too young, and then she moved out. She was on her own for the first time. Well, you were there too, but suddenly she's free to do whatever she wants. And then she moves back in and then she moves back out, again and again. I tried to help, but I think both of you were growing up at the same time. And then…in no time you were off to college, and you never came home again."

Ailie buried her head in her hands. She missed caffeine. This was a very deep conversation to process first thing in the morning.

"I have apologized a lot to your mom over the years, Ailie. We've had time to work out the kinks. And I'm not saying that she'll apologize to you for anything, but maybe she just wants a chance to talk to you about the past. Shit, that's all you do as a mom—apologize for the past. As a matter of fact I still pick up the phone in the middle of the night and call Gloria with apologies."

"You guys live in the same house."

"Yes, but we've got two different phone lines, silly. She says I'm a social butterfly. I go out a lot." She winked at Ailie. "Hell, I've probably apologized for that too." Vivien turned her attention back to the sunrise before she spoke again, "Do you ever ask your mom about your dad?"

"Well, sometimes. Kind of, I guess. I don't know, grandma, we talk about other things. I'm always here for such a short time."

"That's just it, Ailie, you're always here for such a short time."

Their conversation was interrupted when Ailie's phone unexpectedly made a noise. "Where is that coming from?" She patted her clothes and located her phone in one of the deep pockets of her cardigan. "What? I have a message. But I've got no bars." She held the phone up, moving it from side to side to find a signal. "It says Ruby left a message… and she called me…a few times, but I can't get more than a bar and it only lasts about a second."

"Can you listen to your messages from my room phone? It's just inside the door." Vivien pointed toward the house.

Eager to find out why Ruby called repeatedly, Ailie dialed her number instead of listening to the message. It would be close to 10 a.m. on the east coast, and Ailie wondered if she might be in a meeting.

"Boy, have I been trying to get a hold of you," Ruby said, answering after the first ring. "I was about to call your mom's house but figured it was too early."

"We're up now. What's going on?"

"Someone else is supposed to join us any minute now. Hang on, let me put Francoise on the phone."

"Wait. Where are you? Who's Francoise?"

"My interior designer."

"Why would I talk to your decorator? When did you get a decorator?"

"Interior designer," Ruby corrected her. "Didn't I tell you? It was Barry's birthday gift—we're getting part of the downstairs re-done this month. But that's not the point. Francoise has been in this business for years, and when I told him your story, about Levi, he thinks he recognizes the name! Hang on…"

"You shared my story with your designer?"

"Hey darlin'," Francoise responded in a soft tenor. With a name like Francoise, Ailie was expecting a thick French accent; instead, she detected a slight southern twang. "Don't you worry, we were just havin' an innocent conversation, nothin' more. I can assure you, Ruby spoke out of love."

"Oh. Well…then…thank you." Ailie sat down on the bed.

"So let's get down to the nitty gritty because we don't have a lot of time here. Ruby's got a beautiful space, and we're goin' over some beautiful ideas."

"Fine."

"Fine?"

"I mean, go ahead. I'm listening."

"Sounds like you been pining after Levi way too long. Let's see if we cain't get y'all hooked up."

"R…right," Ailie responded, apprehensively.

"Let's see," he began, "about ten years ago…or…was it ten years? Gosh, I can't believe a decade goes by so fast. Anyway, I did this big re-design for a woman named Margo. She wanted everything tore up—the kitchen, the fireplace, her ex-husband—she was goin' through a divorce, you see. She had a lot of money to play with, and she was a piece of work, let me tell ya. Constantly changing her mind…"

"U-huh." Ailie hung on every word.

"Anyway, Miss Margo collected antiques, too, and so did her husband. I want to say the feller's name was Roger."

"Sure."

"Now, you understand, darlin', normally I try not to pry into the lives of my clients."

"Of course."

"But, Margo, she came home one day and was all a flutter about this 'hot antiques dealer.' She would not stop talkin' about him, and I swear that if I recall correctly, which I often do, his name was Sommerfeld. Now, Ailie, you might be askin' yerself—how does he remember this after all these years?"

"Yep. That's what I'm askin'."

"See, she was so excited about this guy, Levi, that she tried to hook him up with her daughter, Myrna. But he wasn't havin' it. I think they only lasted one date. It's not like she was particularly ugly or anything, but I think he just liked to play the field. Ya know what I mean?"

"Oh…" Ailie's back retreated into a slouch.

"After that one date Myrna was heartbroken, and Margo had to find herself a new antiques dealer. Someone said he even closed up shop after that. Gone. Left the city. She was bendin' my ear about it, the whole rest o' the summer."

"Hmm. Okay." Ailie tried not to sound too disappointed.

"But here's where the story picks up again."

"Yay!" She sat up again.

"Margo's new husband, Harold, asked me to come by and do some work last month. He also wanted me to get rid of some leftovers that Margo's ex had in storage. One of 'em was a desk, and inside the desk, I found lotsa business cards…"

"Was Levi's among them?" Ailie slid to the edge of the bed.

"That's what I'm gettin' at—I think it was. I mean, it is. I mean I got it here in my wallet. Would you just hold the phone for me a sec, sugar?"

Ruby took the phone, "Ooh! Isn't this exciting?"

Ailie shouted, "Yes! Yes!"

"Let's see…" It was Francoise again. "Nothin' fancy…on the front it says, 'Sommerfeld,' in big letters. On the back…there's some dates and times, and the name 'Levi,' with a big 'x' over it. Not sure what that 'sposed to mean…."

Her heart raced. "Well, what else does it say?"

"Here we go…there's two addresses: one in San Francisco, and another in Santa Monica. Lemme give you both."

"Thanks, Francoise!" Ailie copied down the addresses. The one near Santa Monica was nearly two hours away.

Ruby returned to the phone, "This is the break you were hoping for, isn't it? Gotta run! I think they're here."

Ailie leapt off the bed and moved her hips side to side in a brief happy dance, and then picked up the phone again.

Olivia answered after just two rings. "Hi beautiful! What's going on?"

"Hi! Listen, what are you doing? Are you busy? Do you have a sec?"

"I do," replied Olivia, calmly. "Except I'm sitting with…my face buried in a large…foam ring…so you're going to have to speak a *little* more slowly. I'm in the middle of my back massage. I'm…relaxing."

Ailie slowed down. "Okay…okay…It's possible…that I might've found Levi."

"Really?" Olivia's voice perked up. "What? Where? How?"

"Ruby's decorator—I mean, designer—told me."

"Francoise?"

"Yes. Have you met him?"

"No, but we talked on the phone the other day. He gave me a delicious recipe for couscous."

Ailie shook her head. "Okay, tell me about that later. Listen, it sounds like he might have a couple of stores here on the west coast, and one of them is kind of nearby. Well…more like two hours away. But he also described him as a 'player.'" She went on to tell Olivia about her conversation with Francoise.

"So?" asked Olivia, eagerly. "That's never stopped you before. Players can be great in bed! They spend all that time *perfecting* their skills! No…wait…that's the old me talking." She paused for a second and then spoke again, calmly. "Levi is an unknown. No matter what happened in the past, people grow a lot in ten years. Besides, we don't know what really took place between him and Margo or Myrna, or whatever that daughter's name was, all those years ago. Maybe she was very homely or too lonely or too talkative. Whatever. You're on vacation. Go down there. Today! Find out if it's *him!*"

Ailie hung up and wondered how easily she could convince her mother to drive two hours south to go antiquing today.

13

We have a lot of wood that is dark.

Gloria sat down at the large kitchen table, a tiny cup of espresso in front of her. "Well, I don't mind going to an antique shop now and again, Ailie. But most of the things I buy are from yard sales. You know I *refurbish* furniture. Sometimes I repurpose it. I look for deals. Sometimes they're antiques, but most often it's just something that's been forgotten. It's fun to find something old *and* cheap and give it new life." Gloria took a sip from the demitasse before continuing. "But you say this place is down near Santa Monica? And what does Olivia want again?"

"She was looking for some kind of tea set, I think." Ailie hated to lie to her mother, but curiosity nagged her. She wanted to find out what was in Santa Monica. Ailie called the shop that Frieda had told her about; no one answered but a machine picked up, providing hours and directions. It had been several weeks since her near encounter with Levi at the museum, and this new lead made her impatient to start her search again. She wanted to sit in the car *now* and drive down to the antique shop and look for him. But the last thing she wanted was an elaborate discussion or lecture against the idea of finding her sperm donor.

She thought about the term 'sperm donor.' He was, after all, just a sperm donor because they'd never truly met or been formally introduced. But she decided that the term was too technical, too unemotional to suit her story. Perhaps 'biological father' was a better description in case she felt the need to explain everything to Gloria and Vivien. Still she worried that her mother or grandmother would try to talk her out of this search, this quest.

In her effort to keep this secret, she forced herself to suppress any excitement or anxiety—such stress would surely lead to nausea. She wanted her mother to come along as a friend, as a source of distraction, and someone who could drive in case anti-nausea pills were necessary. Also, Ailie knew nothing about antiques or yard sales for that matter. She tried to recall the last time she'd been to someone's yard in New York. What qualified as a yard in the city consisted mostly of concrete slabs or tile at the back of the house, like miniature courtyards sandwiched between tall, tightly packed houses. If you were lucky enough you could fit a few chairs and a table in your 'yard.' But most of the 'yard sales' she'd seen took place in front of the house, on sidewalks, streets, and in large alleys, or sometimes inside a home—any place that provided enough room to fit a large number of people…and that place was not often a 'yard.'

"A tea set?" her mother asked, trying to remember the conversations she'd had with Olivia.

"Well, let's just say that Olivia has a certain taste in tea sets. And someone told me I might find something of interest at this particular shop." Separately, neither of these statements were fabrications. Ailie instantly felt less deceitful. "I also took the liberty of looking up some sales that should be nearby. I woke early, so I jumped online and found these." Ailie slid a piece of paper across the table to her mother. On it she'd scribbled a few addresses that promised estate sales, tag sales, and one flea market.

"Oh?" Gloria put on her reading glasses and held the paper in front of her. Vivien looked over her shoulder. "It's been a while since we've visited that area. We could do with a little travel out of town, right mom?" Gloria looked up at Vivien and then over at Ailie. "Let's take a road trip."

***

Ailie requested to drive, knowing that the winding roads and length of the trip might be too much for her stomach if she sat in the passenger seat. She expected that they'd travel in Vivien's beautiful 1960s convertible and tried to hide her disappointment when Vivien pulled up in the battered pick-up truck from the backyard. Ailie had always assumed it was a permanent fixture among the tall grasses. Vivien parked the pick-up in front of her, hopped out gingerly and patted the hood of the car. "Ailie, this is Bessie. She comes with us on all our treasure hunts. She came with the property. Old but reliable, and she can carry a ton."

The old pick-up puttered down the driveway with the three women sitting side by side in the front seat. Ailie drove, Vivien sat by the passenger-side window, and Gloria sat in the center, knitting.

Vivien nodded off about ten minutes into the drive, while Gloria focused on the pattern in front of her, so Ailie used the quiet time to figure out a strategy for her arrival to Levi's shop. *Let's say he's actually there—which could be a long shot—but what do I say? What do I do? Do I walk around his shop first, observing him from afar? Like a lioness, going in for the kill. That's terrible.* Ailie's heart began to race. *Shake it off, Ailie. We do NOT get nervous about meeting new people. We LOVE meeting new people.* Her lips felt cold. *Crap, the last time I got nervous in front of someone I froze. That seems like a lifetime ago.*

She remembered her senior year when Dwain Keller, a football player, asked her out. She had no idea what to talk about, so when they arrived to the movies she bought a huge tub of popcorn, with way too much butter, consuming all of it in the short span of ten minutes. Halfway through the movie she threw up—all over the floor and on the seat next to her. She was mortified; she couldn't move. Ailie stayed in her seat and stared at the screen as if nothing had happened. Finally, Dwain stood up to tell the theater manager.

Ailie thought again about Levi. *If I get too nervous I should just walk around the shop, loading my cart with things, until the feeling goes away. But then I'd have to pay for all these things…or put them all back.* Sweat formed between her palms and the steering wheel. She grabbed a tissue from a small box tucked into the dashboard. *I should just be upfront with him, 'Hello Levi, I'm not here to buy anything but a minute of your time.'*

"Are you okay, honey?" asked Gloria, setting down her knitting needles. "I'm worried. Your face is a bit pale. Should we go home?"

"No!" Ailie's loud response woke Vivien. "No," she said more quietly. "I just…let's talk about something. The weather. Anything. I just need a distraction…to get my mind off work."

"Oh! Not a problem! I get so excited on days like this, when we're out looking for things." Vivien broke into a smile and began talking about the old guns she'd been collecting lately.

At last—and to Ailie's relief, after listening to 90 minutes of frontier history—the women pulled into a parking lot, at the address that Frieda had given to Ailie. Gloria and Vivien hopped out of the truck, gingerly walking to the front door. Ailie trailed behind them, stalling as she pretended to check her phone messages. She looked up at the store sign, *Adrift ~ Architectural Salvage*. Once again her pulse raced. She looked down at her hands, balling them into fists as they trembled. *Stop! Stop*. But as soon as she had control of her hands, her legs felt disjointed. Breathing down into her stomach, she finally opened the door and walked in.

Inside, the store was made up of two enormous bays, separated by red brick walls. Furniture, pottery, immense ceramic vases, hand-carved statues, wooden boxes, musical instruments, and vintage posters—all displayed in rows along a distressed concrete floor. Smaller items were stacked neatly on top of the larger furniture, and brighter elements were carefully placed between darker items, giving the seemingly-haphazard arrangements a very elegant look. Skylights, at the end of each aisle, brightened the farthest corners of the shop, inviting the curious to explore the most remote sections of the store.

"This great, Ailie!" Gloria whispered. "We might be here a while." She winked at Ailie before walking off to find Vivien who had already disappeared somewhere.

Ailie surveyed the space before she began to explore. Up and down each row, customers were poking around, lifting items, inspecting them. She expected to see mostly older women and men, of which there were plenty—dressed in jeans and t-shirts, ready to pick through items no matter what their condition—but she also saw a number of young couples, strolling around together, two of which just arrived to the shop on their bicycles. Noticing Ailie's contemplative gaze, an employee tapped her on the shoulder and asked her if she needed any assistance. "Yes," Ailie responded, her hands cold, and her lips heavy and numb. "I…I'm looking for someone named Levi. Does he work here?"

"Levi?" The girl tapped her finger on her chin as she thought. An older man, with an enormous belly, walked by and the girl turned to him. "Joe, is there a Levi here?"

"Oh, I know who she's talkin' about. Come with me." He waved for Ailie to follow him as he ambled to the back of the shop. They stood in an enormous doorway, and he pointed to the opposite corner of the back lot. "Just follow this path, go right, then left, then straight, and down to the back. He's in the shop."

Ailie followed a dirt path lined with leaning stacks of barn doors, regular doors, reclaimed wood, stone, and window frames. Twice she stumbled on small bits of wood that jutted out into the trail, she was so focused on the possibility that she might see Levi around the next corner. She was visibly nervous with anticipation: halting to rub her hands together because they were still cold and shaking; stopping again to slap her cheeks to bring the color back into her face; standing in place to move her mouth around, like she was warming up to sing, so that she could bring some feeling back into her lips. She wanted to find Levi, to be done with this search, but she couldn't think of a thing to say to him.

At last she arrived at the end of the short trail, where she found a small building with garage doors open on two sides. Backed up to the garage door farthest from her was a small truck, loaded with pieces similar to those she'd seen in the store. And there he was, through the garage door closest to her. There he was—Levi, Leevi, Lehvi, who knows—unloading and examining a couple of large items. Cautiously, she stopped a few feet outside of the door. She wasn't sure if her legs could move any further. Her limbs felt clumsy, her breath short, but her eyes were steady, completely fixed on him. He hadn't seen her yet, so she took the opportunity to watch him, if only a few minutes.

Levi wore faded jeans, a brown, leather belt and work boots. His shirt hung on the wall beside him. Ailie's eyes traced the lines of the muscles on his chest and forearms. He looked incredibly fit. He wiped his brow with his arm. His skin was tanned but not too tanned and if you looked closely—and Ailie leaned as closely as she could without falling over—you could spot a thin layer of sweat that had begun to form, catching the light with every movement. His hair was dark at the roots, but looked blonder on the edges and a little longer than what she recalled from the museum. She was mesmerized, her mouth agape. She watched him move back and forth between the workbench and a desk. He was building something or repairing something, Ailie wasn't sure. He was focused on a project. Every time he leaned over to look at something on the table, she watched how his body moved inside his jeans.

Ailie was startled when he became aware of her presence, and he turned and looked at her. "Oh, I'm so sorry," he said, reaching for his shirt and draping it over himself to button up. His cheeks became rosy. He looked back up at her, so he could see her better, as she entered the shop.

Ailie was glad she'd worn a tan summer dress; the color perfectly accentuated her chestnut hair, which fell in long tresses around her neck and down her shoulders, a few locks curled by her breasts. The dress was stylish but comfortable, with an empire waist that emphasized her curves and growing cleavage. *The first benefit of pregnancy*, she thought. She noticed that he watched her intently as she approached. She walked toward him feeling a mixture of confidence and unsettled nerves.

Stopping just couple of feet in front of him, she didn't expect him to gaze at her, but she loved the feeling it produced, like everything around them had disappeared, and it was just the two of them. Their eyes stayed fixed on one another.

Standing so close, she was completely taken in by him. She could smell his cologne. Ailie resisted the impulse to reach out and touch him; his face was now so familiar to her. He stood about three or four inches taller than her.

Perfect, she thought. She noticed a few fine lines that had developed since that black and white photo was printed more than a decade ago. That photo was still in her purse. After realizing this, she clutched her purse tightly to her chest. Neither of them said anything, waiting for the other one to speak.

"Hi," they both said at the same time. Ailie was uncertain, but for a moment she thought he vaguely recognized her.

"I'm sorry, you go," he said.

"No you go," she replied, politely.

"Okay," he said, as though thinking about what he should say next. "Um…Is there anything I can help you with?" He asked, gently, smiling at her.

She was still unprepared for questions. Swallowing hard, her throat was dry. *Oh no*, she thought, *please don't vomit, please don't vomit, please don't vomit.* "Yes!" Ailie replied, surprised by her own volume. "There is…something you can help me with." She stumbled on her words, trying to form a sentence. "My friend…my friend said that a man named Levi…. I assume that's you?" She giggled nervously but didn't wait for him to respond. "A man *here*, could help me with…" Ailie looked around for something small. "A chair…that I need for my…desk."

"A chair?" he asked, perhaps noticing the uncertainty in her voice.

"A chair," she replied in an unsure, quivery tone, as if asking a question.

"Okay." He paused to look around. "Well, is there a particular style you're looking for? Is this chair for comfort or more for display?"

Her smile ached. She straightened her back and attempted a more professional demeanor. "What I meant to say is that I need a chair…that…" Ailie thought about the type of furniture her mother had around her house. "Is wooden… and it should match…an…older look. We have a lot of wood that is dark…around the house."

"There you are!" Ailie heard her mother's voice behind her. "When I couldn't find you in the store, that kindly old man told me I might find you back here, and…" Gloria observed Levi. "Well, hello!" She walked over carrying a basket full of small items.

Ailie breathed a momentary sigh of relief as Gloria's interruption diverted the conversation.

Vivien appeared behind Gloria. "Hi!" She leaned in, extending her hand. "Boy, aren't you a tall glass of water. I'm Vivien, this gorgeous, young lady's grandmother."

He shook Vivien's hand. By now his face was almost as flush as Ailie's.

Before the women could say anything else, the older man from inside the store, came over to address Levi. "Son, the school called again on the store phone. They really need you to call back today. We've got plenty of people here now, and Steve's here too, so he can help with whatever needs liftin'."

"Oh yeah," Levi responded, scratching his head. "I keep meaning to call them back. Okay…" He bit his lower lip, looking at Ailie as though he needed to make a quick decision. "Okay," he said again, more quietly. "Joe, I'll just go to the coffee shop and call them back on my phone." And then he turned to Ailie. "Um…well, I guess Joe can probably help you. It was nice to meet you…" He prompted her for her name.

"Ailie," she replied. "Ailie Faulkner."

"Well, Ailie Faulkner," he smiled at her again. "I'm going to go across the street, to that coffee shop, and make a phone call…" He indicated the café on the corner.

"That's okay, that's okay," Ailie said gently, trying to hide her disappointment, her mild panic, the feeling of nausea that bubbled in her stomach.

"Thanks again, Joe." Levi patted the older man on the back, and then looked at Ailie before he turned to go. Ailie watched him through the window of the shop as he crossed the street to the café.

"Joe, can I ask you a question?" asked Vivien. "It's about a piece I saw in the store."

Ailie didn't turn away from the window. She barely heard her grandmother and Joe chatting away in the background, when she sensed that her mother was standing next to her, staring at her.

Ailie turned to her. "What?"

"Who was *that*?"

"Levi," Ailie answered quietly, looking out the window again. "Just a guy…named Levi."

"Ailie, I know we haven't spent a ton of time together in the last… however many years, but I can tell when you *like* something."

"What? What do you mean?" Ailie asked.

"You were absolutely smitten by that guy. You were giddy. I watched you…"

"You were watching us? Mom…"

"Yes, I watched you because I rarely get the chance to see you with someone. It was nice. It was refreshing! You should go over there. Talk to him." Gloria nudged Ailie in the direction of the café. "I think he might've wanted you to."

"What's going on?" Vivien asked curiously before heading back into the store. She held a small, antique pistol in one hand.

"Nothing, grandma. It's nothing." Ailie kept her eyes on the café.

"I'm telling her to go over to that coffee shop and talk to that guy again."
Gloria turned to Vivien. "Did you see the way they looked at each other?
The way she was staring at him, and how he was smiling at her? Good
heavens. Ailie, don't worry about us. At this rate grandma and I will be here
a while longer. And I haven't seen a single tea set here, honey."

"Tea set?" Ailie asked.

"Go on," Vivien insisted. "Go to over there and buy yourself whatever
pregnant people drink these days. We'll be here." She winked and said more
quietly, "That baby won't find a daddy on its own, you know."

14

This is what it's like resting on a giant baby flamingo.

Ailie crossed the street, her sense of adventure restored. Though her mother's nudging embarrassed her, it encouraged her too. Entering the coffee shop, nearly every table was occupied—people on their laptops, reading on their phones, a few groups talking excitedly, huddled around small tables. One person sat on a beanbag, reading a book. On the left side of the café a couple of floor to ceiling windows opened onto the sidewalk, a soft breeze floated through the room. Ailie caught sight of Levi at a table near the sidewalk, talking on his phone. She walked up to the counter and placed her order and stood by, waiting for the barista. She scanned the store for some bookshelves or merchandise or any additional excuse to be there.

"Hi." Ailie turned to see that Levi was speaking to her. She walked over to his table. "I'm sorry I had to run out like that, but I had to make that call."

"That's okay!" Ailie giggled, nervously, "I... had to come over here too. Still trying to wake up. I haven't had my coffee."

"Decaf latte!" the barista announced. "A decaf latte for Ally!"

"Would you excuse me for just a moment?" She trotted over to the bar, and leaned over the counter to the barista. "My name is pronounced *Ayyyleee.* Please." She grabbed her drink, turned to go, but then turned around again and cheerfully added, "Thank you!"

Ailie walked back over and stood at Levi's table. The two of them grinned at one another. He stood up. "Oh, I'm sorry. Please, sit down. I'm sure I have a few minutes before Joe calls me back."

"Sure. Okay." Ailie sat down quickly, perhaps too quickly, she thought. "So…is that your dad in there? I noticed he called you 'son.'"

"No, that's just Joe. He calls everyone son."

"And, is that your store? Is that what you do? Here? Antiquing?"

"I'm part owner, actually. My friend's family owned a lot of land in the area a long time ago, and when they sold the last of it, this is what was left. It was an old warehouse, and we converted it. Slowly."

Wow, he's got nice eyes, she thought, resting her chin in her palm. *They're a brilliant blue in this light.*

"Feels like it took forever," he recalled. "But the store does good business these days." He smiled at her. "But it's not just antiques, it's a lot of salvaging too…"

He hasn't shaved. He looks great that way.

"…Sometimes I make furniture, or I help with hard to find items. And, when there's time I also help restore houses…or fix them up for resale…"

Oh shit, she thought, *I know nothing about any of these things. Olivia watches HGTV. I should call her.*

He flashed another grin. "And…Miss Faulkner, what do you do? Do you work around here too? I feel like we've met before."

126

Ailie hesitated. She couldn't take her eyes off of him. It was an effort for her to ease her smile. Her cheeks ached. She wasn't sure if he might recall seeing her in New York. "I work in advertising. On the east coast. I'm out here visiting my mom and grandma, who, of course, you just met. I got here a few days ago, and…they enjoy looking at bargains and sales and they restore things sometimes. But they love to look. They like cheap stuff. So we thought we'd try your shop. Not that we thought your shop is cheap. But they hadn't been there before. So we thought we'd start here."

Though she was still nervous, throughout the conversation she relished the fact that he looked at her so intently. As Ailie spoke she became aware that he kept glancing at her lips. Several of her past boyfriends had complimented her lips, describing them as 'full' and 'strawberry-colored.' She was delighted that he seemed to notice too. It helped her relax, as she slowly regained her confidence.

"And, I assume you might be working while you're out here," he said. "After all, you've got a desk…that needs a chair." He grinned playfully.

"Yes, I do have a desk, without a chair. But I have a laptop, so I can make it work… And I am on vacation while I'm out here, so it's not urgent."

Levi's phone beeped. He looked at the message and then at Ailie. "Sorry, Joe needs help with something." He played with his napkin for a second. "But…if you're in the area, and you're interested in looking at more furniture, I'm helping out at an estate sale tomorrow. Do you have a pen? I can write the address down for you."

Ailie scrambled in her purse for pen. He scribbled the information on his napkin and handed it to her. "Very nice to meet you, Ailie. I hope you can make it."

Watching him walk away, she admired the fit of his jeans again. She squinted and couldn't help but wonder, *Is he wearing Levis right now?* Then she looked down at her untouched decaf latte and went back to the barista to request a chamomile tea instead. Since her flight, she noticed that the agitation in her stomach had declined and the dizzying spells were now very mild. But on a day like today, with so much excitement, she could barely contain the butterflies in her stomach. Ailie wondered if Frieda had a pill for butterflies too. Sitting at a table by the open window, Ailie delighted in the breeze and cautiously sipped her tea. She closed her eyes to reflect on her meeting with Levi. Someone tapped her on the shoulder.

"I hope we're not disturbing you," Gloria said quietly. Ailie opened her eyes to see both Vivien and Gloria standing by her table. "That lovely young man came over to help us load the truck. I hope we didn't steal him away from you."

"It's okay, mom," she replied. Gloria noted that the look on Ailie's face was somewhere between peaceful and delirious—her eyelids relaxed at half-mast and her smile unwavering.

"Do you want to stay here, or are you coming with us to the next place?" Her mother pulled out the slip of paper that Ailie had given to her in the morning, listing all the nearby sales. "We've got a lot of ground to cover if we're going to make all of these places before all the good stuff's gone. Your grandma just bought the loveliest dresser, so there won't be much room for anything else big. But we've come this far, so we might as well see what we can…"

Gloria and Vivien discussed their next stop as they walked back to the truck. Ailie strolled behind them. She glanced over at the shop again, hoping for another glimpse of Levi.

Visiting yard sale after yard sale, the day turned out to be much longer than Ailie anticipated. She felt drained after such a stimulating morning. *Why did I have to write down the address of every sale in the area? It seemed like such a good way to convince my mom to come down here this morning. Now I have to convince them to go home. I want to go home. This would be a perfect time to vomit.*

Finally, Ailie decided to take a break. Their next stop was an estate sale, where she spotted a loveseat made of a very garish fabric. No one stepped near it. She walked over to have a closer look. The bright pink cushions were luxuriously velvety. A couple of throw pillows, in an equally vibrant pink, appeared to be made with soft feathers. She sat down and leaned back. She imagined that this is what it's like resting on a giant baby flamingo. Ailie closed her eyes to relive the moments at the coffee shop. She imagined his eyes, his lips, his eyes staring at *her* lips, his voice. He reached over to hold her hand. Then he pulled her closer and kissed her.

"Ailie, Ailie," Gloria leaned over her daughter, fanning her with a folded piece of paper. "Sweetie, are you okay?"

"Mom! What?" Ailie opened her eyes, but then closed them again.

Gloria nudged Ailie to get her attention. She opened her eyes again, and her mom motioned for her to look to the left. Ailie saw an old man standing close by. He wore a bowling shirt, long shorts, a belt looped just over where his belly button might be, his socks pulled up close to his knees, and oversized glasses emphasized his tired eyes. He stood with his arms akimbo, glaring at her disapprovingly.

Gloria and Vivien each took one of Ailie's hands and shoulders and gently propped her up. "Let's get you to the car. We can't sleep on the furniture, darling. It's meant to be sold."

Ailie stared at the man as she stood up. "I'm sorry, mom. Did I get us in trouble?"

Gloria spoke to Ailie reassuringly as they walked to their truck. "I keep forgetting that you might not have your usual energy. Pregnancy can be hard on the body, there's so much going on in there right now. You should be resting more."

It was a long, quiet ride home. Vivien drove, Ailie slept with her head on her mother's shoulder, Gloria sat in the center, knitting.

***

That night, Ailie finished at least three bowls of her grandmother's soup, without the need to run to the toilet for fear of spitting up. She was elated that this might signal the end of her nausea spells. They sat at the kitchen table, and, after some discussion about their excellent finds in Santa

Monica, Vivien excused herself to have another look at the dresser she'd purchased earlier. Gloria decided to have a better look at her own small acquisitions too, so Ailie went to her room to find her laptop.

It was a hot evening. The winds whisked leaves and dry brush around the courtyard. Ailie ran from the kitchen to her bedroom. The doors closed softly behind her. It was hot in her bedroom so she turned on a fan, then she pulled out the napkin with Levi's handwriting. She held it up to her nose to see if there was any discernable smell that might elicit images from this morning. But nothing happened. She looked at the address. *He has good handwriting.*

She opened her laptop and plugged in the location of tomorrow's estate sale. After that she checked her all three of her personal inboxes, her work mail, glanced at a creative brief, updated her iCalendar, answered an Evite, a Facebook request, a few LinkedIn connections, flagged a Punchbowl invitation, favorite some tweets, liked several Instagrams, accepted four meetings, declined a lunch, and then skimmed her blog feed and the news. For the first time since visiting her mother's house, she was relieved that her cell phone couldn't connect to texts or voicemail.

As she read through her inboxes and apps and web pages she found it very difficult to concentrate because even the smallest tasks sparked thoughts of Levi. Clicking on her work calendar she remembered that he wore a watch, which led to reflections about his forearms, and shoulders, and his chest; when she declined the lunch, she thought about food, and then remembered his lips and hands.

It was late evening by the time Ailie felt sleepy again. At first her thoughts drifted to the café. Once again she was sitting across from Levi. Then, as she lay in her bed, in this small, undisturbed space, she felt free to let her fantasies run wild. *She stood outside his shop again, watching him. The next minute she was standing beside him. His forearms glistened with sweat. She ran her fingers across his chest.* Ailie opened her eyes. *Wait,* she thought, *that shop would be uncomfortable. All those tools.* She closed her eyes and started over. *He took her to his bedroom, somewhere beside a lake. The electricity was out, so he had to light candles. Lots of them. Because it's very dark. No. Hang on. That would take a while.*

In front of the fireplace, he ripped her dress off. She tore his shirt off. Somehow they made it to the bed in a heated, passionate fury of lips and hands and heavy breathing....

Ailie slept blissfully, paying no attention to the winds howling outside or the branch that rapped lightly on her window.

15

It's all in the delivery.

Ailie awoke early again, but this time it wasn't the jetlag. It felt more like the
return of her nausea. She tiptoed around the kitchen. They'd forgotten to
buy more chamomile while they were out yesterday, so she hoped that her
mother or grandmother stocked ginger. It was hours before the start of the
estate sale that Levi had told her about, but she was already worried that the
ill feeling in her stomach would keep her from attending. At last she found
some ginger root in the freezer. She chopped off a few small pieces and
then steeped them in boiling water. After she finished her drink she ate a
bowl of cheerios without milk, and then took her medication. She lay down
in her bed again, hoping she would feel better after some more sleep.

But Ailie felt worse. Gloria came by to check on her. "Maybe yesterday was
a bit much. You should really take it easy today."

Ailie lay in bed, miserably, either staring at the ceiling or peering at the
corner of her room where the wall whistled on occasion when the wind
gusted. She mustered up just enough energy to prop herself up against a

pillow, check her email, read the headlines, and fall asleep again. As the hours passed, her dizziness began to improve. By early afternoon she felt confident enough to eat more and take a short walk.

When Ailie returned she quickly ducked into her bedroom, but then reappeared ten minutes later. She had changed into a long, brown, linen-blend skirt, slit high on the sides, showing off her slim legs as she walked. She'd also chosen a white V-neck top that was slightly loose, ending below her waist. Gloria stopped her work in the garden and looked up at her. "You look beautiful!" she commented. "I can barely tell that you were sick just a little bit ago, the color's really come back to your face."

"I feel so much better, mom…back to myself." Ailie combed her fingers through her hair briefly. "Um…hopefully this isn't premature…but I'm going to go back down to Santa Monica… to meet that guy. From yesterday. He told me about an estate sale that he'll be at today…so I thought I'd…"

"Oh, he was such a cutie!" Gloria's eyes widened with excitement. "But are you sure you're well enough? That's a bit far…Do you need me to drive you? Not that I want to drive all that far. But… should you really go?"

"No, no, no mom. I'll be fine. I'll be fine, really. If I don't feel well, I'll pull over. I can call you."

Of course within minutes Vivien had joined the conversation. Her hands stained with motor oil. "Are you sure? That's a long way. He better make it worth your time." She winked at Ailie.

"Why don't I call you guys when I get there," Ailie smiled, reassuringly. She already had her purse and keys in hand.

"Back in my day, I would've asked the man to drive up here if he was interested," suggested Vivien.

"It's okay. Seriously. This is all very casual. It's not a date. He's working. I'm looking at furniture. I'm just showing an interest in what he does. We'll see how it goes." Ailie waved goodbye, trotted through the house and hopped into her rental car.

The GPS navigated while Ailie ruminated. *What should I do once I arrive to the sale?* As far as Ailie considered it, dating was no longer a complicated affair after so many years of going through the motions: a lunch or dinner or coffee, and a routine list of questions. But this wouldn't be an official date; this rendezvous, she concluded, was more of a feeler, a test. "It'll be like a dance," she said to herself as she drove. "I'll have to ask questions about the items on sale and he'll provide answers. And then…somehow I'll have to segue into more personal topics, while still feigning interest in…whatever's on sale. Or, better yet, maybe he'll volunteer information, while we look at things. Together. So…furniture could lead to conversations about what happens when we're *not* sitting on furniture, such as favorite activities or hobbies. A bike or a baseball or toys could introduce questions about childhood. And if they have *clothing*…" Ailie blushed and giggled. She fanned her face with her hand and conjured up her best Scarlett O'Hara imitation, "Hello, Mr. Sommerfeld, tell me what you like to do when you're *not* wearing clothing."

By the time she arrived Ailie worried that the event might be over. Fortunately there were still items littered across the lawn and driveway. People packed boxes, others lifted larger pieces into their trucks or vans. She spotted a woman holding a clipboard and writing things down. Ailie walked over to her. "Hi, I'm looking for Levi. Is he still here?"

"Levi?" The woman tapped the pen on the clipboard as she thought for a minute.

Just then Ailie spotted him coming around the corner at one end of the house. She yelled over to him. "Hi!"

He strode right over, grinning at Ailie. "I didn't think you'd come." His face, again slightly unshaven, glistened from the day's work. He wore workman's gloves, jeans, and a plain white t-shirt, just tight enough, for Ailie's liking, to perfectly display his torso and arms. He wiped the sweat from his brow, a gesture with which Ailie was pleased to now be somewhat familiar. Ailie inhaled deeply as she admired his physique. He looked back at her, slightly self-conscious. "Sorry. I'm a bit sweaty. I've been here, helping out all day."

"Oh, no! You look good! You look good!" Ailie thought that by now her cheeks were crimson.

"And so do you," he said. Both of them laughed nervously.

The woman with the clipboard still stood between them. "I'm just going to…walk over there." She wandered to another part of the lawn and found a bench that hadn't been put away yet.

Ailie surveyed the yard. "Well, it looks like I'm a bit late. I'm sorry. I tried to get away earlier, and it just wasn't going to work. Um…hmmm…" She bit her lower lip as she watched the workers put the last items in the trucks.

"I'm nearly done," said Levi. "I need to go home and shower, and I'm starving."

"Me too. I'm actually hungrier than I expected."

"What are you… in the mood for?"

"I eat just about anything." Ailie felt fine at the moment but prayed that her stomach wouldn't betray her at a time like this.

"It's not too far to the beach, and there's a great place near the pier." He gave her the address, and she pulled out her phone and found the directions.

"Thanks!" replied Ailie. She paused before asking, "And, just to clarify, will you be there too… at the same restaurant? We're eating…together?"

"Yeah," he laughed. "That was the idea."

"Sounds good! Sounds good. What time should we meet there?"

"Gimme an hour?"

Ailie hopped back in her car. It was another hot evening, so she turned on the AC and as she pulled away. She drove less than half a block before letting out an ecstatic high-pitched shriek. "I have to call someone! I have to call someone! I should call Ruby. But I should pull over first." She looked out windows of her car as she drove down another residential street. "I have no idea where I am. I should figure out where to go first, and then I'll call Ruby." Ailie parked her car by the side of the road and searched online for places nearby. She found a second hand bookstore located fairly close to the restaurant where she planned to meet Levi.

She wanted plenty of time to talk to Ruby and tried to not run too many red lights in her hurry to get to the store.

Ailie paced back and forth outside *The Second Shot: Coffee, Beer, and Used Books*, talking excitedly on her phone. She had just finished telling Ruby all about her conversation with Frieda, the trip to the antique shop, then the coffee shop, and now her anticipated dinner with Levi.

"And what does he say about *everything?*" asked Ruby.

"Everything?"

"The baby."

"The baby?"

"Can you hear me okay over there?" Ruby checked her phone to see how many bars she was getting.

Ailie's heart sank at the thought of telling Levi *everything*. She had no answers for Ruby. "I don't know. I seriously don't know if I can tell him right now. I've been so thrilled about this idea of finding him. And now…I'm going on an actual date with him? Can you believe it?"

"I believe it."

"Seriously, I can't believe it. It's happening so fast! I haven't thought about any of this."

"I believe that part too. I think we should talk this thing through…"

Ailie checked her hair in the café window. "Ruby, it's so bizarre. I don't even know how to wrap my head around what's about to happen. This man existed in a photo—a piece of *paper*—for over a decade. But in my imagination…I was like a little kid, I made up stories about him, about how we'd meet and fall in love. But it was just a game or a *dream*. I didn't think it would *happen*. I know, you'd hardly guess since I'm married to my work. But…all that aside, it's like overnight this guy went from a 2D image to this living, breathing thing that I can *touch*. But I haven't touched him yet. Cause he hasn't asked me to. But I could if I wanted to. And if he asks me I will."

"Slow down. If you weren't pregnant I'd *make* you drink a glass of wine. Right now."

"And he actually *likes* me!" Ailie went on. "They way he looks at me…or maybe it's the way I look at him. Hmmm. Well, maybe I'm being a little presumptuous, but he's meeting me here tonight…and I feel like a little girl." Ailie pulled the phone away from her ear to check the time. "Shit. He'll be here soon. And I really do think he likes me. What do I *do*?" Ailie looked at herself in the window again. "I am cute."

"You *are* cute. You are very cute," Ruby responded. "Lord, I have never heard you talk like this before…"

"I know. I need to get it together."

"Hell yeah. If I was standing right in front of you I'd have slapped you by now. Let me think. We need to strategize. As your best friend I need to be the voice of reason, if only for a second. First of all, there is *a lot* riding on the table here. Put your work hat on."

"Work hat?"

"Yes, practice what you've learned in the boardroom. You need to tell him before you're in too deep. And remember—it's all in the delivery. No pun intended."

"It's *in* the delivery," Ailie repeated.

"That's right. You've got to tell him at the right time and in the right place. These are all the little things that we forget to do when we're in love and our brains get hijacked by emotions and hormones—the messy stuff. Cause if I didn't know any better, I'd think you're in love." Ruby waited for a response. "Ailie...are you even listening to me?" Ailie was reapplying her lipstick in the store window.

"I am! I am. I hear you. I really need to be clear-headed about this." She paced back and forth on the sidewalk again. "I need to figure out a strategy."

"I just gave you a strategy."

"Okay, I'll stick with that plan. If I want this to be a successful endeavor, then we need complete transparency to make it work..."

"*Full* disclosure," Ruby interjected, firmly.

"Full disclosure," Ailie repeated. "And...If...I mean, *when* I present this additional information, I need to think about my delivery...." Ailie caught sight of another attractive man crossing the street. She sighed. "Ruby, he looked so sexy after working in that yard all day. Oh my god, you don't understand how much I just wanted to take him, right there. And he's got these forearms that I could just...I wanna *lick* them. But I won't. That would be weird."

"Ailie..."

"And his butt! I actually felt this *need* to slap his ass. Have you ever felt that before?"

"Ailie!" Ruby exclaimed, laughing. "I know it's been a while, but you're losing focus again."

"I know, I know. Maybe it's this pregnancy? Or maybe…maybe this is what happens after a decade of pent up energy? But I am *so* turned on right now. I mean not *right* now, cause I'm talking to you, but…"

"Hold up. Hold up. Your brain keeps gettin' hijacked. Reel it in, Ailie. Stay on task. Is tonight when you plan to tell him? Or you gonna feel out the situation and then tell him? Maybe much later tonight? But soon?"

Ailie sighed. "I want to tell him everything. But then I don't want to ruin anything, so I don't want tell him a thing." She stared at her belly. "I wish we'd met before all this. I wish we'd met the *normal* way."

"What?" Ruby said, bewildered. "Forget normal! Normal is not always exciting. And as far as he knows, you *did* meet him the normal way. I mean, he doesn't know you followed him. Twice." She looked through the bedroom door at Barry, her live-in boyfriend, arranging his ties on the bed. "Lord knows *I* could use some adventure right now. Look, Ailie, the desire to get out of the normal is what got you here in the first place. This is what can happen when you actually leave the office! Now go enjoy this really… you know, bizarre situation you've created for yourself. I'm kinda jealous. Well, not the pregnancy part but all the rest. Go have fun! But don't scare him and try not to throw yourself at him on the first date. Gotta save something for later. But try not to fuck up the delivery! Seriously, enjoy yourself! But *tell him.*"

After a few more words of encouragement from Ruby, Ailie hung up the phone. She checked her reflection in the window one more time, and walked toward the restaurant. Cute.

16

That's worse than a jellyfish!

Ailie and Levi arrived at the same time. They were a little early for dinner, so they didn't have much trouble requesting an outside table.

"I hope you didn't have to wait too long," he said as they sat down.

"Not at all." *Ten years,* she thought. Ailie took in the scent of his cologne, which brought her directly back to the previous day, when she first smelled it at the coffee shop. He dressed in another t-shirt, but this was a dark grey v-neck. The nighttime version of what he wore earlier. It wasn't quite as tight as the earlier shirt, but it exhibited his muscular frame all the same. Her mind drifted as she imagined him hoisting a giant log over his shoulder.

"So tell me more about what you do," he said.

Ailie forced herself back from her daydreams. She thought about how to summarize the last few years. "Well…like I mentioned the other day, I work in advertising. The online market is very competitive, and I've done well in that area. I was Executive Creative Director for a while, lots to do.

Lots of pressure with office politics and drama…but…last year I stepped back from that role…and somehow I always end up back in that role again. There were some other options, but…I've been reconsidering what…I don't know, where I want to go. Maybe start my own business, but I'm not sure. I'm not tired of it. I don't think. At the same time I feel like I should take a step back. I've had a hard time focusing lately." She played with her napkin, pensively, and then smiled at Levi. "Still, there are not a lot of women at the top of my field. I should consider myself lucky to be where I am."

"Sounds like you're burned out. Like you've got a lot to think about," he said, softly.

"Oh yes."

The waiter stopped by to light the candle at their table and take their order. Levi ordered an ale and grilled Hawaiian pork chops. Ailie was very tempted by several of the entrees, but the possibility of nausea still loomed at the back of her mind, so she considered ordering seltzer water and soup. But then she began to worry that he might think she's dieting, so quickly changed her mind to a burger and fries—foods that, in the past, had served her well after a long night of drinking. She took a chance and figured if burger and fries worked for a hangover, they might do the trick if she began to feel any sickness.

After ordering, she discretely placed her hands on her knees and then her stomach, just to be sure it wasn't visibly shaking. She could tell that he was also a little nervous as he put his hand on his chest, straightening out his shirt, and then combed his fingers through his hair.

Their anxieties dissipated quickly. The two engaged in lengthy conversation after conversation, over dinner, and then dessert. They discussed books and movies, favorite foods and places they'd traveled.

Her introduction to books was the Brontë sisters, and as a kid he'd read everything by Jack London. They'd both read *Watership Down* more than once. These days she was reading a lot of memoirs, and he was into science fiction and adventure, but he hadn't picked a book up in months. The last book he'd read, Bill Bryson's *A Walk in the Woods*, turned out to be one of his favorites; she hadn't read it, but she'd walked portions of the Appalachian Trail, over the course of several years.

They were both fans of movies about aliens, space, and adventure. *The Abyss, Contact,* and *Goonies* were early favorites, but they disagreed over the movie *E.T.*—it was one he cherished as a kid, but she didn't care for it. They also loved the original *Star Wars* trilogies, and they laughed as she explained how much of an impact Darth Vader's death had on her as a child. "I just couldn't believe he was dead," she said. "I cried for hours. Seriously, I'm sure my mom had to sit with me the next day too, consoling me."

He replied teasingly, "So hang on, you mean that Darth Vader, the most evil, most feared person in the entire galaxy, the guy who sucked the life out of everything...you actually mourned him...but you couldn't find any way to connect with an adorable creature who just wanted to be friends and brought flowers back to life?"

"No, it wasn't like that," she explained, still laughing. "It's just that...Darth Vader was so evil, and there was so much reason to hate him. But then...the minute he turns around and acknowledges his child and tells him that he loves him...or...did he say he loved him? I only saw the movie once—I couldn't bring myself to see it again. Anyway, I can't remember, but the point is that they had about two minutes to enjoy this...this coming together, this father and son moment. It could've been something awesome, you know? Think about that—when *everything* from the past, *all* is forgiven and everything is right in the universe, for just a few minutes, between parent and child." She stopped for a second. "Sorry, I know I'm way over-analyzing this. But then...that was it. At the end of the film he was gone. Done. Dead. Worst of all, they didn't even get to share a hug...because of that suit."

"I think we'll have to see that one together sometime because I'm not sure we're talking about the same movie," he said, laughing. "And you cried for how long?"

"Several hours...two days at most." Ailie sipped her water. She was taken by the fact that he watched her so closely as she talked. Every time their eyes met, it was tough for her to concentrate on her story. "So did you cry at all as a kid when you watched movies? Or…you strike me as someone who hasn't watched anything more romantic than a baseball movie."

"I don't remember much crying." Levi placed his hand closer to hers on the table. "But, as for romances, I hate to admit that…well…sadly, I have watched *a lot* of romantic movies. But not by choice," he confided, smiling confidently.

"Oh?" Her eyes lit up as she pulled her chair closer to the table. She moved her hand nearer to his, but didn't want to appear obvious, so she placed it on a flower vase that sat between them. Without taking her eyes off him, she slowly ran one finger back and forth across the base of the vase.

"It's not like I watched them willingly," he confessed. "But…I didn't want to play ice hockey, so…"

"What?" Ailie interrupted. "You didn't like ice hockey so you watched chick flicks? And you made fun of me about Darth Vader…" Her tone was playful, and without waiting for him to respond, she asked, "Did you see *An Officer and a Gentleman?*"

He nodded.

"*The Way We Were? Roman Holiday? Casablanca? Breakfast at Tiffany's? The Graduate?*"

He nodded again and again. "That last one wasn't just a romance…I probably saw it more than once." He protested, lightheartedly, "But my family only had one TV."

"Wow." She grinned, wide-eyed, straightening up her back. "So do you still watch them?"

He shrugged, responding cheekily, "Now I have my own TV."

Ailie laughed. "You didn't answer the question."

"I should finish my story first though...I didn't say I didn't *like* ice hockey. Don't get me wrong. I love sports—soccer, lacrosse, skiing, baseball, football, whatever. And I love watching ice hockey. But, man, it can be brutal. Fists and missing teeth. I mean, we were young, so it wasn't that bad, but there were some...*mean* guys on the team...in and out of the locker room. Sometimes we'd play on this pond that froze up. I still have part of a scar here." He indicated his bicep.

"I can just imagine what that might look like," she replied, staring at his bicep.

He continued, "...and some of them had mean brothers too. So on the nights my brothers played ice hockey I stayed home with my mom. And the agreement was that I *had* to help her in the kitchen, cooking, putting dinner together, whatever. And whenever we got done with that, if there was any time left, which there always was, and if I'd finished my homework, which I usually did, she'd put a movie in the VCR or DVD player, whatever we had at the time. And, guaranteed, it was usually a romance. And, like I said, we only had one TV, so if I wanted to watch TV, that's what I *had to* watch."

"Your mom taught you how to cook?" Ailie asked, curiously, tilting her head. *He's perfect.*

"Yeah, cooking, baking, whatever." He waved his hand, nonchalantly. "My mom wasn't the most patient person, but...you know, cooking can be interesting. It's like a science. The more you play with ingredients, the more you learn."

"So do you cook from...recipes or just...? I mean...do you enjoy it?"

"I don't often use recipes, but I'll look at some here and there. And most of the time I enjoy it. After a long day, sometimes it's nice to just...throw stuff together," he said, casually. "Most of the time the ingredients work out—sometimes really well..."

He cooks. I could kiss him right now. His hands...his lips. Her mouth hung open slightly as she listened, undressing him with her eyes. She wondered if he'd been doing the same when she was talking.

Levi's smile widened. He stopped midsentence, glancing at Ailie's hand. "You must really like lilies…I mean, you've only got three fingers on that vase, but the way they keep traveling up and down…"

"Oh!" Ailie gave a soft shriek, embarrassed, instantly pulling her fingers off the stem of the vase, as though it burned. She spoke hurriedly. "It feels nice cause it's ribbed. I mean, etched. I like the etching. I mean, the vase is nice." She covered her eyes with her hand, laughing and blushing. "I mean…it was a nice vase to touch." She stopped to collect her thoughts. "Okay, what I mean is, sometimes you see something, and it's nice to the touch, does that make sense?"

"Yes," he replied, laughing and taking her hand. "But I'm sure that vase wants a cigarette." She shook her head, her cheeks still red.

He held her hand, caressing her palm, softly touching her wrist, lacing his fingers between hers, as they conversed, until their entrees arrived.

For dessert Levi ordered himself chocolate cake. Ailie declined any sweets, declaring she was full. The cake arrived and he'd nearly finished his plate when Ailie asked if she could try a piece. "Sorry, I don't think I could finish a whole cake," she explained. "But could I just have a little bite? It looks so good."

"Of course." He picked up the last piece, intending to hand Ailie the fork, but she mistakenly assumed he was going to feed her the cake. The fork and cake fell to the floor, but not before a small amount smeared above Ailie's lip, close to her cheek. "Shit, I'm sorry," he apologized, retrieving the fork. "My fault. I thought you were…"

"That's okay," Ailie laughed, searching the table for a napkin. "But I think our server took both our napkins."

"Okay, just go like this," said Levi, motioning with his hand. "Just take your finger or your tongue, and it's right up there." Ailie tried to lick the chocolate but couldn't reach it.

"Really?" he said, tilting his head. "I was sure you'd be able to reach that. I guess your tongue's shorter than I thought."

"I don't have a short tongue."

"There's nothing wrong with a short tongue." He grinned, his tone flirtatious. "You can still do a lot with a short tongue."

"But I don't *have* a short tongue," she insisted, smiling back at him, playfully.

"Well, here, let me get it for you," he offered, reaching across the table. "But first I just have to move your hair, a little."

They both pulled their chairs closer to the table. *Don't go crazy,* she thought. *But I love this.* She closed her eyes. *Don't act sex-crazed.* His hand brushed her cheek as he moved her hair. *Don't act sex-deprived...* Her breath faltered. *It's only been a year... and a few months.* Her hair stood on end; she could feel her temperature rising, as his fingers traced her ear. *Who am I kidding? When I checked the calendar the other day, it's been 471 days since my last date.* Then he placed his hand close to her lips, removing the chocolate, delicately with one finger.

She opened her eyes, their faces still so close. *I want him. I want to have him. I want to have his babies... Wait...I AM having his baby!* She saw that he was about to lick the chocolate off his finger. "Wait," she said, nonchalantly. "I didn't get the chance to taste it yet."

Without waiting for him to respond, she took his hand, gently nibbling on the tip of his finger and then placing it in her mouth. She closed her lips and slowly rotated her tongue. Their server came by, stopping momentarily. "I'll just get you the check," he said, raising his eyebrows. Levi slid his credit card to the edge of the table, without taking his eyes off Ailie.

A few seconds later Ailie pulled Levi's—cleaned—finger out of her mouth. "I'm glad you liked the cake," he said, quietly, looking down at his hand, and then back up at her.

"See? I told you I don't have a short tongue," responded Ailie, just as quietly.

Levi placed his hand on her cheek and softly kissed her lips.

The waiter popped by. "Sorry! Me again. I know. Bad timing." His face flushed with embarrassment. Ailie sighed. He continued, "I…I just wanted to show you that I accidentally charged you for this wrong check, and then I re-ran the card for the right check, so then I had to credit you back for this one…" He set several strips of paper down, in front of Levi, handing him a pen. "It might take a few days for you to see the credit. But can you sign this one and this one? And I'll need that one. These over here are yours to keep. I can staple them if you'd like. Looks like you had a fantastic time. Here's a link at the bottom if you want to fill it out our online survey…you know—how'd I do? Stuff like that."

After a three-hour dinner, and signing several receipts, Levi took Ailie's hand and led her through a small crowd. They hid their shoes near the steps and walked onto the beach. A fat crescent moon emerged as the sun set, the Santa Monica pier off in the distance; lights from the amusement park and shops bobbed on the water like floating lanterns. As they strolled along the water's edge he told her about his family, going to summer camps with his brothers, and growing up in upstate New York. "I love it," he said. "I absolutely love it. The lakes, the rivers… it's so green and you don't realize it till you take yourself out of that scene and then go back home again. If I could, I'd be back there in a heartbeat."

"So…any reason you haven't moved back?" she asked.

He picked up a stone and threw it across the water before answering. "Life. The business, I guess… It's going really well. Everything's here now, you know? You move somewhere and before you know it you're putting down roots. A year passes and then another year, you get so busy. It's hard to step back and think sometimes."

"That's true," she said, thinking about how many years she'd been in New York at this point. They strolled quietly for a few minutes. She noticed his hand on her lower back at first, and then across her waist; she slid her fingers into a loophole at the back of his jeans. As they walked, it was one of those welcome, comfortable quiets. Not a moment of awkwardness between them.

She thought about her own childhood and told him about her life as a young, single child, moving from house to house with her mother, and sometimes her grandmother. "They are a very loving, but eccentric pair," she said fondly.

"I can't imagine that was easy, moving around so often. Making new friends every year."

Ailie nodded. "It wasn't. And we didn't have a lot of money, so that didn't help." The ocean breeze played gently as they walked, and she stopped to tuck some hair behind her ear. "But in retrospect it made me a much stronger person. I think I improved with every move—I had a better idea of how to make friends and who to trust. Sometimes it worked and sometimes it didn't. But, like they say, kids are resilient. I wasn't the person with the most friends, but I formed some great, long-lasting friendships. We could be the outcasts. We could be free to think, to act…to focus. I became an entrepreneur at a very early age. But that was temporary. Once I tapped into my creative side, I…I just felt free. I didn't look back. I just knew what I wanted to do." They stopped walking and she pushed the sand around with her feet. "Once I got to my teens I thought of each move as an opportunity. To recreate myself or better myself. It's like with each new place you can strip yourself of your history and you can start over, every time. Well, this was before the internet." They both laughed. "What about you? It must've been comforting to live in the same town for your entire childhood. You probably knew everyone."

"We knew all our neighbors, that's for sure. So if we did anything wrong, my mom knew about it before we got home. That really sucked when you wanted to do something daring." He smiled. "One of our friends had this video recorder. Remember those things, how big they were?"

Ailie laughed. "Yeah, I think we rented one from the library once. They were huge!"

"Well, we'd video ourselves anytime we thought we were being really cool. So one day we built our own ski jump on this tiny cliff—maybe it was more like a ledge now that I think about it. It was near the house and my mom was on the scene before we even got to try it out."

"I'm jealous. I'd have loved to grow up in one town, one place to really call home. The support of friends and neighbors."

"Well…every place has its drawbacks. There were bullies in our school too. My dad tried to teach me how to fight, but…but if things got real bad, my brothers always stuck up for me. That was a benefit to being the youngest..." He trailed off, looking at the water as they walked, holding her hand again.

"Ow!" Ailie stumbled and quickly limped away from spot where she'd just stepped. "Shit! I stepped on a jellyfish. It felt like it bit me! Do they have beaks?"

"A jellyfish?" Levi peered down at the sand, through the limited light of the moon. He knelt down for a closer look and then looked over at Ailie. "Are you okay? Are you bleeding?"

"I don't think there's any blood," replied Ailie, also trying to use the moonlight to examine the bottom of her foot, holding her long skirt up with both hands. "But there's something on here, and it's oozing down my foot," she said in a shaky tone. "I really think part of the jellyfish is still on me. Should I put it in the water? Or…I think someone once told me that urine is supposed to help?"

"Are you saying one of us has to pee on your foot?" Levi asked, laughing. "Shouldn't we save that kind of magic for the third or fourth date?"

He was still kneeling above the spot where she tripped. He turned on his phone's light and took a small army knife out of his pocket, pushing the sand around.

"Okay, well maybe you can look it up on your phone? I don't want to let go of my skirt down right now. This stuff might get on my clothes." She stood still, poised like a garden flamingo—resting on one leg, and the other one bent, with toes pointing down to the sand.

"Okay…I found it." He said, chuckling. He poked at the items, and then looked back at her. "By the way, you have gorgeous legs."

"Oh…okay, thank you," Ailie replied, trying to maintain her balance. She wasn't sure if he was laughing or smiling at her, it was tough to discern with all the shadows. "So what is it?" She asked again. "It doesn't hurt anymore, but this feels so disgusting and the restaurant looks so far away right now."

"Don't worry—the good news is you didn't step on a jellyfish. You stepped on a bottle cap. I can't believe people are still drinking Natural Light. Looks like they didn't know it was a twist-off."

"I stepped on a bottle cap?" Ailie was more confused than stunned, looking down at her foot again.

"Yeah, who knew that stuff was still available in bottles," Levi replied, pushing the sand back with his feet.

"Well…then what is this?" Ailie peered again at her foot.

"Oh, sorry, it looks like you stepped on a used condom, so that other stuff…"

Ailie didn't wait for Levi to finish his sentence; she raced toward the surf, screaming. "Oh gross! That's worse than a jellyfish! That's much worse! That's so much worse!" She ran knee-deep into the water, dragging her 'tainted' foot through the squishy sand below, declaring several times, "This is so disgusting!" She considered for a moment telling Levi about the chicken condom incident but decided against it.

Levi caught up with her, his jeans soaked. Ailie began to giggle. She turned to look at him, her skirt billowing between her legs, moving back and forth with the tide.

"Oh my god, this water's so cold," she said as he pulled her close, wrapping his arms around her.

She could feel his chest rapidly rising and falling, after their mad dash to the water. Ailie looked up at him, about to kiss him—she'd quickly forgotten about her foot and the chilly water—all of a sudden he picked her up as though she were his bride going over the threshold and carried her out of the water.

He set her down on the beach and held her, their eyes met again. "This is better, much better," she whispered just before their lips touched.

A loud ring broke their embrace; Ailie automatically answered the call. *I should've just let it go to voicemail,* she thought, with the phone at her ear. Her mother started to speak before Ailie had the chance to say hello. "I'm so sorry, sweetie, I really hope we're not interrupting. But when you didn't call... Honey, it's nearly midnight. I just got a little nervous."

"Oh! I'm so sorry, mom!" Ailie glanced at the screen of her phone. "But....mom, it's not even eleven yet. It's 10:30." She saw Levi glance at his watch.

"Well, dear, we just wanted to be sure everything's ok," Gloria replied. "Is everything going ok? Are you having fun?"

"Yes, mom. A lot. Thank you." She hung up after a couple of 'I love yous' and 'I will, I will.'

Levi brushed his fingers through his hair. "I'm so sorry, Ailie, but I lost track of time. I was supposed to be somewhere at 10, and it's already 10:30."

"Oh." Ailie detected disappointment in her own voice. "That's okay! That's ok," she added. They turned back to the restaurant. "Wow, I can't believe five hours went by so fast."

"I've...it's been, great. Seriously, I've had such a good time," he said, sincerely. "Can...is it okay if I call you? I have to fly to San Francisco for the day tomorrow, but I'll be back tomorrow night."

"Yeah! Okay! Sure." Then she thought for a moment. "I'll have to give you my mom's number. Their house isn't very remote, but I can never get a good signal there." He handed her his phone and she entered the number.

By now they stood at the top of the steps. "My car's this way," he said.

"My car's this way." Ailie pointed in the opposite direction.

Levi offered to walk her to her car, and then his phone rang. He looked at the number and his smile faded slightly. He sighed. "Sorry, I should take this."

"That's fine." Ailie gestured that it was okay and he answered the phone. She waved good-bye.

She was absolutely giddy. Giddy enough to want to skip all the way to her car, but thought that might look funny coming from a grown woman, and at this time of the night. The smile on her face remained, got bigger; it definitely wasn't fading any time soon. By the time she sat in her car it was already 11 o'clock. *Ruby!* she thought, *I need to call Ruby. Wait, the time difference.* Ailie bit her lower lip as she considered the hour. Then she remembered her conversation with Ruby earlier in the evening. She leaned back in her seat, staring at the ceiling. "Even if she's up I can't call her yet. I haven't told him about the baby. The baby...I need to tell him everything. I just...I should just say it." She put her phone back down and started the long drive to her mother's house.

Ailie danced in her seat to the Go-Go's "Head Over Heels" and then the Proclaimers "I'm Gonna Be;" she tuned in to every love song she could find on the radio. It was dark, but the road before her felt welcoming—it was no longer this cold, concrete network, laid out in unfamiliar directions—it became an inviting pathway, an intimate link connecting her (other) home to Levi's.

17

Back in my day we all looked like teepees.

This shift in perception, this change in how she viewed her surroundings, extended into the morning—Ailie felt so alive, like she'd been revived after decades of sleep. When she took her morning walk, the hills, which used to appear dusty and lifeless, took on a golden hue, a color that she'd previously only read about in books. She stopped to admire the tall, sunbaked grasses, bending in the breeze. Enchanted by their rich color she was reminded of fields in Spain. Spain—where she'd gone backpacking when she was 26, with barely a penny to her name—gleefully roaming the countryside. Hot and summery Spain where she'd met handsome Stefan who lived on the outskirts of Paris. They'd talked on the train all the way from Barcelona to Paris. *All we did was talk? Hmm…I never kissed him. I think he wanted me to kiss him. But I had an itinerary to keep. But why didn't I kiss him? Because he wasn't on the itinerary?* She shook her head and watched the grasses undulate, like soft waves. Soft waves like sunny Venice, with its colorful gondolas and gondoliers…singing songs about the sun and the sea and love. *I LOVED last night with Levi…being in his arms, touching his lips. Today. This place. California. Everything feels so magical. I don't want to be anywhere else right now.*

Ailie caught herself humming a tune, like some sort of enchanted Disney princess, as she washed some eggplants later that morning. She'd just picked them from the garden. Gloria sat at the kitchen table, reading a newspaper.

Levi probably wouldn't call until evening, so to pass the time Ailie volunteered for as much housework as possible.

"I'm guessing it went well last night?" Vivien asked as she sauntered into the kitchen.

Ailie chopped some tomatoes. "It did. Yes. Very well." Then she set everything down and turned around to face Vivien. "Oh my god, grandma, I had so much fun. I mean, I…like him. Am I just infatuated? I mean, I *really* like him. I just want to see him again."

Gloria's eyes widened, she set down her cup and broke into a smile. She looked at Vivien. "My baby's falling in love. I can't believe it."

Vivien looked at Gloria. "We didn't think it could happen, did we? I mean, shit, that took a long time, but it's finally happening."

Both Gloria and Vivien strode over to Ailie, sandwiching her in a group hug. Ailie pushed back playfully. "Thank you. Thank you, mom. Thank you, grandma. I love hugs, but what I need now more than anything else is distraction. I just can't stop thinking about him and how much we talked last night and when he might call and….I just, I've never been like this before. I can't figure out what to do with myself." Ailie turned around and scrubbed the vegetables some more.

"Forget the vegetables, honey." Gloria put her hand gently on Ailie's arm. "Let's go to town. I saw some really cute maternity clothes. I wanted to show them to you, see what you think. And maybe we can get you to try some on for us before you head back to New York?"

"Maternity outfits?" Ailie nearly dropped the items from her hands.

"What's…well, yes, you'll need them at some point. And when I looked at them the other day, sweetie, well…maternity wear has really improved over the years. There's so much more to choose from than when I was pregnant."

Vivien added, "Back in my day we all looked like teepees. Walking teepees. Probably made by the same bastards who made those awful tents we used to go camping in."

"Of course," Ailie said slowly, placing her hand on her belly. "I just forget that at some point this is going to get bigger. I mean, I know it will. But it's been so many weeks, and you still can't see it in some of my clothes. I guess I'm getting used to it being this size."

"Some of these clothes are gorgeous, honey," Gloria replied, gently. "Consider yourself lucky. Your new boyfriend probably won't know the difference between your old clothes and your new clothes."

***

Several hours later, Ailie, Gloria and Vivien arrived back at the house, each woman laden with shopping bags that contained maternity clothes, baby clothes, a few soft toys, and a pile of books.

"As much as you know about everything, and I mean that in the nicest way possible, Ailie, because you really are well read, but I really think you could benefit from reading that top book." Gloria pointed to the stack that lay on the kitchen table as they emptied the contents of each bag. "You know, there's just so much that happens in the first year of a baby's life."

"Thanks, mom, it'll give me something to read before I go home next week." Ailie said those words and then thought about what the sentence meant. Next week she would fly back to New York, back to her own home, back to see her obstetrician, back to her office, her career. These were additional details that Ailie had yet to tell Levi… after she explained to him about the baby….and how she found him….here and in New York. She closed her eyes, rubbing her temples, the weight of all this information causing her to feel feverish. *Are these hot spells from pregnancy or am I panicking? Or maybe it's both?* She sat down on the couch.

Vivien pulled out some pots and pans to start cooking dinner when Gloria re-entered the room. She looked over at Ailie, who appeared somewhat sad, hugging a cushion. "He hasn't called yet. I'm not sure I have the patience for this."

"For what," asked Gloria. "Dating?"

"Yes. It's too emotional. I'm not used to feeling this emotional."

Gloria smiled, walked over to Ailie and began to rub her back.

Just then, the phone rang.

***

Ailie jumped up to answer the phone.

"Ah, ah, ah." Vivien looked up from the meat she was cutting and shook her head at Ailie. "Let your mother answer, Ailie. You don't want to look anxious. Let him think you're occupied."

"She can answer the phone, mom," Gloria countered. "If he really cares about her, then he'll be happy that she's excited to hear from him."

The phone continued to ring.

"Well, we don't want him to think she's gushing all over him, now do we?" Vivien said.

"It shouldn't matter if she's gushing. She should be able to truly express her feelings to him. It's a good foundation to a healthy relationship."

"Could I just answer the phone? Excuse me. Mom?" Ailie tried to step around Gloria but the coffee table was in the way.

Gloria turned around and walked to the hallway where the phone called out impatiently. She picked up. "Hello? Why, yes, she's here. May I ask whose calling, please? Oh?" Gloria smiled. "It's for you." She handed the phone to Ailie. Ailie rolled her eyes at the formalities.

"Hi!" Ailie said in a breathy voice. Her heart felt like it was jumping through hoops.

"Hey! How are you? I was about to hang up. I didn't think anyone was there."

Just by the sound of his voice, Ailie's thoughts were immediately transported back to the beach, to the kiss. "Well then I'm glad someone picked up! I had a really great time last night."

"Me too," he responded. "I'm so sorry I had to cut it short. I had…something I had to get done. But, hey, I was thinking, that maybe, if you're up for it, maybe you could come by the house tomorrow. In the evening? After I'm done with work?"

"Your house?"

"Yes, my house. I'll cook us something."

Ailie quietly jumped up and down with excitement. And in the process forgot to speak.

"Hello?"

Ailie stood still again. "I'm here. I'm here. Sorry, my mom said something."

"So…does that sound like something you might want to do? Or…maybe, is it too soon? Am I being too forward? I promise it'll just be dinner. But tell me if I'm going too fast."

Too fast? Ailie's mind flooded with memories of dinners that she might've rushed through because her date was hotter than she expected, or maybe it had been too long between relationships, and on occasion there had been the odd sloppy drunken one-night stand; very few of those experiences actually led to longer relationships. She closed her eyes and promised herself not to act like an over-sexed hyena. "I'd love to come over. I'm looking forward to it."

After that, she asked him about his trip to San Francisco. She'd been there several times on business, and a few times with her mother and grandmother. He'd been to three of the coffee shops she mentioned, and they talked about some of their favorite neighborhoods—and of course restaurants, there were endless restaurants. "I'd love to go there with you," he said. "At some point. I think that'd be fun."

He added that today was unseasonably hot in the city, so after his meeting he visited a few streets he hadn't been to before. Halfway through the conversation Ailie's legs began to tire, so her mother brought her a chair. By the time he said he had to go she realized nearly two hours had passed.

Before they hung up Ailie wrote down his address and phone number. "Do you need me to bring anything?" Ailie was about to offer to bring wine, but then decided against it since she wouldn't be drinking. *But…there are so many articles debating whether or not it's okay to have a small amount of wine when pregnant.* She tossed around the idea.

"No, just bring yourself. I've got plenty to drink here," he said.

"Okay, I'll see you tomorrow. I just hope I haven't talked your ear off already, and that we haven't exhausted every topic."

"Not at all," he replied. "I can't wait to see you again."

Ailie set down the phone and looked up to see her mother and grandmother peering at her, expectantly, from the kitchen.

18

Just throw yourself at him.

Ailie fussed in front of the mirror for a considerable number of hours over her choice of clothing, make-up and hairstyle. First she tried on several dresses. Then she tried on some of her pants, but none fit very well anymore. They were all skinny and tight and meant for someone less—or not at all—pregnant; they showed that she had a growing belly, even before she tried, with little success, to button them. But she really wanted to wear one of her favorite t-shirts, one that accentuated her breasts. At some point she collapsed on her bed, in a heap of clothing, when Gloria walked in and asked her what was the matter. "I want to look good, but I don't want to look like a tramp," she explained to her mother.

"Oh my," replied Gloria. "Well, your grandmother and I were just wondering what on earth you've been doing all this time. Honey, seriously, you look fine with whatever you're in."

"No I don't," Ailie said, covering her eyes with her hands, in mild anguish. "I look like shit."

"Well, you know, your body is changing, but then it bounces back after the baby's born. Slowly. But it will."

"Yes, but I don't want to *look* pregnant just yet. I just want tonight to be about him and me and…" she trailed off as she thought about what she was saying. Ailie looked in the mirror again. "I can't decide if my hips are wider today or if my stomach is pooching out more. I actually looked good in a pair of those pants last week," she said, pointing to the pile of miscellaneous clothes on her bed. "But now all I see is this…this muffin top."

"I have an idea. Why don't you take a look in my closet? Don't roll your eyes. I know I'm a bit more old-fashioned when it comes to taste…"

"Well, no…it's not bad, it's just a bit more…bohemian than my style, mom."

"Okay, but you've always said that I've got some gorgeous peasant blouses, and I think they'd cover your stomach quite nicely. You know, just pick one that kind of billows over the top and then cinches underneath."

An hour later Ailie jumped in the car, wearing a short skirt that tied loosely around her waist, once again showing off her legs, and a peasant blouse that cinched just at the right spot. She smiled and waved at her mother and Vivien as she drove from the house.

As soon as she got to the bottom of the hill her phone beeped several times, indicating new messages. Ailie pulled over and saw texts from both Ruby and Olivia, asking her to call them 'ASAP.' The last message was from Ruby. After she found her earpiece she dialed her number and got back on the road.

"Oh good!" Ruby exclaimed, as soon as she picked up. "I was about to dial your mom's house, but didn't have time for a long conversation. Olivia is in labor!" She said the last word in an elated, sing-song fashion.

"*What?!*" Ailie exclaimed, equally elated. "But her due date's not until two weeks from now! And I was supposed to *be* there. I thought her doctor said there's no way she'd be early."

"Well, she can tell you the story. So you've got to call her. Now."

"Oh? She wants to talk to me now? Isn't she at the hospital, doing…the whole birthing thing?"

Ruby spoke quickly. "No. But that's only part of the story. We went to the hospital, and the doctors told her to go back home. The baby's big, but she's barely dilated. So she's back at the house. Mathéo's out of town, which is why she called me. But then she didn't want me to see her vagina or something. I don't know. I'm over it. She's at home. Call her! Oh, by the way, did you tell him?"

"What? No, I didn't. Wait, what?" Ailie was trying to pay attention to the conversation and the road at the same time. She pulled over again.

"Okay, hang up and call Olivia. And then call me back!"

"Okay, but…" Before Ailie could finish, Ruby hung up. Ailie dialed Olivia's number and then got back on the road.

"Ailie!" Olivia howled cheerfully, somewhat out of breath, pacing around the room, holding her back with her other hand. "I'm in labor! This is crazy, but it's happening! Slowly. Maybe too slowly." She sat down on her bed and then lay down on her side, speaking serenely. "Oh, this feels so good. A break between contractions."

"I heard! I heard!" Ailie responded. "I just got off the phone with Ruby! She said Mathéo's out of town, but you don't want her there…because you don't want her to see your girly bits?"

Still laying on her side, Olivia took a couple of long breaths before calmly replying. "Okay, that's *not* exactly how the conversation went… Look, you know how Ruby is? She doesn't drive stick, so she can't drive my car. And she likes her jeans washed in a particular way. Maybe she gets them pressed too, who knows. But her clothes and her car are spotless. She's very clean. I can't have a baby around all that. What if my water breaks, spilling onto those leather seats? What if my labor doesn't progress until the next rush hour and we have to pull over and have it in the car? I was so stressed out thinking about those things... I need my body to relax. If I relax, then all the bits and pieces relax. It'll be easier. I need to be calm so my baby feels *welcome*."

"So... is there anyone with you now?"

"Yes. Anna's here now."

"Anna the accountant?"

"Anna the mom! She's had babies so many times, Ailie. She's an expert."

"Oh...and you find her calming?"

"No, but she's quiet. And I can pretty much ignore her when I need to."

"Really? What're you guys doing now?"

"I'm in the bedroom, trying to maintain a positive energy flow. Every time there's a contraction I'm supposed to 'embrace the wave.' It *sucks*."

"And Anna?"

"She's downstairs—watching TV, drinking."

"Drinking?"

"Relax. I think she's only had one glass, maybe two. She has five kids, remember? This is a vacation for her." Olivia winced and grumbled in pain.

"Okay, I should let you go..." said Ailie, looking up to read a highway sign.

"Wait! I think that was just the baby moving..." replied Olivia, elevating herself with one arm and then standing back up, pacing around the room.

"Ruby tells me you actually found *him* after our talk," she said, smiling. "So before you go, let me give you a piece of advice: if you haven't told him yet that you're pregnant—then don't. *Not yet.* The start of a relationship is the honeymoon period. Sample the goods. Just…throw yourself at him. Get it out of the way. Do it in every room of the house—like every day—before you fly back. Then you've got him. You'll be in love and he'll be in love. And then…I don't know, email him the rest of your story from the plane or something. Trust me on this one."

"Okay, thanks Olivia," laughed Ailie, thinking it was a tease.

"I'm serious!" she countered. "Look, Ruby and I were talking about it the other day…and, I have never seen you actually chase after a guy before, and I have no idea what it's like to dream about a guy for like ten years and then actually get the chance to meet him. But, I'm sure you must feel a certain amount of pressure about the whole situation, so just give *in* to those positive feelings. Build on it. Just enjoy your time as much as you can. Let nature take its course. I mean, you don't have to go on an actual honeymoon in order to feel like you're in love, but if you don't start with that feeling of the honeymoon—the fireworks and the romance—you won't have the foundation for a lasting relationship." Ailie was about to speak but Olivia continued, "Look, your baby's no bigger than a kumquat right now. I just looked it up the other day, after our last conversation. Just suck it in a little if he sees you standing up."

Pausing briefly, Olivia walked over to the open door of her bedroom and closed it slightly, before speaking in a lower voice. "Did you know that Mathéo stopped having sex with me the *minute* he found out we were pregnant? He said it was like this sacred thing, my body…growing this life. We used to have this fabulous sex life…it was almost…tantric. Wild. And then bam! Just like that. Shut off for eight months. It's not like I wanted it all the time, but it would've been nice every once in a while."

"Wow, you've never mentioned this before…"

"I know…which is why I'm telling you now. Then you remember last month my back started hurting? And every week it got worse. It's like overnight I was pregnant and celibate and in pain. It was depressing. But here's the thing—part of Mathéo's work is helping people ease their pain, without pills, you know. So I told him we *had* to have sex—the orgasms would relieve my back pain. I had to convince him it was medically necessary. And every day this week has been awesome. And then…he boarded his flight this morning, and, of course, that's when I go into labor, but he should be back in a couple of hours."

"Oh fantastic!"

Olivia let out a whimper. "Shit. I can feel another contraction coming on. You know, if it were up to Mathéo, I'd be having this kid in a field somewhere, with flowers in my hair, surrounded by goats or something. No drugs. But I have got to tell you I can't wait for some heavy narcotics. I gotta go. I love you! Do yourself a favor. Don't tell Levi just yet. Have your honeymoon first. You'll thank me later!"

As she hung up, Ailie thought about Olivia's insight. She suddenly felt very confused about the right time to tell Levi her secret. She also wondered if it was possible that she and Levi weren't sexually compatible. If so, was it selfish to find out before telling him about the pregnancy?

She considered Olivia's message for a good half hour when her phone rang—it was Ruby again. "So? What did you say to him?"

"Well…about that…" began Ailie, sheepishly. "It just wasn't a good time to tell him the other day at dinner…or on the beach. And yesterday all we did was talk on the phone, so that *really* wasn't a good time."

"You haven't told him."

"No. But now I also have new advice to consider, you know. I was just talking to Olivia, and…"

Ruby sighed audibly. "Olivia? Do tell me what our born again tree hugger told you to do?"

"What? Are you still mad at her for sending you home?"

"No…no. I'm over it. I'm over it. What did she say?"

"Well, it's kind of private, so please don't tell her I told you, but it weighs so heavily on my mind right now. She said she didn't have sex for like eight months because Mathéo didn't want to once they found out they were pregnant. That's a big deal. I mean, as much as some people downplay the role of sex in a relationship, it's…it's important to *me*. And I'm assuming it's important to him. I mean…it's not like I'd feel like a fraud without it. But I just wouldn't feel like myself if I couldn't act on my feelings. Does that make sense? And right now I feel like I've got this thing with Levi, it's happening so, you know…organically…"

"Oh, she had you on the phone for a while…"

"And if I tell him about the pregnancy…I just don't want to spoil it. Not until I know where it goes first. And I'm so tempted… So, she basically said I probably shouldn't tell him right away…not till I've…given him a test drive. For several days."

"Well of course Olivia is going to say that. She's been crying about being sex-deprived for the last eight months. Every week it's, 'Mathéo this and Mathéo that—he won't touch me.' I finally told her to look online for some inspiration."

"What? She's been talking to you about Mathéo the *whole time*?" Ailie asked, feeling somewhat hurt and excluded from some part of their friendship. "She never said a thing to me."

"I thought you just said she told you."

"Well, *now*, but…"

"Then you're all caught up. Now listen, this is a very significant piece of information that you carry with you—that you're pregnant. And I know that you already know this, so I don't need to remind you, but I will—you need to earn his trust in order to achieve the kind of deep and meaningful relationship that Olivia is complaining about right now. But in order to do that, you *know* that you should tell him that you're carrying his baby, *before* you try to sleep with him… As odd as that sentence sounds."

"Okay, okay…I know…you're right, Ruby. You're right." Ailie felt a small amount of determination return.

After several more words of encouragement Ailie hung up with Ruby, and then realized she was on the wrong road. She exited the highway and stopped her car, once again, but this time it was to check her GPS. Fortunately, it turned out she was not very far off track, and, in the end, she arrived at Levi's address right on time.

***

Ailie looked around as she stepped out of the car. None of the homes on his street were audaciously large or questionably small, but every one had its own unique structure and exterior. His house, renovated with a stone facade, and a porch that ran the length of the front of the home, reminded her of something she'd find in New England. She walked up the steps to find outdoor wooden furniture decorated with soft cushions, and large, painted terra cotta containers with tropical plants at either end of the porch. A truck and a motorcycle sat in the driveway.

Levi opened the screen door. "Hey! Come in! Come in. Did you find it okay? I hope the drive over wasn't too bad. Is it a long drive? I forgot to ask where your mom lives."

"It was fine," replied Ailie, her heart fluttering again. She could barely contain her smile, as she walked up the steps. She was delighted, noticing in her periphery that he looked at her, up and down, as she entered the house. They were both unsure of how to greet one another, so they hugged. Although the hug wasn't awkward, the moment after it was, because they still had their arms around each other, but they'd separated just enough to look into one another's eyes, as though they should go in for a kiss.

But then they both blushed and turned. He immediately put his hand on the small of her back to give her a quick tour of the house. The kitchen, living room and dining area took up most of the downstairs with a semi-open floor plan. The dining room lanai doors opened out onto a low deck, and beyond that there was a small garden boasting enormous ferns, fragrant herbs, and flowers of every color. He stood somewhat behind her as he pointed out the various features of the backyard. She could feel his chest by her back and his thigh by her hand.

"Wow!" said Ailie, turning her attention to the yard again. "This is all you? I mean, I know you do this for a living, but I guess you bring your work home with you."

Levi laughed. "I've been here nearly eight years. It didn't always look like this." He explained, as they walked back to the kitchen, that when he bought the house it was in a rather forgotten state. But he needed somewhere to live so he moved in, with only a mattress to sleep on, as soon as he signed the papers. Starting with repairs to the plumbing and electricity, he first renovated his bedroom, and then the other rooms upstairs. Finally he tore down the kitchen, knocked down some of the walls that divided the downstairs space, and rebuilt the entire first floor. It wasn't until late last year that he had the energy to tackle the backyard. "Friends helped out with some of the bigger jobs. It's tiring doing this at work, and then coming home to do it again. After finishing the backyard I told myself I wouldn't touch another inch of this house again. But, wait a few months, and I'm sure I'll find something."

She sat down on a stool by the counter. A cat unexpectedly jumped in her lap to greet her. Ailie nearly leapt out of her chair with fright. Levi hurried over, "Sorry, that's Sadie. She loves people."

He walked over and gave Sadie a gentle push and then used his hand to brush the cat's hair from Ailie's lap. "Oh, sorry," he said, pulling his hand away from her thighs, smiling bashfully. "Sorry, I didn't mean to…I don't randomly touch people's thighs. It's just so automatic—you have a cat…and then you see hair. My bad." He laughed, embarrassed.

"Oh no, it's fine, I'm fine," insisted Ailie, also laughing. "You can touch…I mean… Whatever. It's fine." Her face flush, she took a deep breath.

As he walked back to the stove, Levi added, playfully, "If I do feel the need to touch your thighs again, which…it might happen by accident again, I don't know. I promise I'll ask first."

Ailie giggled and then observed him at work. She could tell that he knew he was being watched because he was smiling, but trying not to look at her. Finally he said, bashfully, "Okay, I'm just going to have to turn my back to you so I can concentrate here."

Ailie stared at his butt and shoulders, her conversation with Ruby fading from memory.

Sadie arched her back against Ailie's legs. Ailie knelt down to pet her, thankful for the distraction.

"I hope you don't mind," he said. "I'm making a simple pasta and salad. I wanted to cook something fancier, but I forgot to ask if you're allergic to anything or what you might want to eat tonight. I didn't have the number for your cell, and by the time I called your mom's house you'd already left."

"I *love* pasta." Really, he could've handed her two pieces of cardboard with cheese in the center and she would've tried it.

They sat down at a large harvest table on the deck. "And did you build this table?" Ailie asked, teasingly.

"Yes, as a matter of fact I did."

"And the chairs?"

"No," he smiled. "Not the chairs. Or the cushions. I don't have the patience to sew. My mom sews, and she's wanted to teach me, but…no."

As Levi served them the food, Ailie realized how much she'd been looking forward to this evening. She was ecstatic, giddy again. She'd been feeling happy and light all day, and now she was here, with *him*, at his house. She wanted this feeling to last forever; she didn't want the day to end.

Levi noticed the joyful look on her face. "I'm really glad you could make it," he said.

"And I'm glad you asked me over." Her cheeks turned rosy as she looked down at her food. "It's just...I feel so comfortable with you, and it's only been..." She turned to Levi again. "I mean it doesn't feel like it's only been a few days or hours."

"Me too," he said, grinning back at her, taking a small bite of pasta. "I've had a good time."

She pushed the food around on her plate, playing with her fork. "So...that day at your shop...did you ask me to the café that day? Did you want me to...come with you?"

"The café..." He considered it. "It's possible I was hinting." He blushed again, and then added, teasingly, "But...I also thought it was adorable that you found your way to the back of the shop...without actually seeing any chairs."

"Oh...okay..." Ailie laughed, her cheeks crimson. "But...you've got to remember that I probably couldn't see very well, considering your...glistening chest... What with the angle of the light, or maybe it was the sun...your torso was just...beaming."

This time his face burned with embarrassment and he laughed looking down at his plate again. "Okay...I have no idea how to respond to that."

As they ate Ailie took small sips from the glass of wine he had poured for her, telling him, causally, that she wanted to pace herself. Halfway through the meal she asked him about what he liked to cook when he was at home and then asked what dish he might've prepared for this evening. "So if you had gotten in touch with me," she said, "before I left the house, what were you thinking of cooking?"

"Tonight?" he asked. "Oh, well I probably would've just asked you what you wanted me to make...and then checked the fridge I guess, and then improvised if I didn't have everything...something like that."

"Anything?" she asked, impressed, still playing with her fork.

"Anything. Well, within reason. Probably anything."

"Lobster? Venison? Bear?"

"Bear?" he asked, in a perplexed tone. "You'd ask me to cook bear for you?"

"No," she giggled. "I just read an article about it once. I'm kidding. I don't want to eat bear."

He looked at her, curiously. "So...I noticed you get kind of excited when we talk about food." And then asked in an earnest but good-natured tone, "you don't have some kind of strange food fetish do you?"

She laughed, protesting, "No, no, no, it's nothing like that..."

"Okay, okay, just wanted to be sure..." he said, laughing. He took a sip from his beer. "I suddenly had this image...that you were going to...I don't know...ask me to rub pancakes and syrup all over your body later on or something."

"No! No! Oh god no," she said, still giggling. "I have absolutely no...no fetishes."

"Good, because I was going to tell you we are totally out of maple syrup."

Ailie fanned her face with her hand. "Wow, no...no, I'm sorry, I can see how that looked. No...I eat off a plate...regular meal times."

Ailie wiped her eyes after she'd stopped laughing and looked at him. She noticed that he'd been staring at her lips again. Unexpectedly she felt very hot. She wasn't sure if it was a surge of pregnancy hormones, or the heat of the evening, or that she really couldn't get her mind off of him—she guessed it was probably all three. Removing her cardigan, she was proud of the way the peasant blouse showed off her cleavage. With one hand Ailie held most of her hair off her shoulders, this time fanning herself with a napkin.

Levi stood up and asked her if she needed anything. As he walked past her he brushed his hand across her upper arm and shoulder, stopping to give her a gentle kiss on the neck, before walking into the kitchen for a second beer. She closed her eyes—the same sensation engulfing her as at the restaurant, when he'd touched her ear—her whole body flooding with anticipation.

Levi returned. He looked around the table for the bottle opener, but it took him a few minutes to find it as he kept glancing over at Ailie. She still held her hair and used her free hand to retrieve a piece of ice from her glass, rubbing it across the bottom of her neck. The ice formed delicate beads of water, rolling down her chest, pooling now and then. Ailie noticed that Levi wasn't touching his food either. She giggled briefly.

"What?" asked Levi, curiously, watching her blouse cling to her skin, wherever the water settled.

"It's nothing," she said, selecting another cube of ice. "I'm just thinking about what you said a few minutes ago." Her eyes met his. "About me…I'm flattered that you were thinking about…my body."

"Oh…you caught that…" He combed his fingers through his hair, and then smiled as he picked at the label on his beer.

"And…well." Ailie ran her finger around the rim of her glass. "I thought…since you put me in the hot seat earlier, asking me that question about a food fetish…I thought I could ask you a question. You seem like a confident man," she said, flirtatiously.

He grinned, mischievously. "I probably shouldn't agree to this, but I'm curious what you're going to ask…so…okay."

For the next several minutes, they glanced frequently at one another, Ailie cooling her neck and chest with small pieces of ice, as he scratched at the label on his beer. Several times they fought the urge to laugh as they talked and smiled through their flirtatious exchange. Ailie spoke first. "I want to know more about what you'd been thinking. Because…you mentioned something about *later*?"

"Oh…*later*…" He took a swig from his beer.

"Yes…you were thinking…about the two of us…what did you have in mind?"

Levi cleared his throat. "I see…so you want to know what I want to do…tonight?"

Ailie nodded, giggling.

"Because…you look like the kind of woman who's *not* interested in…crocheting…or helping me organize the toolshed, right…things I'd normally do on a date?" He tried to maintain a straight face.

Ailie shook her head, hiding her smile with one hand.

"Well…" he replied, fixing his shirt, clearing his throat again. "We could…hmm." He tapped his finger on the edge of his plate.

"Okay, don't worry about it," Ailie said, laughing. "You don't have to answer that. I just wanted to see how far I could take the question."

He took a sip from his beer and stretched his arms. "No, no. It's okay…I got this…I got this. I can handle it. Your question was what do *I* want to do…right here, right now, with you…I'm assuming you're referring to…the sexual tension."

Ailie nodded again, trying to appear steadfast, still attempting to hide her smile.

He combed his fingers through his hair again and said, slowly, "Well…I thought we'd start by rubbing…hot lather over your…" He paused for a second. "Dishes."

172

Ailie started to giggle and was about to say something, but Levi continued, "Wait, wait…it gets better. Because…I can tell just by looking at you right now…that you are very excited…that you're a woman who likes a challenge…something hard…" he paused again for effect. "So when you get the urge…I thought we could relax on that soft rug in the living room and play…with my…" He shrugged and said casually, "…Videogames."

"Oh." Ailie beamed, fighting the urge to hurl the plates to the floor and pull him across the table. In the most serious tone she could muster, she replied, "Well, you're in luck then…because I know how to handle a stick…so I'm up for all kinds of games."

"Well we can just go straight to the videogames then," he said with a wave of his hand, setting down his bottle, the beer head gushing through the top and down the glass.

Both of them sat still, staring at each other, as though waiting for the other one to make the first move. Ailie motioned with her eyes toward the house.

Levi blushed. "Let's…stay out here for a little longer because I don't think I should stand up right now. I just need a minute…for things to…calm down."

"What?" Ailie said, giggling, pushing herself up with her arms, trying to peer at his lap over the edge of the table.

"No, no! Stay there." He laughed, stretching his arm forward, indicating for her to sit back down.

"We don't have to go inside, I'm sure that chair could hold us both," insisted Ailie, eagerly, ready to leap across the table and slide down onto his lap.

Levi studied the chair at first, and then he looked back up at her, and then at the table. Ailie became confused because he suddenly appeared very pensive. He said in an earnest tone, "Okay…I really want to tell you something, before we go any further. I just want to be honest with you…tell you some things that are important to me." He rubbed his temple with one hand. "Sorry, I didn't mean to rush and then stop…because I'm so into…what's happening here…"

The words 'honest' and 'need to tell you something' were a jarring reminder to Ailie. She sighed, looked down at the table, placing her palm on her forehead. *Crap! I have to tell him my secret too…right now, before anything happens! But would this really qualify as the right time to say I'm pregnant with his child? I mean, Ruby said it was all in the delivery, but a good delivery is also based on timing…and she didn't mention anything about the right timing for a smooth delivery. Does heavy petting count as sex? What's a good opening line?*

Levi detected the change in her demeanor. He said in a concerned voice, "Don't worry, I'm not going to say something really shocking. At least I don't think it is. And I can talk quickly."

Ailie shook her head and replied gently, "No…it's okay. I…actually have something that I should tell you too."

Ailie stalled, opened her mouth to speak, but then Levi started. "So…" he began, and then uncrossed his arms and leaned forward in his chair. He looked directly at her and spoke carefully. "I should say again…I have had…" He stopped and started again. "The last day or so has been…amazing."

Ailie's eyes brightened, her heart raced. *I'll just listen to what he has to say first.* She knew she shouldn't delay any further, but she held her breath. She didn't dare move because it looked like he was searching for the right words and she was dying to hear what he might say next.

He fidgeted. "I'm not exactly good at this. As a matter of fact, I haven't done this very much." He shifted again, nervously in his seat. "Look, I haven't gone on that many dates in the last…well, it's been a long time. And I don't really get the chance to meet a lot of single women in my line of work…"

That's totally okay. I'm fine with that.

He stopped and thought for a second. "Actually, that's not true, I meet a lot of women. But I don't always meet a lot of women that I…like *a lot*." He smiled again at Ailie. "And when I first saw you at the store, I was…I thought, 'here's a gorgeous woman and she wants to ask me some questions,' and I wanted to talk to you more, and then you came to the café…but I never figured…Well, don't get me wrong, I *have* been on dates, lots of dates, but I don't always have the time, or take the time, to get to know someone, and… "

Ailie reached forward and took his hand. "It's okay," she said. "I think I know where you're going."

"Well, I do have some things that I want to tell you." He still held her hand. "Like we were saying earlier, I feel like we've gotten to know each other pretty well. And I can't believe I just met you a couple of days ago. But I'm having such a great time. I don't know if it's too soon to assume that you feel the same way I do, but I know I feel something."

Ailie nodded. *Yes, yes. Go on.*

"Like I said, I just wanted to tell you more about me…"

Ailie was on edge, her throat tightened. *Wait, is he going to tell me he's married? Shit, his wife is probably the one who actually decorated this place. Or maybe he's only got a few months to live. I hope he's never done time. Is that why he's not on Facebook?* She dabbed her napkin against the sweat that beaded on her forehead. *Crap. Why is it so hot out here?*

Levi looked at her. "You look a little nervous. I don't mean to make you nervous."

"I'm not nervous. Do you think it's hot? Because it feels like it just got hotter. I'm okay. Go on."

"Um. Okay. So…what I wanted to tell you is that I have a daughter." He stopped to gauge Ailie's reaction. Ailie sat still. "And that obviously means that I have an ex. Not an ex-wife, but…girlfriend…"

Sigh. I don't want to meet her...

He glanced at her, and then resumed. "We were young. We didn't have a lot in common. She's a great person. She's a great mom. We met about ten years ago, when I was going through a turbulent time. But, like I said, there wasn't much to the relationship... well, besides sex I guess. Well, a lot of sex actually. I mean, it's almost like the whole relationship was about sex really."

"Yep, I got it." *I need to meet her.*

"And then we had our daughter. It didn't last long after that... It was a long time ago."

"What's your daughter's name? How old is she?"

"She's nine. Her name is Fiona." He smiled as he thought about her. "Little Fi. And she takes up a good chunk of my time, between school, sports, theater on the weekends. I used to have her here almost every weekend, but now she's a little more independent, and she wants to spend more time with her friends. Now she comes over just about every other weekend. Fiona is probably the only reason I never moved back to the east coast." He cleared his throat. "You had asked me before why I don't move back to the east coast, and this is why. I just wasn't ready to tell you yet."

"Wow, I'd love to meet her some time," said Ailie, sincerely.

Levi smiled, affectionately. "Kids are...hard work. So I spent a few hours cleaning this place before you got here. It was so hot too. I think I showered twice today. It's easier now than it was five years ago. I don't know how many toys a kid needs, but...this place is sometimes out of control. She's got a huge personality." He chuckled. "And that cat...that poor cat. Sadie's great with Fiona, but Fi wanted to name her 'Boner' when we first found her because she was eating chicken bones out of our garbage can. To this day she sometimes still throws a fit when she hears me call the cat 'Sadie.' At some point she'll get it...and then I'll have to start worrying about other things." Ailie laughed. "She's funny, she's quirky, and very determined. And, yes, I'd love to introduce you to her sometime. She'll be here this weekend."

Ailie let a couple of minutes pass as they held hands and looked at one another, amorously, exchanging smiles. *Okay, now my turn. MY TURN. I will say it! No…I can't. I really don't want to. I have never been less eager for it to be my turn.* At last she found the nerve to speak. "Levi…"

But before she could utter another word, he interrupted, "Okay, so that reminds me of the other thing I should mention."

"I'm sorry?" said Ailie, confused.

"Levi… is not my name."

"What?"

"Finnian is my name. Levi…is a name that my twin brother used to use." He let go of her hand and sat back in his chair before he spoke again. "I told you the other day that I have two brothers….one is a couple of years older, and the other was my twin. We were identical twins. Sometimes people got us confused. Lots of people got us confused." He looked at Ailie whose eyes were as wide as saucers. Her mouth hung open.

What? How could I end up with the wrong brother?

"I'm sorry, I should've told you earlier. But, it's not something I talk about all the time."

What am I supposed to do now? Am I supposed to ask him where his brother is?

"He died. He died ten years ago. He was my best friend. Someone I looked up to when I was growing up. He was the older one. He was strong one, the more confident one, the one who always took everything to the next level. His real name was actually Garret." He rolled his eyes and laughed. "He hated that name. But my parents refused to let him change it, so when we were kids he started asking everyone to call him 'Levi,' and by the time we were teenagers the name really stuck. I don't know if he thought the name was cool, or tough, or just better than Garret."

Well, if you really think about it, he had a point. I mean, right now I'm wrestling with the fact that I'm carrying your dead brother's kid, but…Levi is a much sexier name than Garret.

He paused again. "After Levi and I graduated we worked together. We built up a small business. Well, it was his idea. He always came up with the ideas. My grandparents loaned us the money and my dad guided us. We were young, we had no idea what was involved in setting up a business. But after a few months we had regular customers, and a couple of years later we were dealing with people in other cities. At first, when people accidentally called me Levi I'd make it a habit to correct them, but after a while it was useless. It was a business, and I never saw half those people again, so it didn't really matter who they thought I was. Levi was the dynamic one, the one who knew how to talk to clients, bring 'em in. At some point I stopped saying anything because it was just easier *not* to correct people. So I got used to it. And sometimes I still run into clients from back in the day, especially in New York…and sometimes I find that I still don't have the energy… or maybe I don't have the desire to explain what happened…you know, that my brother's dead. Shit, it's been ten years, and if they haven't heard about it by now… And….sometimes it makes me feel good to be called Levi, like somehow he's here, with me…again."

Ailie placed her hand over her mouth disbelievingly. "I know I should've mentioned it the other day, Ailie, but then I forgot. And…I mean, it's only been how many hours since we met? I guess I got carried away. It's my fault. I'm sorry. I should've said something at the café…" He took a deep breath. "But I could've sworn that I gave *my* name when your mom picked up the phone yesterday…"

Ailie set her chin on her palm, her eyes unfocused, fixed straight ahead. *I feel like I've been saying your name—I mean, HIS name—at least once an hour.*

Finn pulled his chair closer. "Like I said, I really didn't think we'd hit it off like this…you know, everything's happened so fast. It's been great! I just didn't expect us…that I'd feel…right now, like this…"

Ailie spoke between her fingers, almost in a whisper. "How? How did he…"

"In a plane accident. He was…he was cocky. He could be really cocky sometimes, and he loved adrenaline. He taught me how to ride a motorcycle. One day he'd want to go skydiving, the next day he'd be kayaking down a waterfall. It didn't leave much time for the business. At some point I was watching after things more often than he was. My mom said he'd give her a heart attack one day. She was so right…" He stared at the table as though he might find the right words in front of him. "And when it happened, when he died, I left. I didn't know where to go. I got on my motorcycle and just kept…going."

"Is that why you moved out here?"

"Looking back…yeah. I came out here to escape, to be numb, to be somewhere else. I certainly didn't come out here to find myself. Instead I found Lorelei. My ex. Back then she was wild. We'd be out drinking, smoking, whatever all night. I thought she was the best thing. She was sexy."

"Of course." *Now I'm dying to meet this woman.*

His smile returned. "I'm sorry, we're going *way* off topic here. The point is, please call me Finnian. Some people call me Finn or Finch. I should've told you sooner. I just didn't think that I might see you again… and again…. and again."

Ailie put one hand on her temple and rubbed slowly.

He became concerned again. "So…did I say something? Well, I know I said a lot. But I hope all this doesn't change anything. It's probably a lot of details for one night. I guess I didn't realize how complicated this might look."

Ailie responded softly, "No, no. Believe me, I understand complicated." She took a deep breath, placed both of her hands firmly on the table and looked him squarely in the eyes. "I need to tell you something and I just need to say it. Here goes." A large lump developed in her throat, dry and chalky as she swallowed. "Your brother. Levi. He donated sperm. Apparently before he died. I then bought that sperm. I am now pregnant with his child."

As if suddenly uncomfortable, he leaned back in his chair, and then leaned forward again to rest his arms on the table. "Wait...come again?"

She took a deep breath. Her stomach twisted and her heart raced. She repeated, "I am pregnant. Your brother Levi is, I mean was, the... biological father."

Finnian looked away, as if trying to digest everything that she'd just said, and then he turned back to her. He reclined again, crossing his arms behind his head, and let out a slow soft whistle. After what felt like an eternity to Ailie, he spoke. "That is definitely not the story I was expecting. How...did this happen? He died ten years ago. And then why...what...you came out here to find him?"

"Um...well, that was two questions." Her thoughts came quickly, but her lips felt slow and awkward. "To your first question, they can do a lot these days with storage, sperm and eggs and things. But about Levi....well, originally yes. It did start off that way. I looked for him. But...then I found you. Of course I thought you were him...but...now I know it's you."

He stared at her, almost vacantly. He didn't look angry, but she wasn't sure if he was thinking or stunned. Then he stood up and walked into the house. Ailie heard the clanking of bottles coming from the kitchen. She turned her head. "What...what are you doing?"

"I'm just going to to pour myself a small amount of scotch."

He returned to the table with a glass three quarters full. He swallowed a mouthful and coughed, pounding his chest a couple of times with his fist. His voice was hoarse. "This one's not as smooth as I remember."

"Are you going to drink *all* of that?"

"Want some?"

Ailie shot him a look.

Finnian smiled. "I'm sorry. Bad joke."

Ailie sighed. "I could probably drink a whole bottle right now."

He set the glass down. "Okay, so take me through this again. Because…well, you've got to understand why I'm a little…" He scratched his head. "Hell, I don't even know what to think right now. I know we've just met…but Ailie I…and now this, this story…."

"Well, it's not a story…it's my life," Ailie asserted. "People donate sperm all the time. People who can't get pregnant or are waiting to have children later in life get IVF all the time. Separately, all these things are not unusual. But…but yeah, I guess I see where you're coming from. I waited a while to use the… *product* that I bought."

"Ten years?"

"It wasn't ten years like that. It was ten years of building a career, it was ten years of deliberating and not knowing when might be the right time to do it. It was ten years of *life*. A decade, figuring out my future."

"And, you came out here because…now it needs a father?"

"No, no, that's not it at all. I came out here because of curiosity, because I had always wondered… '*What If.*' I don't know, I didn't realize I was such a romantic at heart. I didn't think it through. I didn't even think I'd *find* you."

"Find Levi."

"Yes, Levi. I didn't think I'd find Levi. And now it turns out that I didn't find him. I found you. I asked you about a chair and… now here we are."

"Here we are." He sat in his chair, silently, looking around the yard as though searching for answers. He turned back to her. "When is the baby due?"

"At the beginning of May. May 7th. Maybe earlier. Right now it's May 7th."

Finnian grew quiet again. Ailie's hands felt clammy, she rubbed them together. Even now she couldn't take her eyes off him. She didn't want to look anywhere else, as though waiting for an answer from him, fearing it might be the last time she would see him.

Eventually, he spoke. "I'm sorry. This is just a lot of information, a lot to process. I want to believe you, I really do...but it just doesn't sound like something my brother would've done. I loved him, he was my best friend, but...he never thought about consequences, he wasn't a planner. He just thought about things and did them. He could barely keep a girlfriend. I'm not sure he ever had a girlfriend. He just slept with people. He was an ass that way. Sometimes he'd drink or party hard and things would get out of hand. He was too busy going from woman to woman. He wasn't the kind of person to donate...anything. It just doesn't sound like something he'd do."

Again they sat quietly. This time they didn't look at one another. Neither of them moved.

Finally, Finn broke the silence. "I invited you over, thinking it would just be the two of us...and now...There's three of us...almost four if you count Levi since we keep talking about him." He closed his eyes and rubbed his forehead. "I really need some time. I need to think."

"Okay, I understand." Ailie said quietly. Both of them rose from their chairs, slowly. As he walked past her she reached into her purse and pulled out the tattered piece of paper with Levi's profile. Without saying anything to him she placed it on the table for him to see later.

He walked her to the front door. Sadie eagerly accompanied them through the house. They stopped on the porch to say good-bye, Sadie brushed up against their legs, seeking attention. Flustered, Ailie wondered if this would be her last chance to speak with him. "I'm sorry. I'm so sorry. Maybe I should've said something at the beginning. It's not the best way to introduce yourself to someone you've never met before, but...and then...I just...I got caught up in everything. I loved it. All of it."

She looked into his eyes and then at his lips. "Before I go, I just wanted to see…" She didn't finish her sentence; instead she leaned forward and kissed him. At first he hesitated but then he put his arms around her and leaned in closer. He kissed her lips and her neck and then her mouth again. She put her arms around his waist, and he pulled her closer still. Their collective breath came fast and heavy. She took a step back and pulled him gently with her. Her back pressed against the wall, and she could feel the weight of him on her. She tucked her hands inside the waist of his jeans and then slid them onto his backside.

All of a sudden, came a small screech. They both jumped in surprise in time to see Sadie run back into the house, her tail tucked between her legs.

"Sadie!" uttered Finnian, in a frustrated tone.

Boner… thought Ailie, watching the cat scurry inside. One of them must have stepped on her tail, she guessed.

Ailie straightened her shirt while Finn adjusted his jeans. "Okay, so you'll need some time to think?" she asked quietly.

"Yes." He tucked his hands into the pockets of his jeans and leaned against the frame of the door as he watched her walk to her car.

19

This probably has a lot to do with your mother...

Ailie tried to soften her grip on the steering wheel but the knot in her stomach prevented her from relaxing. She found spa music on satellite radio, but instead of filling her mind with visions of beaches or celestial journeys she became irritated; without taking her eyes off the road, she pushed the radio buttons a couple of times to find new music, but nothing appealed to her. Frustrated, she turned it off and drove in silence for a half hour or more, staring at the road as it disappeared under the beam of her headlights. Highway signs and light posts flashed past as she drove; a half moon hung low above the hills like an expectant belly. The quiet inside the car did nothing to diminish her doubts as she went over what had just happened, again and again. She was vexed by the irony of the situation—it was the pregnancy that brought her to Finn after a decade of longing and dreaming, and hours of searching and planning, and…within the shortest amount of time, after just a few sentences…it's why he asked her to leave. Ailie felt a growing sense of despair, wondering if she'd ever hear from him again.

She considered calling her friends but then remembered that it was far past midnight on the east coast, and Olivia was probably having her baby right now. The last thing she wanted to do was to cry into the ear of a new mother. Besides, she thought, her friends couldn't change anything that had transpired tonight. Her friends couldn't provide for her the one person that she craved, the one person that she'd fallen for and now could not stop thinking about. She wanted desperately to go back his house, to be there with him again, to hear him tell her that this wasn't the end.

Her throat ached. But she was afraid to swallow, because it would certainly trigger tears. She tried to turn the radio back on, but the satellite radio wasn't connecting, and she couldn't figure out what button to push without taking her eyes off the road. Finally she managed to find a local FM station. They were playing Roy Orbison's "I Drove All Night." She turned it down at first, annoyed with the romantic lyrics and the upbeat tempo. But then she began to pay attention to the words:
Nothing erases this feeling…
…I was dying to get to you…

She turned up the radio, listening intently to the desire and urgency in Orbison's voice. Her thoughts drifted back to those last minutes on the porch with Finnian.

When the song was over a female DJ came on, "Now let's listen to Celine's version of the same song. You may remember this one from the Chrysler commercial in 2003."

"I Drove All Night" came back on, and Ailie's throat tightened again. This time she couldn't contain her anguish as Celine Dion belted the highest notes—the same verses about heartache and release. Tears pooled in her lower eyelids, gliding softly past her cheeks. "I should probably turn this off," she said to herself, quietly. But then she turned it up a little louder. "Olivia would tell me to give in to this… so I can free myself…"

The DJ came on again. "And, finally, here's Cindy Lauper's version of 'I Drove All Night.' This is what brought it to the top of the charts back in '89. Let me know which one you like best."

"What? You're kidding me," she said, glancing briefly at the radio buttons. "Again?" But within seconds she put her hand on the volume and turned it up louder. "Fuck it," she said, singing at the top of her voice with Cindy Lauper.

Could taste your sweet kisses...

...this fever for you is just burning me up inside

I drove all night to get to you...

Nothing erases this feeling...

Ailie let Cindy take over the song as her tears formed rivulets, coming faster and faster. Her thoughts went back to Finnian—his lips, his tongue, the kiss. She felt his touch, his body pressed against hers. She felt his hand again, sliding under her shirt, touching her breast. She recalled the warmth of his skin as she ran her hands across his hips. Intoxicated by the yearning and passion of the song, she wanted to go back to him right now, this minute, to see his smile again, to be wanted by him again, to taste his kiss again...so that he could tell her that everything would be okay, that everything would work out.

But when she arrived at her mother's house, when she cut the engine, when the music was gone, she was left with a sobering reality...that she had to wait. She had to wait and see if he wanted to talk to her again. She had to wait and see if he wanted anything else to do with her.

When Ailie entered the house she had no desire to talk to her mother or her grandmother. She just wanted to bury herself in bed and wake up to something else. Fortunately, the main house was dark and Ailie tiptoed to the courtyard. She saw Vivien through one of the French doors, laughing, watching late night TV, bags of chips and chocolates spread out in front of her.

As the doors of her room softly shut behind her, Ailie undressed and then lay down in bed. She closed her eyes, and the words to "I Drove All Night" echoed through her mind. She tried to revive her earlier feelings and fantasized that Finnian was lying beside her, kissing her neck...

"Ailie." Gloria knocked softly on the door.

With her eyes still closed, Ailie flipped to her side and put a pillow over the other ear, trying to re-capture the images she'd been building.

"Ailie." Gloria tapped on the door again.

From under the pillow she yelled, "I'm tired! I just need some sleep, please mom?"
Then she heard the muffled voices her mother and grandmother.

"What'd she say?"

"She said she was tired."

"Oh. Is that a good thing or a bad thing?"

"Well, I'm not sure."

"Should we leave her alone then?"

"Yes!" Ailie yelled. "Yes! Please. I'm tired."

Again one of them spoke. "That's probably a bad thing."

"Poor thing. Let's give her some time."

Ailie closed her eyes again, but this time the moment was gone. She was upset. She went back to her conversation with Finnian again and again, wondering how she could've done things differently. Wondering what she should've done for a different outcome. She couldn't quite tell when it happened, but at some point, her mind became utterly exhausted and she fell asleep. The wind rustled dry brush outside. A tree gently tapped at her window.

***

The weekend came and went, with no word from Levi or Finnian or Finn or Finch. Despite—and because—of all that transpired, Ailie still felt like a teenager. She kept checking the answering machine, fiddling with all of the buttons to see if it was turned on properly, to see if the volume was adjusted correctly. She sulked around the house, looking for things to do, but nothing interested her for very long. Her only successful diversion was to take long walks around the hills surrounding the house.

"How about your cell phone, dear?" her mother asked, encouragingly.

"No. I didn't give it to him that number."

"Why wouldn't you give him your cell phone?"

"Because it doesn't work out here! And then that first night on the beach we'd lost track of time and then he had to go somewhere. I just gave him your number...and, besides, if I gave him two numbers, then it would just confuse him, and then he'd have to pick one to call, and how would I know which one he'd call? I'd have to walk down the hill every hour just to check my voicemail." She threw her hands up in frustration.

"Okay...." said Gloria in a calming voice. "Then *you* should call *him*."

"Call him? Wha...What? I can't."

"Why not?"

"Because."

"Oh," replied Gloria, more confused than before.

Dejectedly, Ailie walked back to her room and closed the doors behind her.

Gloria gave her a couple of hours on her own, but then tried talking to Ailie again. She knocked lightly and entered. Ailie was sitting on the bed, her eyes, nose and lips, swollen from crying. Small pyramids of used tissues littered the room. Gloria sat down on the bed beside her.

Gloria hugged Ailie. "Honey, I've never seen you like this before. But I can't help you if you don't talk to me. I know I was a bit aloof when you were young..."

188

"Very aloof." Ailie was quick to correct her.

"Okay, I wasn't always the best mom, but the point is that we're much closer now. We've done so well. I love you so much." She squeezed Ailie again. "And I want to be here for you. But I can't help you if you don't talk to me. Please talk to me. I want to help. What happened?"

Ailie rolled her eyes. The last thing she wanted to do was to retrace the mistakes of the past week. But she was tired of overanalyzing the situation. She reconsidered that perhaps talking about it was exactly what she needed. "Well, you know I came out here for vacation, right? But then I was told that this person I'd been looking for—someone I really wanted to find—might be out here. His name was Levi."

"Levi?"

"Yes. So you see, when we went down to Santa Monica I was actually looking for this guy, Levi. I know I should've told you guys this, but I wasn't sure if I'd find him. And then I introduced you to that guy at the store. Remember? I told you his name was Levi."

"Well, of course I remember him, but... A-ha!" Gloria appeared to be mentally putting the pieces together. "So this is making more sense to me now. I was so confused the other day. That was Levi at the store. You looked so excited to talk to him. But then the gentleman who called the other day, before you drove back down there... I remember he said his name was Finnian. And I thought, well, this must not be the same man. So I just handed you the phone..." Gloria hugged Ailie again. "Honey, you've been dating two different men? Wow, the way you've been sulking and crying. Are you in love with *both* of them? This is starting to make sense to me now! It's not easy to choose between men, believe me, I've been there!"

"Did I hear that my granddaughter is smitten with two boys?" Vivien asked as she strode into the room. "Holy shit, someone's been busy! You trying to find a dad for that little tyke before it arrives? I want to hear this story!"

Listening to her mother's summary, Ailie had been growing irritated, but now she was ready to explode. "Why can't you just once listen to me talk?"

189

she screamed, looking back and forth between her mother and grandmother, but mostly at her mother. "Just once let me finish what *I* have to say! Without giving me your opinion!"

Gloria and Vivien stared at Ailie in stunned silence. "Mother—for once, this is about me, and someone *I'm* seeing! A man! *One* man! Not two! That *I* am seeing! Not you! This has *nothing* to do with you, mom! Nothing! NO-THING!"

Vivien waited a few seconds and then spoke, softly, "Well…you remember our conversation, Ailie. This actually…probably has *a lot* to do with your mother, so this might be a good segue…And I'm still confused about which guy you're seeing…"

Ailie and her mother shot angry looks at Vivien. Vivien bit her lip.

Ailie closed her eyes and counted to ten, but it didn't work to calm her. Without looking again at her mother or grandmother she stood up and walked out of the room. She could hear her mother or grandmother, or maybe it was both of them, calling after her, but Ailie ignored their pleas. She walked through the house, and the front door, and then found a familiar footpath through the front yard. Eventually she made her way down the long hill to the valley and town below.

An hour after leaving her room she arrived to one of the town's coffee shops and went inside. A thin, young girl, with braces, enormous brown eyes and long blonde hair, was behind the counter, cleaning the floors. "We're closing in a half hour," she announced as Ailie walked in.

"Okay," Ailie responded, halfheartedly, striving to smile. She ordered a chamomile tea and sat down. The café was empty.

The barista brought the steaming cup of tea to Ailie. Ailie asked for some ice cubes to cool it down, but the girl responded that they'd already dumped all the ice for the day. As the barista walked away, Ailie looked out the window. She wore her mother's enormous square-framed sunglasses, the only ones she could find before exiting the house. Her face was puffy; she'd cried for the entire hour that it took to get to town. She wasn't sure if she felt any better. She couldn't recall any other time she'd been this depressed. But whenever she tried to tell herself to think positive, she wondered if it wouldn't be more of a delusion at this point—that Finnian might call or that he might want to see her again.

Ailie thought about Ruby and Olivia. She'd thought about them several times throughout the weekend. But she hadn't called Ruby because she wanted to wait and call her after she heard back from Finnian. She wanted to wait and give Ruby good news…but at this point, without any word from Finnian, it was just as easy to wait and give her the bad news at home, when she returned to New York. And she hadn't called Olivia because Olivia was probably at one of the highest points in her life right now, after the birth of her baby, while Ailie felt like she was experiencing one of the lowest points in hers. So when she received Olivia's birth announcement over the weekend, via email, Ailie responded with a very long congratulatory letter, filling it with lots of happy words, smiley faces, and plenty of exclamation points and x's and o's, in the hopes that it would suffice until she got home to see Olivia for herself.

Abruptly, the music in the café became very loud, blaring Bonnie Tyler's "Total Eclipse of the Heart."

"It's time to go…I know…I know…" Ailie muttered. She closed her eyes, attempting to shut out the romantic lyrics of the song, but instead new tears formed.

Tyler's song ended, and Journey's "Open Arms" blasted over the speakers. Ailie rolled her eyes at the love ballad, feeling irritated again, just as she had before her walk. But she didn't want to yell at the barista. She sat through the first two or three minutes of "Open Arms," and then wiped her eyes and walked to the counter where the girl was stacking cups.

"Hi," said Ailie, forcing a smile. "I know you're only open for another fifteen minutes, but I just wanted to stay for a little longer and finish my drink. Could you possibly…maybe play something other than Bonnie Tyler or Journey?"

"Journey?" asked the girl, looking at her blankly. "Who's...what's...? Do you mean this stuff?" she said, pointing up in the air. Ailie nodded. "Ohhh," replied the barista. "My manager's playing that. She's in the back. I'll go tell her to play something else."

"Okay, thanks," Ailie shouted as the girl walked toward the back. "Just...ask her if, maybe no more 80s...or none of these love songs?"

"Sure!" the girl yelled back as she went behind the swinging door.

Ailie sat down at her table again, sipping her tea when "Heartbeat Song," a more modern love ballad, by Kelly Clarkson, started to play. Ailie closed her eyes and bowed her head, resting her thumb and index finger on the bridge of her nose.

"This ...sucks," she mumbled. *I can't believe some people fall in love more than once in life. This is such a miserable experience. If I weren't pregnant I'd take up smoking... I feel like a piece of shit on the bottom of someone's shoe. A piece of shit I want to throw at that doe-eyed barista. Why am I thinking like this? Stop it.* She shook her head and then realized a headache was coming on.

Ailie threw her tea into the nearest trash bin and walked out the café doors. "Heartbeat Song" continued to play on the speakers, to empty seats outside. She heard the track all the way down the block, until she turned the corner, and started the ascent to her mother's home.

20

I see we've been busy.

Ailie entered the house, and, as expected, Gloria and Vivien waited for her in the living room. Neither of them said a thing as Ailie closed the door, took off her shoes, and sat down between them on the couch.

"Ok," said Ailie, breaking the silence, looking back and forth at her mother and grandmother.

Neither Gloria nor Vivien knew who should speak first or what Ailie was agreeing to. Finally, Gloria asked, "Okay? This means…you've made a decision?"

"Yes," replied Ailie, confidently, her cheeks and nose still inflamed. "I assume he hasn't called…otherwise you guys would've jumped on me the minute I walked through the door. So… *I* will call *him.*"

"Well," said Vivien firmly, "I'm glad you've decided on one of them. But I hope you're not just picking the cuter one. You can never go by looks alone. Your mother can advise you on that one…"

"Shush, mom!" Gloria retorted. "She already told us she'd decided on one man! Whichever one she picked, she doesn't need to explain it to us." And then, turning to Ailie she said, "Just go with your feelings, honey."

"Okay," said Ailie, taking a fresh tissue out of a box on the coffee table. "I'll just need a pen...I'm going to write a few things down, so I don't make an ass of myself."

"Oh good," replied Gloria, standing up to retrieve a pen and paper for Ailie. "I think it'll be great for you to get these things off your chest, and, trust me, you'll feel so much better afterwards."

"If you ask me," added Vivien. "You should ask him to come over. Then we can all get a good look at him, so we can all decide if we like this guy. He's made a mess of my poor granddaughter..."

"Oh please, mom," Gloria interjected. "You'd frighten him." Gloria looked back at Ailie. "Seriously, honey, tell him whatever you need to over the phone. Feel free to express your heart to him. Open up."

"But stick to your principles!" insisted Vivien.

"It's okay to be vulnerable," Gloria said, gently.

"But with confidence," added Vivien.

"Explain how you feel."

"But get to the point. Don't be all wishy-washy."

"That's enough," Ailie replied in a firm voice. "Both of you. I'm ready to do this thing, please don't talk me out of it."

***

An hour later Gloria placed a chair in the hallway for Ailie to sit on while she talked on the phone, and then promised that they would not interfere or listen in on any part of the conversation. Ailie held a small index card

194

with talking points so she wouldn't lose focus. She felt another lump in her throat, but her face and eyes were dry.

Ailie dialed Finn's number. It went to voicemail after the first ring. Ailie hesitated, set down her notes, and then spoke, "Hi. Finn. Sorry, I know you said you need time, and that I'm supposed to wait. Um…I'm leaving…soon. To go home. To New York. New York City, that is. That's home. Did I tell you that? I can't recall…we've talked so much, and… Um…I waited and hoped for you to call. There's so much more I want to tell you." Fresh tears formed. "I didn't expect any of this to happen. Like you said, it happened so fast. But on the beach, and on the phone, and at your house, and at the café too—that was you and me. It was just the two of us." She was already off of her talking points and wasn't sure what to say next.

Vivien appeared at the end of the hallway, creating a small heart shape with her fingers and mouthing the words 'I love you! Tell him you love him!' Ailie spoke into the phone again, "I think I'm in love with you. I know it was just a few days…but sometimes that's all it takes."

Gloria stepped into the hallway, next to Vivien, and whispered, "You *really* love him. Tell him you *really* love him." Ailie motioned for them to go away.

Ailie took a deep breath. "I mean, I *know* that I love you. It probably sounds far-fetched, but now that I've gotten to know you, been near you, I can't imagine being with anyone else but you. When I sleep at night I dream about you. It's you that I want. Finnian."

She was about to speak into the phone again when an automated voice said, "You have thirty seconds to finish your message."

Gloria slid a piece of paper down the hall, it landed at Ailie's feet. On it she wrote, *Your cell number!*

She spoke rapidly into the phone, "Oh, and I totally forgot to give you my number the other night, so here it is. I completely understand if you don't want to call after this really weird message, but if you do, then that would be great. But maybe you like to write? Maybe email? Texts are good too." Ailie ended her message with her phone number and spelled out her email address and then hung up.

She sat there for a couple of minutes staring into space, digesting what she'd just said. Rising slowly from her chair, she proceeded down the hall, a little stunned and unbelieving, still staring straight ahead. *What the hell did I just do?* she thought. *Why don't I feel better? I can't believe I just said all that. He's going to think I'm crazy. But now I've said everything. I've put it all out there. Now I really can't change it. It's all on the line. Now the ball's in his court. But it was already in his court. But now it's really in his court. Shit. I shouldn't have done that. Why did I listen to my mother and grandmother? Out of all people!* Ailie felt a hot flash coming on. She angrily fanned her face with the index card and continued down the hall. *First I'm going to kill my mother and then my grandmother, and then I'm going to fly to New York and kill Ruby...for telling me to listen to old people.*

***

Ailie felt a great sense of relief when her plane touched down in New York. She'd spent half of her time in the air trying to distract herself with work email and plans for upcoming meetings, but she found it difficult to concentrate. The couple next to her seemed like newlyweds, cuddling, intertwining their legs and sometimes their arms, across their seats—so much so that half the time she wasn't sure where one of them ended and the other one began. Her feelings about the couple fluctuated between happiness and disdain. One minute she was delighted for them and imagined what it might be like for her and Finnian on their first flight or first adventure. She was reminded of his playfulness and how relaxed she felt in his company. But the next minute she was annoyed and angry with the couple, their giggling and snuggling, how they seemed so focused on one another, without any considerations for the world around them. It was the first time she wanted to tell two strangers to 'get a room.'

Frustratingly enough, when she wasn't attempting work, and when she wasn't daydreaming about Finnian, she was thinking about Levi. During take off and landing, and a few episodes of turbulence, she wondered about Levi's last flight and how he died. She wondered what kind of person he might be today—could she have fallen for Levi the same way she fell for

Finnian? Every time there was a bump in the flight, she placed her hand on her stomach, reminding her of this permanent connection she had with both brothers. If Finnian never called her again, how easy would it be to forget about him, now that she had this daily reminder, this flesh and blood that they shared? She wondered if the children of identical twins also looked alike and made a mental note to look that up once she was home.

With NYC coming into view through the airplane window, Ailie was finally able to shift gears—she was eager to be back at home, get back to her friends, and get back to some kind of a routine. Back to reality.

It turned out that Ruby had left several messages on her phone, and now, as Ailie walked through the airport, she listened to a new voicemail from her.

Hello? Ailie I have left you so many messages. Where are you? What is going on with you? Olivia said you sent an email, but why aren't you calling us back? If you don't call me soon, I'm going to be forced to call your mother's house, and then they're going to ask me about my life and who I'm dating and…and they might ask me about Levi. Yes, they might ask me about Levi. And if that happens, I cannot promise you a thing. Those women like to ask questions. I say this politely. I know you love them. I love them too. But they can be insistent. So you need to CALL me. CALLLLLL meeee. Call me. Love you!

Ailie sighed. She sent a quick text to Ruby. *Sorry. I'm back home. I'll tell you everything Monday. Miss you. Xx!*

She put her phone back in her pocket and hailed a cab. As she waited, she took a deep breath, inhaling the cool air, relishing October's arrival in New York. Trees flaunted their colors of purple, gold and crimson. This meant brisk evenings and possibly frosty mornings. For a short time sunny days might warm the air, curtailing the sharp, biting effect of a cold autumn. But such days would become less frequent with each passing week. It was officially autumn, the fleeting season.

***

Monday morning came, and Ailie studied her profile in the mirror. She let her stomach relax and placed her hands lovingly on her developing belly, smiling affectionately, thinking about the tiny human inside—which was about the size of a small lemon now. "It's you and me kid." She wore a new dress, from the maternity shop she'd visited with her mother and grandmother. It was a simple dress, with clean lines, and it reached to just an inch above her knees so that she could still show off her legs. Before leaving home she threw on a thick pea coat, and hat and gloves, to keep warm.

After weeks of working from home she planned to re-enter the office today and let the rumors fly about her new belly. Her boss, Geoffrey, would obviously be curious, maybe he'd even have the audacity to start asking questions before she was ready to talk to him about pregnancy and her plan for the next year. So long as the pregnancy wasn't contagious, she thought Geoffrey would eventually respond well.

Ailie didn't have to wait long to speculate. As soon as she stepped off the elevator, jacket in one hand and decaf latte in the other, the receptionist in the lobby—usually a very talkative twenty-something—remained absolutely speechless. Instead of saying 'hello Miss Faulkner' her eyes widened, like saucers, focused on Ailie's changed figure. Her fingers hit the keyboard the second that Ailie walked past her desk.

She went straight to her office and hung up her coat. Before she had the chance to sit down Geoffrey opened the door. "Welcome back Ailie!" He looked her up and down. "I see we've been busy."

"Excuse me?" Ailie responded.

"The Hagar campaign. I know you only helped peripherally, but it was great. Another success." He then smiled, turned around, and closed the door behind him.

The door had barely shut when Ruby gleefully barged in. "Where is she? Let me see!" Ailie stood up from her chair and the two women hugged and squealed and hugged again. Ruby stood back to get a better look at Ailie's belly. "Wow!" She let out a small chuckle, "And it's just going to get bigger."

"Yes, and can you believe I'm nearly a third of the way through now. I have my next appointment lined up. They might be able to tell me if it's a boy or a girl. Want to come?"

"Of course I'm going to be there!" They hugged again. "Now I have to run to a meeting, but before I go, are you up for visit with Olivia tonight?"

Ailie thought about Olivia and her new baby boy. They had so much to catch up on. "Yes! Yes. I'm totally up for it!" she said, elated to be home. It felt like she'd been gone for ages.

***

The end of the work day neared, and Ailie wanted to go home, to bed. She was exhausted. First days back at work were never easy, but this one felt brutal. She hadn't checked her personal inboxes all day, and was disappointed to find nothing from Finnian. She drummed her fingers on the desk and then lay her head down. Her body felt so heavy, she wondered if her belly was larger now than when she entered the office this morning. She and Ruby were meant to head to Olivia's house around 7pm, so she decided to log off work email and tend to personal matters until it was time to go.

There was so much information to digest before the baby's arrival, and several weeks ago she downloaded a pregnancy app, and signed up for alerts from a pregnancy website. Their emails gave expectant mothers an update once a week—illustrating the size of the fetus based on familiar fruits, also explaining what was happening inside and outside of the bodies of mom and baby. All of this information might've helped if she actually took the time to read it, but she was finding it increasingly difficult to be knowledgeable about 'everything' at home and at work, for herself and the baby. Ailie opened the calendar on her phone and set a daily reminder to read her pregnancy app and then set two alarms within two hours of each other so there was less of a chance she might ignore the initial reminder.

She stared at the wall again, her eyelids growing heavy. Then she went online and googled *pregnancy and why the fuck am I so tired.'* She proceeded to read several articles and explanations about the hormones 'surging' through her body and the fetus' need for nourishment, literally feeding off the mother's supply when there wasn't enough for the two of them. At first visions of parasitic little creatures filled her head, but then a mild panic set in. If she was this tired now, how would she feel in a few months?

Ruby knocked lightly and opened the door. "Hey! I just talked to Olivia, and she'd be thrilled to see us now. So would you be opposed to leaving...now?"

"Okay." Ailie brightened up immediately.

***

They passed store windows and displays decorated with gourds, ghosts, witches, and jack-o-lanterns. Twinkling lights, in orange or purple or white, outlined buildings against the dark early evening. Pedestrians huddled deep in their coats as they hurried to their next stop. The chilly air worked to sufficiently wake Ailie by the time they arrived to Olivia's house. She knew her friends would have a thousand questions for her, and that she needed extra energy to recall every detail of her trip. But first, Ailie had a baby to meet.

Ruby, Olivia, and Ailie huddled around a small basket—in it slept a newborn swaddled in off-white, organic cotton. The three of them gazed at him lovingly. Ailie gently touched the soft, tiny hairs on his head. "I can't believe you still haven't named him," she whispered.

"I know, right?" responded Olivia, quietly, looking around the room to check if Mathéo might be standing behind them. "Mathéo wants the baby to help us name him." They stared affectionately at the sleeping baby again. Olivia whispered, "It's not like he's going to start talking anytime soon. I'm not sure what the little guy's supposed to tell us. The people at the hospital were annoyed that we didn't have a name yet, so they just wrote 'Baby Boy' on the birth certificate. Which means I've got to fill out more paperwork once we *do* name him." Olivia sighed. "Oh well. Until then I'm calling him Tiger. Do you see how big he is, Ailie? Ten...pounds. Yep. Took a bit of pushing to get this one out."

"Wow!" Ailie said, in a loud voice. Then she looked back at the baby and said, almost to herself, "That would be a big...parasite." Ailie placed a hand on her own belly. She was so glad she had another few months to get accustomed to the idea of something so large exiting her body. She figured—she hoped—it would not be ten pounds at birth. *I thought newborns were tiny. He looks huge. I have to look this up again.*

Olivia shook her head at him. "I'm so glad they gave me drugs." Then she turned her attention to Ruby and Ailie and motioned for them to follow. "Here, let's go to the other room."

Ailie had barely taken a seat on the couch when Olivia began. "So, I've got about one hour, maybe less, before I have to feed the little tiger again, and then I might not be able to give you my complete attention. So you need to start with your story right away, Ailie. First of all, did you kiss him?"

"What?" Ruby blurted out, looking at Olivia. "We're not in grade school, Olivia. Did you see his picture? Of course she kissed him." Then she quickly turned to Ailie. "You did kiss him, right?" Ailie nodded, Ruby continued, "See? She didn't fly like 4000 miles just to shake hands with him."

Olivia shot back, playfully, "First of all, that was just a photo of his head, Ruby. So I don't know what the rest of his body looked like...not *yet*. We need a complete description from our friend here." And then she turned to Ailie, smiling. "But you need to start with the highlights. Make it quick, like a PowerPoint presentation. I want bullet points only. Please."

"Okay..." replied Ailie, slowly, even though she'd mentally reviewed the events of that night more than a hundred times at this point. "It was pretty hot that day. Oh, and he asked me to an estate sale first. Have you guys ever been to one of those? Some people have the strangest tastes in furniture. Anyway, didn't make it on time to the sale. Which worked in my favor, because then he asked me to dinner. Loved the restaurant. Right by the water. But I'm trying to remember the name..."

Olivia interrupted, "Highlights only, Ailie. Stick to the presentation." Olivia grinned, her hands clenching the arms of the sofa chair, as though hanging on the edge of her seat.

"Okay." Ailie threw her hands up. "I didn't sleep with him. It was just the kiss."

Olivia slumped down in her chair, pouting, giving Ailie her best look of sympathy.

Ruby asked, "And this was before or after you told him everything?"

"This was after," said Ailie, half-heartedly. Olivia was still pouting. "But it wasn't all bad, Olivia. Just for you, I should add that he has a very nice ass. I got to squeeze it and rub my hands all over it." Ailie made small circles in the air with her palms. "Like that time we waxed Ruby's car."

"Yes!" Olivia threw a fist in the air, like she'd scored a touchdown.

Ailie giggled. "And I wish I could tell you that I got to kiss it and eat breakfast off of it, but then I'd be lying."

"That's okay," said Olivia, also giggling. "But so…nothing under the hood? You didn't get to tinker with anything?"

"No…" Ailie responded, playfully hanging her head in disappointment.

"Okay," said Ruby, suppressing laughter. "Now that we've gotten the most important elements of the story out of the way, let's hear all the trivial details. Like…did you connect with him? Hopefully on an intellectual level? Did you have anything in common? And why are you lookin' so sad talking about him?"

Without too many interruptions Ailie recounted every aspect of the trip to her mother's house—trying to find Levi and then meeting Finnian. She ended her story with the voicemail that she left for Finnian on her last day in California.

As soon as she was done both Ruby and Olivia spoke at once, as they regularly did in moments such as these.

"Wow…did you really say that?"

"Hope he's someone who checks his voicemail. I know I hate checking voicemail…"

"That is *a lot* of words."

"And you told him you loved him? I'm gonna cry. That is so sweet."

"Yes," replied Ailie, pensively. "I am in love…or I *was* in love…I don't know."

"Well, you're still in love with him. We can both see that," Ruby said, delicately.

"Well, like they say," added Olivia. "If you love something, let it go…"

Ruby glared at Olivia.

"Well, no, I mean…it's been *proven*," insisted Olivia. "Did you ever see *Dances With Wolves*, Ruby? He fed that wolf, and then it came back to him. It works sometimes. It's a positive film with a positive message…but it's positive for the wolf, not the natives…but then I guess the wolf dies too. Nevermind."

Ailie was barely listening. "I think it's best if I just forget about him at this point," she lamented. "But…it's hard to believe that after ten years of wondering and conceptualizing it feels like it's all come to an abrupt end. I know it wasn't him in that picture, but it was all part of the story, the fantasy. That face… it's etched into my memory…" She stopped speaking as she held back tears. "And now I've touched him, and I can still smell his clothes."

In the other room, little Tiger began to cry.

21

Tell me how much you loved his tacos.

Ailie lay under a gown with her legs in stirrups. Ruby sat by her head, reading a magazine. Frieda had just finished part of the exam, when a technician walked in to help with the ultrasound machine. "Okay, my dear. This might be the day vee get to find out if it's a boy or a girl. I gonna try to make it happen, but if ze baby is not cooperating, vee gonna try another day, ja?"

Frieda covered Ailie's legs with part of the gown and then opened it at the center, over her stomach. She took a tube of gel out of a warmer and squirted it onto her belly and then laid the searching probe onto the gooey liquid. Frieda turned to the monitor and studied the image. "Now zat is interesting."

"What?" asked Ailie, concerned. "What's interesting?"

"Hmm…very interesting." Frieda turned to the technician and whispered something. The two of them looked at the screen, nodding and pointing and whispering. At last Frieda turned back to Ailie. "We gonna go to anozer room, wid a larger monitor. It's a much more sensitive system, and we gonna have another looksee, okay? It's all fine, though, noting to vorry about."

Ailie couldn't help but worry. She remained quiet for the short walk down the hall to a different room. There she undressed again, covered herself with another gown, and waited as Frieda squirted warm gel on her belly again.

This exam room was much larger, an enormous flat-screen hovered in one corner. Again, Frieda laid the probe onto Ailie's belly and looked up at the screen. This time the image was much easier for everyone to see, it was larger and well defined. In spite of the previous ultrasounds Ailie felt like she was viewing her baby for the first time. A minute later Frieda shouted, "A-ha! I knew it!" Ailie's heart skipped a beat, but before she could say anything, Frieda added, "It's tvins! We have tvins, my dear!" Ailie lifted her head and nearly sat up.

"Twins?" Ailie and Ruby asked in unison.

"Ja!"

"Twins?" Ailie repeated.

"Ja, two of zem. Look, zere you can see ze little hand of ze other one. She keeps waiving. Hallo! You little devil, you vere hiding, but I found you. Hallo!" Frieda waived to the little hands moving on the screen.

"Oh… fuck." Ailie put her head back down on the pillow.

"You okay?" Ruby asked, fanning her with a magazine.

"Oh fuck…oh fuck…oh fuck." Ailie repeated.

"It's okay," Ruby replied, still fanning Ailie. "She didn't say they were dead, she just said there's gonna be two of them."

Ailie rocked her head side to side on the pillow. "No, no, no. I only paid for one."

"Well, my dear, I guess tvins run in ze donor's family; although, his record didn't say anyting to zat nature. They both look healthy, so zat's good. Maybe a little small, but ve should have better luck eating now zat your sickness is gone." Again Frieda pushed the probe slowly back and forth across Ailie's belly. "And, my dear, I can tell you now zat it's lookin' like two bouncy little girls."

Frieda excused herself briefly, accompanying her assistant to the hallway.

Ailie spoke under her breath. "Oh my god. I hate you, Levi, I hate you for this shitty mess."

"Now, *he's* the one who's dead." Ruby shook her head at her friend. "Let's not be saying things like that about dead people."

"I know. But none of this is going how it was supposed to," argued Ailie. "What am I going to do?" She laid her head back down on the pillow. "How can this be happening?"

"*I* gonna tell you how it's happening," replied Frieda, walking back into the room. "Cause we're gonna monitor it. Together! But first I need you to download an app, and it'll tell you vat's goin' on in zat belly of yours every veek. You need to read more, Ailie, so you don't panic."

"I already have that app," Ailie rubbed her temples. "And I *do* check it. I looked at it this morning, and it told me my baby is the size of an nectarine right now."

"Vell, now you got two nectarines in your basket. So you're gonna need a different app, one zat tells you about tvins." And with those words Frieda smiled at Ailie and affectionately pinched her cheek.

***

The two women sat in the cab, quietly contemplating what just happened in the doctor's office.

"Boy, I did not see that one coming," Ailie said, staring out the side window.

"Me neither," Ruby replied, looking out the window on her side of the car. Rain began to fall, streams of water drifted across the glass. Ruby took a deep breath and turned to Ailie. "That is a lot of work for one person. You will need help."

"I know, I know."

"I've been your best friend for as long as we've been working, and I'm not going to say how long that is, but you know it's a long time. I would hate to see you go, but this time...this time, I have to tell you that you need to *go*."

Ailie finally looked at Ruby. "I know. I do know. It's just that...this is huge. I haven't lived with my mother and grandmother since I was a teenager. It's like...starting over."

"No, having *twins* is huge," countered Ruby. "If you stay here, can you afford to pay for someone to live with you day and night, to help you with everything? A live-in nanny...or two? You'll need a bigger place if you stay here."

Ailie didn't say anything for a few minutes, observing the buildings and pedestrians they passed.

Ruby spoke again, "Listen, why don't you come over for dinner tonight. Then we can talk more, and I can drive you home later. I think Barry's making tacos tonight. He's got this great recipe. Very spicy though, so you'll need to lay on the sour cream." She nudged Ailie's arm, trying to coax a smile out of her. "The twins 'll love it, I promise."

Ailie giggled. Then she closed her eyes, laid her head back, and sighed. "Okay, okay." Her eyes remained closed as she spoke. "But you'll have to promise to tell me what's in the recipe. This ex-boyfriend of my mom's sometimes made the best tacos, and to this day I can't figure out exactly how he made them. It might've been smoked paprika or…I can never put my finger on it."

Ruby laughed. "Oh yeah? And what was that guy's name?"

"Diego…" said Ailie, casually, opening her eyes again.

"Diego? It's good then that you're not having boys. Diego's a beautiful name."

"And he was a beautiful man," replied Ailie. "And, of course…he could be such a dick."

"No!" protested Ruby, laughing, closing her eyes, and shaking her head. "Just leave it at 'beautiful man!' I had this whole vision going in my head. Don't ruin it for me."

"Okay, okay," said Ailie, giggling again as she looked over at Ruby. "I won't ruin it for you. He was hot. And he wasn't a total dick—not all the time— and he made a good taco."

Ruby laughed again. "Then please tell me about Diego, and how much you *loved* his taco."

By now, both of them were laughing. Ailie punched Ruby lightly in the arm. "My mom loved that taco a lot more than I did. And it wasn't always the best taco because sometimes he'd have too much to drink and he'd mess it up."

Ruby laughed harder. "Why, was it all floppy when he drank too much? Oh, that was bad, that was bad."

"Kind of," replied Ailie, still giggling. "If he got really drunk he wouldn't let either of us touch a taco, because he'd say it wasn't any good."

Ruby wiped her eyes as she finished laughing. "So now you have to tell me. What happened with Diego and the tacos?"

"Oh Diego," Ailie grumbled. "Are you sure you want to hear this story, Ruby? You know my 'mom stories' are always long."

"Of course! I love hearing about your mom's wild days, her sexual revolution or whatever you're calling it these days."

Ailie thought about where to start. "Remember how I said we lived in Georgia before I got to college? With my grandma?" Ruby nodded. "I was graduating high school, and I was so looking forward to just getting to the end of summer—then I'd be stepping out on my own and off to college. So...it's the day before graduation and my mom tells me that she's saved all year to rent this apartment. In Alaska. So that the two of us can spend some time together. You know, it *was* our last summer together. But of course I was pissed—I wanted to spend my last summer at home with a couple of close friends, and my grandma, and maybe take off to college earlier if I could. Plus, at that point my mom and I would argue about the smallest thing."

"Which you...still sometimes do today..."

"Sometimes. Kind of. Anyway...it wasn't a good start to the summer...and when we got to Juneau I didn't make things any easier on my mom. She worked part time, as summer help at this store, but when she had time off she wanted to take me places, so we could enjoy the outdoors. That's what she was always saying, 'enjoy the outdoors!'" Ailie threw her hands up in the air for emphasis. "But I was determined to win this one...I was determined *not* to enjoy myself just because she wanted me to so badly. I was sick of moving, I was sick of introducing myself to more new people. So I'd protest by staying inside and reading books all day. Two or three weeks of this, and of course my mom goes off and does the same thing she always does—she looks for a man."

"Well, you've got to admit she's a pretty woman, Ailie. Which means that she may not always be the one doing the looking, maybe the men are doing the finding."

"Well, I'm not sure how it happened," Ailie replied. "But one day she comes home with Diego...and after that it was *all about Diego*. He was good looking and charming and she fell so hard for him." Ailie shook her head in disapproval. "And like I said that first night he cooked us tacos that weren't from a box, different than anything I'd ever had...which endeared me to him...a little. But day after day after day I began to see that behind all this charm was...a very needy person. All he did was talk about himself and his paintings and his photography and what he needed."

"Probably a momma's boy."

Ailie nodded. "And I noticed that he wouldn't want to do anything for you, even if you asked him politely, unless he was in the right mood. He was that moody. Sometimes it felt like I was talking to a three year-old. So... back to the tacos—he'd make these tacos, and he refused to tell me what was in them. He'd just be reaching for spices here and there, all while talking about himself and what a productive day he had. He was like this giant peacock in our tiny kitchen, with his feathers spread, strutting back and forth between the countertops. And my mom just fed right into him. It's like she was his number one fan. And sometimes he was really mean to my mom, insulting her right in front of me. And she never said a thing. I didn't get it."

"No..." Ruby interjected. "That doesn't sound like your mom. Love...love really gives you blinders..."

"Plus, I had a hunch that he had other girlfriends, but I wasn't positive...No matter what I tried to say to my mom about Diego, we just got into arguments because she claimed he was good to her. And she'd switch the subject, telling me that I wasn't participating at all in this trip that she'd spent such a long time planning, and that now I was trying to ruin her vacation too. I kept encouraging her to try and do something else with her time, besides...Diego."

"Can't get in the way of love," Ruby declared, looking out the window.

"So it's almost August, and I'm reading something in the apartment late at night. My mom's about to head to a midnight movie with Diego, and she tells me to come out because she wants to show me something. We climb this hill, and of course Diego's right behind us because he wants to make sure they're not late to the movies. We sit down on this rock and she shows me… the aurora borealis. It was so beautiful, Ruby."

"What? My travel agent said you can *never* see the aurora borealis in summer. It's too bright out."

"She's right. It's very rare, but it happens. Look online. Anyway, at first I had no idea what it was. I mean, it was always so cloudy, and, like you pointed out the days are so long you usually can't see the northern lights. But then…it was just dark enough…and I saw these intense streaks of neon green, just lighting up the sky. And it could've been this beautiful moment for me and my mom, but Diego would not stop talking about how that aurora borealis was not as great as this other one he'd seen, last spring…or maybe this other time…or this other time. He keeps telling her to hurry up so they can get to the movies. But I'm trying to enjoy this spectacular light display, this *one thing* that my mom and I could share, without arguing. But he wouldn't stop whining. My mom tells him to 'shush' or quiet down a couple of times, but he won't. So I finally stand up and just start yelling at him. I can't remember everything I said, but I basically told him he was an arrogant prick and that he didn't deserve my mom. And as soon as I was done yelling…the light was gone. The aurora was over. That was that."

"Let me guess, that night kind of put a damper on the rest of the summer?"

"Pretty much…I flew home early, said good-bye to my grandma and went off to school. My mom stayed in Alaska, with Diego. She lasted until the New Year or something. I heard about it from my grandma because my mom was pretty upset. When they broke up, she moved back home, back with grandma again, and… I figured she'd get over it, just like she did all the others. But I know she was heartbroken for a long time." Ailie trailed off, reflecting on the arguments from that summer. "That was the last time we lived together…And well…that was Diego—a handsome, self-absorbed lover who wooed me with his taco… But, like I said, I haven't been able to figure out that secret ingredient."

"Maybe it wasn't a secret ingredient," offered Ruby. "Like you said, maybe it's just that his taco didn't come from the same old box."

Ailie spoke quietly, "And I was such a bitch to my mom that summer..."

"Sounds like it. My mom would've slapped me a few times before even thinking about letting me go home early." Ruby looked out the window and then turned back to Ailie. "See now these are the kinds of conversations you should be having with your mom. *You* should be apologizing...*she* should be apologizing...*everyone* should be apologizing."

"I know, I know...it's just so much easier not to talk about things. Neither of us are the person we used to be. I go home...for a short time...and we have fun...most of the time...and then I come back here to New York, and...life is good. I prefer it when we laugh..."

"But like you said, Ailie, so much has changed. Everything has changed, and you're not going back to life the way it used to be. You've seen that you're not going back to that. Your mom is awesome now. She wants to help you, and she'd want to take care of those babies in a heartbeat. I know that from her phone calls..."

"I still can't believe she calls you sometimes," Ailie interjected.

"And I know that from the way you talk about her. She is a very giving, loving person. Just don't be sneakin' around at night or else that kooky grandma of yours might shoot you." Both of them laughed. Ailie's eyes began to water.

"You can work from anywhere, Ailie, you know that."

"I'm not sure what Geoffrey's going to say."

"Oh, don't worry about him. Little Napoleon. Sometimes he's great, and other times he is such an ugly little man. He'd be crazy to let you go. Lots of people are bi-coastal these days. And if that doesn't work, I know you can figure something else out." Ruby took Ailie's hand and squeezed it. "You'll do just fine, Ailie, I know you will." With her other hand Ruby wiped her own tears.

22

Once you're in love, everything seems to be a sign.

Ailie was in her third meeting for the day—her eyes glazed over as she listened to the nasal drone of the human resources assistant. *This is what meditation must feel like when it's working,* she thought.

The next instant, her phone vibrated. Grateful for the interruption, she ducked into the hallway to answer. As with every phone call at this point, Ailie hoped that it was Finnian. But it was Olivia, and she sounded tired or sick, her voice raspy, coughing as she spoke. "I know you're at work, but I need your help. Can you come over for maybe twenty minutes…a half hour at the most?"

"What? I'm in the middle of a meeting right now, and I've got a ton of work to do. What's going on?"

"I'm sick, and I need to go to the doctor. My mom is in the *Bahamas…*" Olivia whimpered. "The doctor says they can get me in this afternoon, but Mathéo can't make it home in time. So could you just cover for a half hour? Until he gets here? *Please?* I am *not* hiring some homeless person off the

Internet to look after my baby. He's still so little. And I don't even want to leave him…with anyone…but the girl at the doctor's office said I shouldn't bring him since he still needs so many shots, and it's flu season, and their waiting room is crowded with sick people. *Pretty please?* I need someone I can trust."

Ailie sighed but gave Olivia's request a second thought—this would be her first time babysitting an actual *baby*. What better way to allay her fears of handling her upcoming role as a mother? "You know what, I'd love a break right now. Okay…I'll be there as fast as I can. I'll think of an excuse."

Ailie stepped into a cluttered scene when she entered Olivia's house—a breast pump was in the center of the living room, large and small c-shaped pillows were on the couches; baby toys, diapers and bottles were on the floors and tables, and various sized cloths littered each room.

"I know it looks like a mess…" Olivia spoke rapidly, supporting Tiger with one arm and blowing her nose with the other hand. "But I'm still trying to figure out how to do all this. You know, do I keep everything in one room where I hang out most of the day? Or do I buy three of everything and keep one station upstairs and one downstairs? But, I swear there's a market for naïve, new moms, because I just bought more stuff, but I'm not even sure half of it's *really* necessary," she said, waving her hand at a couple of bags, filled with unopened items.

Ailie had no idea what Olivia was going on about, but she nodded her head in agreement. "Of course. Of course."

Olivia gently handed Tiger over to Ailie. "Okay. I need to go! I'm late already, but it's really close by. I don't even want to ask you if you know what to do because I could *not* leave this house if you said that you have no idea what to do. Please…nod your head—let me know he'll be okay." Olivia placed her hands on Ailie's shoulders and stared at her earnestly.

"Yeah!" Ailie blurted, grinning. The smile was meant to reassure Olivia, but it also boosted Ailie's determination, somewhat. *Well, I've skimmed the first chapter of all my baby books,* thought Ailie, considering Tiger nervously, her palms sweating. *I've seen lots of commercials about babies. I've signed up for a few websites....so I get emails about motherhood. Sometimes billboards display helpful hints about parenting.*

"He just ate," continued Olivia. "Mathéo should arrive before he needs to eat again. I left five pages of instructions, right here, in case he cries. But don't forget—don't let him roll over. I doubt he can, but don't let him. Don't let him put anything in his mouth. Don't set him down on anything other than in his crib. But don't do that either, because he likes to be held—and nobody wants to feel unloved. Don't put him near water. As a matter of fact there's probably no need for you to use the water while I'm out. Babies don't really *do* much of anything at this stage, so just hold him. Not too tightly. Be gentle but sturdy. Keep your eyes on him at all times." Olivia took a deep breath and again looked very seriously at Ailie.

"Okay...so just...hold him...and...stare at him." Ailie confirmed, in her most confident tone.

"Yes, that's probably the best plan. Bottles are in there, diapers and wipes are right there, but you can find more of everything over there." Olivia pointed in different directions around the room. "You're going to be a mom soon. So much of this is instinctual...or so they say. Do I even need a key right now?" Olivia addressed the question to the floor as she walked around the room, patting her pockets, sneezing and searching for keys. "Okay, just...hang tight for a half hour. An hour tops. I hope it's not more."

"Okay. Got it."

"Mathéo, please be on time. For once," Olivia mumbled, walking to the door.

"Is he smiling? Aw!" Ailie spoke to Tiger lovingly, in a high-pitched voice, her mouth wide.

"Oh, he's got gas," Olivia added, hurriedly. "He hasn't pooped yet, but he should soon. I'll probably call you...a lot. Please tell me he'll be okay." Olivia pleaded again.

"Yes!" Ailie flashed another smile. "Now you go! We'll be fine!"

Olivia had barely been gone a few minutes when Ailie heard and felt a muffled roar coming from Tiger's diaper. "Ohhh…shit," Ailie whispered, using two hands to slowly lift Tiger above her head and assess the damage from all sides. "What the…? Wow." Mustard-colored liquid had erupted from Tiger's diaper covering his entire back and stomach, all the way to his neck, some of it transferring to Ailie's blouse.

"Crap, that is *so* much…crap." Ailie panicked, walking in a circle. "Olivia needs to come back. No! She can't come back. *I* have to handle this. This is what moms do." Examining the dirty baby, episodes of *ER* and *Grey's Anatomy* came to mind. "A paramedic would use scissors to cut a patient out of this filth. But Olivia said we couldn't go near water, so scissors are probably also out of the question."

Without further pause, Ailie switched to emergency mode for her tiny patient. First, she located the changing station between the kitchen and the living room. She laid the slick baby onto the soft, undyed-cotton-covered changing pad and then grabbed an unopened container of eco-friendly, hypoallergenic, fragrance free baby wipes. Ailie managed to unbutton his organic, all-cotton bodysuit and then pinpointed the stack of chlorine free, latex free, compostable diapers on the side table, strategically placing a fresh diaper next to baby as she considered her next step.

Tiger began to cry. "Shhh, shhh," replied Ailie, attempting to pacify him. But he continued to cry. "Ooh, that's gonna be distracting." She promptly retrieved a couple of travel earplugs from her purse and then looked at her patient again. "My voice should be *soothing* to you. And babies like *faces*." She exaggerated her words and motions as she spoke, like a joyful, doting mother, her face inches from his.

Tiger whimpered. "Do you want me to sing to you instead?" she asked, anxiously.

The mustard oozed in and out of his onesie as he squirmed. "Okay, I'll sing. But…but I don't know any lullabies."

Ailie sung the ABC's; Tiger wailed. "Not your cup of tea? Okay, well, let's think about what might be trending in your world…"

Humming the first line of melodies that included words like 'babe,' 'baby,' 'mom,' or 'dad,' she tried everything from "I Got You Babe" to "Stacy's Mom." She switched from tune to tune, gauging his reaction and finally settled on Kelis' "Milkshake," singing the words she knew and improvising where she could.

My milkshake brings all the babies to the yard,
And they're like
Nothin's better than yours
Damn right nothin's better than mommy…

Tiger quieted immediately, distracted by Ailie's animated body movements and facial expressions.

Turning her attention back to the diaper, Ailie feared she might break something if she tried to extract Tiger from his soiled garment—his limbs felt so soft and malleable. Brainstorming, she remembered her eighth grade summer internship with a handsome archaeologist. 'Evaluate the site. Start by delicately removing any large debris and cautiously work your way through the strata.' With that in mind she began the arduous process of excavating the infant—pulling wipe after wipe out of the box, slowly scooping and removing the fecal matter, bit by bit, methodically working left to right, in small movements, on top and then underneath, as she gently lifted the cloth from his skin, section by section.

Tiger lay calmly blowing spit bubbles, as Ailie danced, sang and cleaned her way across his tummy and up his neck, slowly rolling the bodysuit.

Twenty-eight minutes later (she frequently checked the clock on the wall, hoping for Mathéo's timely appearance), Ailie wiped her brow. She was now wearing one of Olivia's t-shirts and had gone through an entire box of wipes. "I probably didn't do that right," she said to herself, observing the sack-full of dirty cloths. Ailie proudly held the spotless baby in her arms; however, he was swaddled in a blanket because she was too afraid to put a new outfit on him…in case he pooped again.

Nestled on the couch, Ailie cradled Tiger as he slumbered, tenderly kissing him on the forehead. Gentle but sturdy.

She looked around the room, observing the mess again, and noticed a pair of Levis draped over a mound of dirty laundry. "It's a *sign*," she grumbled. "Once you're in love, everything seems to be a sign, Tiger. And if there is one lesson I should teach you today…it's that you'll get all kinds of reminders about the mistakes you've made. Especially the big ones."

Tiger wiggled without opening his eyes. "You're right, I won't say Levi was a mistake." Ailie spoke to the baby as though they were in deep conversation. "Please don't get me wrong, Tiger. Levi gave me something *wonderful*. I am so excited to be on this journey. Honestly, I wouldn't have it any other way. But…but right now I'm trying to forget about Finnian, and I can't do that if I'm constantly reminded about Levi. So I'm angry with both of them for hanging out in my head. See how that works?"

With one thumb Ailie gently held Tiger's plump hand, counting this chubby little fingers. "And since we're on the topic…can I level with you for a second? I have a lot on my mind right now, and…I feel like I can talk freely with you. I trust you won't tell anyone."

Tiger pursed his lips suckling the air as he slept. "Good," she continued. "Sometimes I wonder, *what if* Levi were still alive. What if I might've met him instead of Finn? What would he be like today? And I need to be perfectly honest with you…and with myself. When I dream about Levi, I adore him; I'm still enamored by this fantasy that I created in my mind. But when I'm awake I…I find that I'm much more critical."

Tiger twitched. "Well, let me explain. You see, Finn basically described Levi as a *real mess*—a total thrill seeker—partying and sleeping around. He was a charmer and an adrenaline junkie. He probably devoured dates like he devoured life. But it doesn't sound like the women ever stopped coming, so he must've been doing something well." Ailie's eyes lit up. "Which is probably why I fell in love with his photo ten years ago."

Tiger's tiny tongue showed between his lips. "But I've changed since then. And I say this because *you* have a wonderful dad. I can vouch for him.

Mathéo is *the best*. He'll be here for you, no matter what. But would Levi have changed? Would he have been a good dad? All I have is Finn's description, so does that make me a bad person for asking these questions?"

Tiger yawned and let out a small fart. "I know," responded Ailie. "We shouldn't talk about the dead like that. Ruby reminds me all the time. But people like Levi—the bad boys—do they ever change?"

Tiger farted again and smiled, still dozing. "You're right." Ailie shrugged. "It's possible he might've turned out differently. But...if he didn't can you imagine what he'd be like today? I think of Val Kilmer—the older one, not the younger one—arrogant and angry. Or, have you seen Ehrlich on HBO's *Silicon Valley*? No, you probably haven't, but the point is I sometimes picture Levi today as this cavalier douchebag with a beer gut."

Tiger's arm twitched. He opened his eyes for a second and then closed them again. Ailie caressed his cheek. "I bet he would've run for the hills if I'd have shown up at his house, pregnant. He definitely wouldn't have called me back. Much less send an email." She giggled. "If Levi was still a womanizer, I'll tell you what he would have done—*if* he was interested—I bet he would've sent me a dick pic." Ailie giggled again. "Of course, at this point I wouldn't mind it if Finn texted me a picture of his junk, just so I know he's alive." She sighed. "Tiger, you are way too young to learn about the perils of sexting, but at some point your mom will have to explain..."

Ailie stopped short, stifled by the realization that a nanny cam was possibly installed somewhere in the room.

"Olivia? Matheo?" she asked, timidly, scanning the toys and furniture for anything that might hold a tiny surveillance unit. "Are you...out there?"

23

Now that's gonna make for an interesting text.

Ailie dialed her mother's number, a few days later, and told her the news—
that she was expecting twins, that she'd hired a moving company, that she
would sell her home in New York and move in with them in California. But
this would all happen the weekend after Thanksgiving, once they'd held
Olivia's baby shower. Ailie had spent many hours and sleepless nights
deliberating and weighing her options. A winter in New York, with her best
friends, but possibly surrounded by deep snow and under the weight of a
giant belly…or sunny walks in California surrounded by very few
acquaintances, and two very lively, inquisitive women.

"Oh my goodness!" Gloria tried not to shout into the phone, but she
couldn't hide her elation. "And that'll be just in time for Christmas! I can't
believe it! I mean, I can tell you don't sound thrilled, but…honey, this is
just such a blessing for all of us. I just knew that somehow this would all
work out, and it did. Those little girls are going to need a family, and we'll
be here to help you in any way we can."

"Thanks, mom. I don't mean to sound so disappointed. I'm not. Really. But it's just…so unexpected. All of it. Everything. It's such a change. I'm just trying to process it all."

"I'll pick a room and get it ready for you. Now let me find some paper so I can write this all down…and when you get out here we can figure out a better arrangement, and move things around, for you and the babies. Oh, there's so much to be done. How exciting! We can go shopping for cribs and blankets…."

"Okay, okay, mom, I am very excited about the *same* things, so I just wanted to say a few things here."

"Sure, go ahead, dear."

"I don't know how long I will stay with you guys, at your house. Maybe a short time, maybe a long time, it's tough to say because I will probably need your help…a lot. *But*, I am raising these babies the way I decide."

"Of course, dear."

"And you'll need to let me make mistakes. I'm not saying you can't give me advice, but, you know, when I was little you were…" Ailie had a difficult time searching for the right words. "Kind of…an absentee mom, sometimes, you know, and now you…well, you've gone in the opposite direction, and, well, I just have to say that… sometimes you can be a bit overbearing. And I mean that in the nicest way."

"That's okay, I can handle it. We promise to stay out of your way when you get annoyed. Well, at least I promise. But I can't say the same thing for your grandmother. You'll have to have a long discussion with her when you get here."

"I'm here!" Vivien interrupted. "I'll be good, I promise. I picked the phone up in the hallway. This is great!"

Ailie sighed and laughed. "Okay, well, since I've got you both on the phone, I do have something else that I want to tell you about. And please promise me that you won't interrupt. Either of you. Please."

For the next hour Ailie recounted her tale about Levi, searching for her sperm donor, and finding Finnian. With only a few interruptions, and less than two-dozen questions, she told her mother and grandmother her entire story—the correct story, and not the one that Gloria and Vivien had assumed. She finished by telling them that she hadn't heard from Finnian since that night at his house.

"Oh, honey bear," Gloria replied. "I'm so sorry."

"I can't believe that," said Vivien, incensed. "He's got a responsibility."

"It's not his child, mom," retorted Gloria.

"It doesn't matter, Gloria. Family is family."

"But he wasn't put in this position by choice, mom. Maybe fate has other plans," replied Gloria.

Ailie imagined Vivien's eyes rolling in response to such a comment. Gloria and Vivien argued for another minute until Ailie interrupted. "Okay! Both of you, stop. You can have this conversation after I hang up. But you must promise me that neither of you will interfere with any of this when I move home."

"Fine," they responded in unison.

Ailie laughed. "I'm looking forward to moving out there."

***

Two days passed and Ailie was at home, *her* home, sitting on the couch responding to work mail, when she noticed she had a new email in one of her personal inboxes. She clicked on the icon and her heart skipped a beat. The new message was from Finnian. It's was titled "a Chair."

Hi Ailie,

I got your messages. Where to begin…

My very adventurous daughter snuck into the garage and tried to build a chair while I wasn't paying attention. She nearly drove a nail through her foot (she found the nail gun), but luckily I got there in time. Here's a photo of the chair. I think she built it for her doll, but it made me think of you and the day we met.

Fiona's mom broke her foot the day after you came by the house. She's doing better now, but it was easier for Fiona to stay here full time for a while. She's still here for another week, I think. Maybe more. Depends on what the doctor says. It's been great, but I'm so tired. She asks a lot of questions. We talk a lot. We cook a lot. We're in and out of the car all the time. I haven't slept much.

I hope you're not pissed. I'm sorry it took me this long to write (I rewrote this a few times).

Finnian

Ailie looked at the photo in the email. Fiona had achieved the look of a chair with several small, flat boards, and a few sticks. They were bound together with glue and string, and some nails. It was adorable, Ailie thought. Then she re-read the email again and again and again, looking for any words she might've missed.

She was about to reply when she pushed the laptop away. She decided she should wait at least one hour before sending anything. She paced in front of the couch. "If I wait an hour then it'll look like I'm at lunch or maybe at a meeting. But then he might think that I rushed back to my computer as soon as I see a message from him. He'll think I'm eager." She chewed her lower lip as she paced. "A good lunch might even take two hours."

In the end she couldn't bear waiting longer than one minute past an hour. She hurriedly typed.

Hi,

No worries.

Her fingers stopped and she reviewed the words. "Okay, that sounds chill. That sounds like I'm relaxed. I'm like whatever. Everything's great."

Please tell Fiona that's a beautiful chair, and that it looks like she wants to take after her daddy. (Maybe you should buy her some tools for Christmas!)

Ailie stopped typing again. "Is she too young for tools?" She chewed her lower lip again.

I miss you.

She stared at the last three words. Stood up, walked around the couch, sat back down. Delete. Delete. Delete.

Great to hear from you! Ailie

She hit the send button. Then she stood up again. She stared at her laptop as if it might speak to her. She walked around the couch two more times, into the kitchen to find a chocolate bar, and then went out to the deck. Without a jacket the cold air felt good on her skin. After about ten minutes she ducked back inside and checked her email again. No reply. Suddenly her phone buzzed with a new text message. It was him.

Sorry! I forgot to ask you how you're doing. How's the baby?

"Now that's gonna make for an interesting text." Ailie attempted to write an email instead, but every time she started typing it became lengthy and she went off topic. Her sentences were full of sentiment, and just as quickly as she typed them she'd change her mind and delete them. She was torn about the message that she should send. She missed him. She wanted to tell him about the *babies* and her tough decision to move, but every time she looked at her words she decided she came across as too emotional. Ailie deliberated for over an hour. Finally she picked up her phone and replied with a text that was short and to the point.

Twins. It's going to be twins. We're doing well.

"Ha!" She threw her hands up triumphantly. "Let's see what he does with that text." Dropping her phone on the couch, she walked into the kitchen for some water. Ailie drank from her glass slowly, eyeing the screen of her phone from the kitchen. As soon as she put the glass down she ran back to the couch to check her messages. Nothing.

Two hours went by before she received a text from Finn again.

Just finished putting Fiona to bed. Will you be out here for Thanksgiving?

The idea of flying to California earlier than planned appealed to Ailie. But then the finality of her move set in. This would be her last Thanksgiving with her friends in New York, before motherhood started. That, and Olivia's baby shower, would be their final get-together before she left.

No. I'll be here for Thanksgiving :)

Ailie assumed her text would lead to a lengthy thread—several back and forth messages, catching up on each other's lives—but she didn't hear back from him. Not that night, or the next morning. She looked at her last text message again and again, wondering if she should've added something or deleted something or maybe it was the smiley face. She looked closely at the type of emoticon smiley face she'd chosen and wondered if perhaps the eyes or the curve of the lips made it look a little too smug, or, in the worst case, even a little fiendish. She studied the smiley face for so long that she was almost convinced that it was staring back at her, menacingly, taunting her, and wondered if Finnian might've interpreted her message as a quick, cheerful, 'fuck-off, I've got better plans over here on the east coast.'

Ailie contemplated texting him to ask him what *he* was doing for Thanksgiving, but twelve hours had already gone by, so she figured that the question might look a bit odd or apathetic at this point. Finally, she knew she'd spent an inordinate amount of time overthinking her actions, so she buried her cell phone at the bottom of her bag for an entire work day, telling her friends and colleagues that she'd misplaced it.

It wasn't until she got home in the evening—after an entire day of not staring at or analyzing her own text—that she could muster the confidence to send him another text.

I'm so sorry! My phone ran out of juice after my last text, and then really busy day at the office. I should've asked what you were doing for Thanksgiving. I guess you'll be their? I meant *there

She drummed her fingers on her laptop and then wrote again.

How's Fiona?

Three days passed, and Ailie frequently checked her inboxes and texts and voice messages. At last, late in the evening Friday, a text came through from Finnian.

Blablablablabla Bla Bla

Ailie was delighted to see his name show up on her phone, but she had no idea what to make of the message, except that he might've accidentally pressed some keys; although the letters looked like a pattern rather than ad-hoc gibberish. She stared at the message for a minute and then wrote back.

? Was this meant to go to me?

He responded twenty minutes later.

So sorry! Fiona got a hold of my phone. Had to change the code. I talked to her about it. Been a bit crazy. Hosting a sleepover. 10 screaming pre-tweens. Shoot me now. Promise I'll email soon.

Ailie giggled, reading the message over and over again. "Email soon…" she repeated to herself. She wondered if she could last *that* long, not knowing what 'soon' meant. But the message perked her up for a day or so, knowing that she would hear from him 'soon.'

More days passed and she began to have doubts again. Every time she sulked she fought the urge to pick up the phone and call him. Her feelings vacillated from unhappiness to annoyance to anger and then back to hope. One minute she wanted to call him and then next minute she felt a sense of pride that prevented her from doing so. What could she say, she thought, that she hadn't blatantly said in her voice mail from weeks ago? If he really wanted to talk, or hear her voice, he would call her instead of sending an email or simple texts. Her head ached from continuously examining the messages and wondering what she should do or not do, and there were so many things to take care of before the move.

24

You go! You can make it momma!

It was late in the evening on the Friday before Thanksgiving, and Ailie's last day at the New York office. She had just finished packing some small boxes that were piled on her desk, when she noticed the snow falling outside her window. She stopped to admire the view.

Ruby peeked in and knocked lightly on the door. "What are you still doing here?"

"I just want to take in the view from my office one last time," replied Ailie. Ruby joined her by the window. "It's my favorite time of year. The Christmas decorations, the lights, the music, and then…sometimes we get this beautiful layer of snow. Hopefully I can share this with my kids someday. The city feels so magical when it's like this."

"Yeah, but then there's the cold and the wet and walking through freezing rain. You have to put on a hundred layers just to go outside, and then take them off when you get back inside. It's a big mess," Ruby said, waving her hand at the scene in front of them.

Ailie looked over at Ruby. "Would you ever move from the city?"

"Hell no," Ruby shot back. "I just wanna make you feel better about your decision."

Both of them watched the snow again. The flakes were larger now, coming down faster.

Ruby smiled and touched Ailie's belly. "So how big are they this week? What do you have in there now—potatoes? Some kind of winter squash?"

Ailie giggled. "This week, they are the size of avocados. But probably not the Florida kind…probably smaller, like Haas." She stared pensively at her stomach.

Ruby smiled. "So…you feeling okay? Lately I can't decide if you're happy or sad about this whole thing."

"I'm actually doing really well," she replied, cheerfully.

"What? Did something happen? Forget to give me some news?"

"No, no, nothing like that," she responded quietly. "It's just this feeling," she said, her tone more upbeat, "that started as I packed up all my…shit. These things, these boxes of stuff…my whole life is getting packed in boxes. And the things that I no longer want I toss in the trash or donate. It feels so cleansing. And now the idea of starting over…starting over after twenty years here…I don't know, it's… it's liberating. The other day I realized that I've been trying so hard to hold on to everything here, trying to control everything. And now…it's lifting, the weight of it all is lifting. I don't know, maybe it's temporary, maybe it's the hormones. But at some point I started to let go. I can't pinpoint exactly when. Maybe it was with this pregnancy, or when I came back from California. I know I was uncomfortable with it at first, but now…the more I pack and unload, the happier I am. When I get to California I'll spend more time with my mom and my grandma. I'll get to know everyone in town." She took a deep breath. "Did you know there are lots of people who've walked away from success, and been ok with it? Like…that comedian Dave Chappelle just walked off the set one day and left. In the middle of his career."

"He got on a plane and flew to Africa…you're…you know…moving in with your mom," Ruby said playfully.

"I know…"

"Okay, just wanted to be sure you're fully aware of the situation. Because overnight you've turned from an anxious momma, who had issues with her own momma, into this Zen-like creature so…"

"That's true. I *was* a bit nervous. I still am a bit nervous. But…I've put a lot of thought into it, and…you've met those two—I won't have to worry about taking care of a house or cooking or cleaning. I can focus on the baby. I can focus on myself. I'll have all this time to read pregnancy books and baby blogs."

"I know I've asked you this before but…are you gonna quit?" asked Ruby.

"No…probably not…. No… I don't think so." Ailie shook her head.

Ruby squinted, looking at Ailie suspiciously. Ailie looked right back her, imitating her expression.

Ruby changed the subject. "So what's next? Looks like you're all done packing here. The movers are coming next week, right? Have you talked to Finn again?"

"No, not after he texted that he'd 'email soon.'" Ailie threw her coat over her shoulders. "Haven't heard a peep from him since," she said wistfully. She stretched the fabric of her coat and tried to button the front, but her belly got in the way. Ailie frowned. "I could button it this morning…and this was one of my skinny coats too."

"Ailie, you should call him if you really need to talk to him before you move out there. Does he even know you're moving out there?"

"No. Of course not. He didn't ask."

Ruby rolled her eyes. "He's not going to know that he's supposed ask that question. You know that. You said he was tired because his daughter's been over there full time. So cut him some slack, maybe he really is tired."

"I *am* cutting him slack." Ailie threw her hands up in frustration. "But I have so many things to do in the next couple of weeks… because I'm trying to pay attention to what I eat, and how my body is changing. The doctor said I should eat more, but the good fats, not the bad ones, the natural sugars, not the processed ones, the tiny fish, not the big ones, the home-cut deli-meats, not the pre-sliced packaged ones, the hard cheeses, not the soft ones. Oh, and I'm supposed to lie on my side and not on my back; stand by the sink and not by the microwave. Maybe I should pee standing up because the toilet water could splash back, all the way into my vagina, threatening my life, that of my unborn children, and possibly everyone on the planet. Seriously, I've never thought this much about anything in my whole life. And while I'm at it—I'm actually packing up my *whole life*. So I don't have time to play these email and text games."

Ailie walked back to her desk and flopped into her chair. "You know, I can focus very well when I'm not thinking about him…so now you're asking me about him…and now I'm getting emotional again…I get so excited when he writes to me and then I don't hear back from him for days. And I know he's probably tired…and I'm tired too." Ruby handed her a tissue. "I poured my heart out to him, Ruby…in that stupid, stupid voice mail. I felt like such an idiot after leaving that message." Ailie choked back tears. "It's hard enough being pregnant, because I *feel so much*…I mean, it's bizarre— I've gotten tears in my eyes just picking out vegetables at the grocery store, Ruby. Vegetables! Because some of them are tinier than the other ones…they're like baby vegetables."

Ruby put her arm around Ailie as she blew her nose. "And don't even get me started about videos of kittens or puppies. And the other day I was watching this lonely opossum, struggling to cross the road, and I began crying when I realized that she was walking so slowly because all these babies were clinging to her stomach. And she was doing it all, on her own. And I found myself saying, 'You go! You can make it momma!'"

"I was waiting for something like this..." Ruby handed Ailie another tissue.

"And I can't help it. As long as I'm carrying Levi's babies, there will always be a connection to Finn...and it doesn't matter which one I think about at this point. Obviously they're two different people, but sometimes, when I'm really tired and when I close my eyes at night, he's with me again, in the room, lying beside me or I can feel him coursing through my blood. I don't know which one it is—it feels like they're the same person—reminding me that I can't let go. No matter what, they're still there, always a part of me..."

"Okay...okay..." Ruby replied, quietly, rubbing Ailie's back. Then she said, encouragingly, "Well...he's supposed to write or call or something soon, right? And...you said he's a great guy and... maybe he's just as nervous as you are when you're around him and...maybe he has a lot to say. If you're annoyed by what he's said or maybe what he hasn't said, then...maybe it's time you call him again. But don't leave a message this time, make sure you get him on the phone first."

Ailie didn't say anything. Ruby continued, "I could be wrong, but maybe he found your message flattering. Or oddly charming. You don't know what he's thinking, and it's probably best if you ask him in a conversation. Or better yet, have a pleasant, nonchalant conversation just to, you know, get back into the grove. Flirt a little." Ruby stopped again, but Ailie still didn't say anything. "If you don't get that email soon, call him. It's been more than a month since you left that voicemail. Maybe you need to have some normal conversation because he's not sure what to say."

They walked together to the elevator, in the comfortable silence of old friends.

"I'll bring those boxes by your house when I stop by this weekend, okay?" said Ruby, hugging Ailie. The two of them stood, without saying a word, staring into the open elevator for a few seconds. Finally Ruby spoke again, "I can't believe I won't see you around this office anymore. But I'm glad Geoffrey's agreed to give the long-distance thing a try."

"It won't be the same," Ailie said, fondly.

"Yeah, but it means I can still nag you about deadlines and we can still gossip about clients." They hugged again.

Outside the snow began to layer. The thick flakes clung to every surface, softening the sounds of the city. Ailie listened to her own footsteps crunching through the fresh powder as she made her way to the subway.

***

The following morning Ailie began making (more) lists—lists of items that would go into storage, lists of items that should go to her mother's house, lists of things that had to be done before the movers arrived, and lists of people she had to contact before leaving. She also wrote a list of the additional lists that she should make later.

She placed a few bags and boxes of supplies out by the doorway for donation, and then sat back down on the couch and opened her laptop. She reviewed Olivia's wish list of organic baby items, when a noise startled her. Ailie sat up, but couldn't determine the source of the sound. Suddenly she noticed someone in her periphery. Ailie turned her head further to see Finnian standing in the open doorway.

"Hi," he said, calmly. Except for his winter coat, he looked the same as when she'd left him on their last night together, leaning against the doorframe with his hands in his jean pockets.

Startled, Ailie stood up quickly. Her laptop dropped to the floor. "Shit! Ouch." She glanced at her toes for a second but then back up at him. She was shocked, almost speechless. Quietly she replied, "Hi."

"Can I come in?" he asked, gently, smiling at her.

"Yes. Yes, of course," she replied. At this point it dawned on her that the man she'd been desperate to see, to hear from, to touch, to be with, was suddenly standing in front of her. She was elated, albeit utterly confused, and tried to contain the huge smile she felt brimming underneath. "What…are you doing here?"

"I had to see you," he said.

"I…I was expecting an email," she said quietly, almost to herself.

"I can go back…" he said, chuckling.

"No!" she exclaimed, and then more quietly, "No, no, this is…perfect."

He wandered into her apartment, observing the various boxes stacked in corners and lying on the floor. She stood in place. Her legs felt like rubber.

Neither of them said anything for a good minute. They smiled at one another, shyly, flirtatiously, waiting for the other one to say something. Finally he spoke, "I see you're packing."

"Yes," she answered softly.

"You're moving?"

"Yes."

"To California?"

"Yes."

"Oh." He looked at her and then down at her belly as their coquettish exchange carried on. "So there's two of them in there?"

"Yes," she said, smiling back.

"Not triplets….or quadruplets…or, there's not like eight of them in there, right?"

"No," she said, trying not to laugh.

By now he was standing directly in front of her, by the couch. He stood so close that she was sure he could hear her heart racing. She wanted desperately to kiss him, but she was nervous to make the first move, and she imagined that he felt that same way because he could not stop smiling. But she stood still, grinning at him, waiting for him. He looked down at her lips and then at her eyes. "I got your voicemail."

"Oh?" she said, embarrassed. Her cheeks became hot. "Did you…listen to it?" At this point she was still embarrassed by her voicemail, but their playful banter broke the tension.

"Yes. *Several* times. I even played it for the cat a couple of times."

Ailie rolled her eyes, suppressing a giggle. "I hardly remember what I said."

"Well, I still have it on my phone. Wanna listen to it?"

"No!" she exclaimed. They both laughed. She blushed and buried her face in her hands, and then looked back up at him. He was about to speak again, but Ailie interrupted. "Just stop talking." She leaned forward and kissed him.

They began to kiss feverishly. She pulled his jacket off, as he kissed her neck and shoulders, then he picked her up and she wrapped her legs around him.

Oh, we're not gonna be able to do that move for much longer, she thought, as he held her.

They settled on the couch with her on his lap. She wanted to remember everything about this moment—that he was actually here, with her, right now. She became intensely aware of the scent of his cologne and the taste of his tongue, and his touch as he moved his hands along her thighs, her hips, and her lower back, pulling her to him.

"I…missed…you," she said, softly, between kisses.

They stopped to take a breath. "I missed you too," he whispered, as he kissed her again.

After several minutes, between shorter kisses he spoke. "We should… do this… but… I need to… get somewhere…and I want to…take you with me…. today."

"Um…Ok." Ailie stopped to catch her breath. She sat up eagerly, combing her hair with her fingers. "What? Where?" She started fixing her shirt.

"It's a secret. You'll just have to trust me." He smiled, fixing his own shirt. "But there's more snow rolling in, and I want to get on the road before it's here."

"But where are we going?" she asked again, swiftly pulling off her sweatpants and an old t-shirt as she dashed to the bedroom.

"You'll see when we get there. You'll like it," he reassured her, watching as she undressed and disappeared behind the doorway. "But we've got a few hours of driving. And bring a small bag because we won't be back till tomorrow."

Ailie immediately picked an outfit that she deemed sensible for 'any' situation—soft black flats, stylish jeans, a white blouse and a cardigan. She also assembled a small bag with overnight items. After years of traveling for work and preparing for various international adventures she was a pro at getting ready in minutes.

She looked at herself in the mirror once she was done changing. The jeans she chose had a small elastic waist that was covered by her blouse, and they were made of flexible cotton that hugged her figure and legs comfortably, giving them the appearance of skinny jeans. Her belly had grown, but she was still small for carrying twins. Frieda assured her that she would probably put on weight more quickly now that her morning sickness appeared to be gone. Ailie rubbed her stomach and smiled at her reflection.

Ten minutes later the two of them were outside, walking to his car.

"Wait. Finn…how did you know my address?"

"Get in," he replied. "I'll tell you on the way. We'll have plenty of time to talk."

***

The drive through the city was slow, as expected. They crossed the river and headed north watching as the metal and concrete of urban surroundings gave way to pastureland and farm fields, divided by forest-covered hills, lofty plateaus and meandering valleys. Based on the signage and their current route, Ailie knew that they were heading to the Catskills. This was one of her favorite areas outside of the city. She had been here on many occasions with old boyfriends and friends, but more often she came here whenever she wanted a quick escape. She cherished the area's quiet hiking trails, winding through dense woodlands, and the scenic vistas featuring majestic landscapes unchanged for more than a millennia—a welcome juxtaposition to the noisy sidewalks and constant changes of urban life.

As they drove he asked her about her decision to move to California and where she'd be living. Ailie told him about her mother's place and segued to the story about how her mother and grandmother acquired Arthur Filbert's house, and all of his books.

As Finn drove, he put a hand in his pocket and pulled out a crumpled piece of paper. "By the way, I think this belongs to you."

"What is it?" Ailie took the paper and smoothed it out. She recognized Ruby's note from several months ago: *My name is Ailie Faulkner. If I pass out please call Ruby De la Vega for assistance.*

"You forgot your sweater the night you came over. It was in one of the pockets." He looked at Ailie to gauge her reaction. She hid her eyes behind one hand and shook her head from embarrassment. "So you realize that once I saw that note I had to call her to find out more."

"You called her to ask about the note?" Ailie raised her voice slightly—a mixture of disbelief and humiliation—the thought of her best friend telling

Finn that the police had to wake her when she fell asleep on a bench in the park.

He laughed. "I'm kidding. But you mentioned several times that she was one of your best friends, so I called her to find out when you'd be home and how I could find you."

Ailie grinned, blushing. "I can't believe you called her. How long did you talk? And what did you ask her? *She* was in on this?" She wondered how long Ruby had been harboring this secret.

"Well, between work and Fiona's schedule, I wasn't sure when I could get out here. Feels like I've been trying to plan this trip for weeks. So I called her after I bought my ticket…and, you know, she reassured me you weren't crazy." Ailie gave him a friendly slap on the arm. "Don't worry. We only talked for a short time. She said you guys were about to go out to lunch, so the rest was texting. She was happy to help."

Ailie beamed. Several times in the past month she'd seen Ruby glancing over her shoulder while texting, often stashing her phone the minute Ailie entered the room. She had assumed it was all to do with her moving-away party, but perhaps the covert messaging was with Finn. Her smile grew also remembering that the last time she and Ruby went to lunch was the day Ailie had 'misplaced' her cellphone. Which meant that while Ailie had spent the whole day turning a blind eye to thoughts of Finnian, he'd spend most of the day, or at least part of it, completely focused on her.

"So how is Fiona?" Ailie asked, after several seconds of contented reflection.

"She's good, she's great! And I'm so sorry I didn't call or…message you more."

"That's okay," Ailie responded. "But yeah, so…you didn't have a lot of time?"

"Not at all. I wanted to talk to you. So I wrote. But then I knew there was more…to talk about. But I knew it wouldn't be just a small conversation, you know. Lots to discuss. Things like that. And then Fiona's school is like an hour away, sometimes more, depending on traffic."

"Oh, that's a lot of commuting," Ailie said, watching his hand gestures. *He looks so cute when he's trying to explain himself.*

"It is. So I didn't want to call you when Fiona was in the car. That...wouldn't have worked. And then I had to use all my extra time in the car to make calls for work, and scheduling, since I never got anywhere on time. Fiona's school used to be closer, but they moved when Lorelei's husband switched jobs."

Perfect—I'm so glad she's married.

"And I've never prepared so many meals in my life. The first day Fiona wakes up and asks me where her lunch is, so I give her some money to buy lunch. But then she comes home and tells me she likes it better when *I* make her lunch. And you can't say no to something like that. Not when your kid's growing up so fast and you feel like you see them less and less. But she didn't want just a sandwich. So every night she's picking out recipes and we were cooking together. It was fun."

I want him. Right now. Where are we driving again?

He finished by telling Ailie about Fiona's weekend acting classes, soccer, figuring out her math lessons; arguments about homework, arguments about bedtime, phone time, computer time, and questions about boys. Exhausted, he collapsed in bed nearly every night, around 9 p.m..

A short period of thoughtful silence ensued. Ailie imagined how many calendars and lists she'd prepare in the future, for work, for home, for herself, for the kids.

Finn spoke, with a far away look in his eyes, "So twins...it's like Fiona...times two..." He said the statement as though it had just dawned on him.

"Yes. Two," echoed Ailie, pensively, staring at the horizon. Another minute of silence.

Ailie turned to Finn. "So...you must be an expert."

"Um...well...with...?" he asked, unsure of her question.

"Twins."

"Ohhh..." He scratched his chin. "I was part of a set. I can try to answer your questions...but I have no idea how to actually *parent* two...at the same time. Two babies. And two girls at that. I guess you just do...more...of...all of it."

"Yeah, I should look that one up." Only now did it occur to her that she was a bit lost on the subject of raising twins, but it never crossed her mind that he wouldn't know much about it either. "I've been so busy with this move, but I should look up 'parenting twins' or something."

"Probably a good idea," he confirmed. "Maybe people just...buy two of everything?"

She shifted in her seat. "So is this a good time for me to ask you again where we're going?"

"Sure!" he replied, laughing—seemingly relieved—paying extra attention to the road as the snow began to fall.

"Well then, are we going on a treasure hunt for one of your clients? Or are we building a barn? What does a guy like you do on the weekends? What's the plan?" she asked, enthusiastically.

"I thought we could do something a little more romantic than a barn raising. My parents have this inn. And they have this pre-Thanksgiving dinner every year, with all their neighbors and friends. My family's owned this land for generations, so they know just about everybody in town."

Ailie sat up. "What? You're introducing me to your parents? Now?"

Finn laughed. "No… In like twenty minutes."

She pinched him on his shoulder. "I can't believe you didn't say anything. I'm not prepared for this, at all." Grinning, she checked her hair and face in the passenger side mirror.

"You're gorgeous," he said, glancing at her again. "You're a talker, and you're the one who told me that you're always meeting new people. You'll be fine."

"And the whole neighborhood's going to be there?" Ailie asked, looking down at her shirt and pants and shoes, taking account of the outfit she'd put on before they left her house.

"I have no idea how many will be there. But it's usually a big event, with lots of people we know from the neighborhood or from town. My parents started the tradition when Fiona was just a baby. I'd come home and show her off to all the people I grew up with. Then, at some point, everyone started to retire. A lot of their friends went away for the winter, or they moved down to Florida or out to Arizona. So it was an excuse to get together before everyone goes away for the season, or an excuse for some of them to fly home and see everyone. This year I didn't bring Fiona because she's back with her mom."

He saw that Ailie was still fretting over her hair in the mirror. "Seriously, you look beautiful." He placed a reassuring hand on her knee. "And don't worry about any of these people, they're very down to earth. They'll love you."

25

What kind of books are you reading at book club?

They pulled into a long driveway that led to an enormous Victorian country home, with a porch that wrapped around three sides of the building. Part of the porch at the front of the house was enclosed, illuminated by Christmas lights. Behind the house there appeared to be a forest, and in front, where there was usually an expansive green lawn, there was now a thick carpet of snow. A few stately trees were spaced evenly around the yard, one stood before the steps that led to the front door. All of the windows, as far as Ailie could see, were brightly lit from within. In spite of its grand size, the house looked very cozy on this winter day.

"Wow," whistled Ailie. "How many kids did your parents have again?"

Finn laughed. "Just three. But, like I said, the house has been in the family for generations. My great grandparents lived in the city, but at some point someone fell in love with this area and bought the land. Between my great grandparents and my grandparents there were a lot of kids that grew up in this house. My granddad still lives with us, and my grandmother passed away a couple of years ago. Now that we've all moved out, and my dad retired, my parents operate a B&B throughout the year. They live full time in a smaller part of the house. But they're always closed for this weekend every year so that all the rooms are available for whoever wants to stay overnight. Even so, you'll probably see people sleeping on the couch or on a mattress on the floor when you wake up tomorrow morning."

They drove past a smaller carriage house with three garage doors and pulled up to the main house. He parked in the circular driveway by the entrance.

With the engine turned off, and snow coming down heavily all around them, they sat, quietly, in the warm car. Finally, Ailie turned to him, with a nervous look on her face. "Okay so…"

But before she had time to finish her sentence Finn leaned over the center console and kissed her, slowly, softly. When he pulled away, he noticed her eyes were still anxiously alert. "Are you still nervous?" he asked.

"No. Okay yeah. But— " Ailie started to climb out of the car. "Do your parents even know about me?" She wrapped her coat tightly around herself. It felt colder here than in the city, she thought.

"Well, I haven't talked to them in a few weeks," he said as they walked to the front door. "Or maybe a few months? I can't remember. But my mom sent an email and I let them know I'd be here." He tried to open the door, but it was locked so he rang the doorbell.

He responded to an email? Ailie wondered how few words Finn would write to his mother in an email, 'Sure, I'll be there.' Or perhaps he was able to respond in one word, 'Yep.' *They know nothing about me, or the babies,* she thought, her anxieties building. *But why should they? Finn and I have barely talked. Why would he call his parents and tell them anything about me when the two of us still have to figure it all out?*

Within minutes a woman opened the door. Ailie recognized her long hair from that day at the train station. "Did those kids lock the door again?" the woman said, looking back inside to see if she could find the culprits. Then she turned to Finnian again, beaming. "Hi!" she said in a big voice.

"Hi Mom," replied Finnian, as they embraced.

"Oh my god, it's so good to see you!" She hugged him tightly again, then immediately noticed Ailie standing next to him. "What?" she blurted. "Honey! Why didn't you tell me you were bringing someone?"

I knew it! He's going to have to do all the talking, because I have no idea what I should say. I'll be shy.

"Tell you what?" shouted an elderly voice from inside the house. "What's he done now?"

"He's brought a woman!" announced Finn's mother.

"A what?" yelled the elderly voice from inside.

"A woman!" shouted Finn's mother.

"Hey!" A different man, with a younger voice, appeared at the doorway and stood beside Finn's mother. "Wow, you brought someone!"

"Come in! Come in." The woman motioned for Ailie and Finn to come inside the house. "It's cold out there."

The enticing scents of roasting turkey, vegetables, and pumpkin greeted them upon entry.

Finn introduced everyone. "Ailie, this is my mom, Susan, and my older brother, Michael." Everyone greeted each other with wide smiles and 'nice to meet you.' To Ailie's surprise, Susan embraced her tightly.

An elderly man with a walker joined them in the entry room. Ailie noticed he wore hearing aids. Finn shouted, "Grandpa! This is Ailie!" Then he turned to Ailie and said, "This is Grandpa Ned."

Grandpa Ned peered at Ailie through his thick glasses. "It's a woman!" he declared. He turned to Susan, "It's a woman!" Then he looked at Finn, "Don't sit in my chair."

"Yes, dad!" replied Susan.

Grandpa Ned took one more look at Ailie and then turned around, gradually, disappearing into another room.

Susan spoke, "You've got time to freshen up before everyone gets here. They'll all start arriving in about an hour. And let's try to sit down for just a few minutes and talk too."

Ailie was reminded of a ski lodge as she looked around. The entrance to the house was a fair-sized room adorned with wide, dark leather sitting chairs and a small sofa. Placed among the furniture were lodgepole side tables, and a few floor lamps, decorated with small alpine stencils of conifers and bear paws and snow flakes. An L-shaped, wooden desk with live edges sat in the corner of the room, for guests checking into the bed and breakfast. Above them hung a circular chandelier composed of many electric lanterns; it was suspended from one of the three thick beams of wood that spanned the room just below the loft ceiling.

Finnian took off his coat and waited as Ailie looked around the room, slowly unbuttoning her own. Susan was in the middle of giving some instructions to Michael, whose immediate task was to check on the caterers, when she caught sight of Ailie's belly and she stopped in mid sentence. Her eyes flew open. "Oh," she said, quietly. Without taking her eyes off Ailie she continued, "You know what, Michael, forget the caterers. Instead, I want you to call your father. He might still be at the store. Tell him we're going to need more wine."

"What? We've already got plenty of wine, mom." Michael continued down the hall, toward the kitchen.

"Michael!" she shouted.

He turned around and strolled back to the entrance. "What?" He said calmly, and then looked in the same direction as his mother. Ailie stood close to Finn, clenching his hand, embarrassed by all the attention. "Ohh. I see," said Michael, regarding Ailie's pregnant form. "Oh, okay."

All at once Michael and Susan broke into broad grins. They spoke in unison as they approached Finn and Ailie.

"We've got something to celebrate!"

"This is great!"

"Congratulations!"

Ailie wasn't sure if her face was pale or crimson with nerves and embarrassment, surprising these people that she'd never met, with babies they weren't expecting, whose embryos had probably been in storage longer than most of the wine bottles in their collection. Everyone exchanged hugs again. Susan whispered in Finn's ear, "I can't believe you didn't say anything!"

"I'm sorry, mom," he replied. "This was all last-minute planning."

"Yes, but there's nothing last minute about that." Susan indicated with a discrete tilt of her head in the direction of Ailie, who was now conversing with Michael.

"I know…but I can explain later," Finn insisted. "Right now it looks like you've got your hands full with the dinner and everything. We'll be here for breakfast tomorrow, and we can talk then. Everything's great. I'm so happy to finally be here."

"Okay," replied Susan, gently but stubbornly. Finn recognized her tone. It meant that the conversation was not over and that there would be many questions later.

Susan turned her attention so she could speak to both Ailie and Finn. "Why don't you guys take the large bedroom at the end of the hall tonight, okay? The one you and Garret used to like for your sleepovers. But listen, right now I think they're still cleaning that room, so take the one in the corner, to the left, at the end. You can freshen up in that room and then come down to the kitchen."

As soon as she was done speaking Susan darted off to the kitchen with Michael following closely behind. Ailie breathed a quiet sigh of relief, watching them walk down the hall.

Finn gave her an express tour of the first floor. Walking through the doorway to the left of the entry, they came to an entertainment room. A long, wooden bar, stocked with liquors, sat on one side of the room, and several circular tables surrounded it in another L-shape, with a couple of flat screens mounted to the walls. Next came the library, which had a door linked to a sunroom. The room was small, containing just a couple of reading chairs, but it was well-stocked with used books. A sign above each exit read *If You Take One, Leave One.*

From the library they stepped behind a door marked *Staff Only*, which led to a tiled pantry area, with neatly stocked shelves on both sides. Through the pantry they arrived to a large, open kitchen. Ailie saw caterers and cooks fussing over the gas ranges and a large island that stood in the center of the room. Susan sat at a small breakfast nook in one corner, by the windows, she looked up from her laptop and smiled and waved as Finn and Ailie quickly walked across the kitchen and ducked through a swinging doorway.

They entered the dining area, where the main event would take place. An immense, stone fireplace seemed to heat the entire room. Perpendicular to the fireplace, three long tables divided the room. Two were covered with white tablecloths, festive Thanksgiving plates, and wine and water glasses, with small tabletop displays of candles and tiny pumpkins. The center table was set for food and drink, prepared with small burners and ice buckets. A couple of caterers tended to final preparations, polishing silverware and cleaning chairs, before the visitors arrived. Michael's two young sons, Dallas and Miles, ran in and out the doorways, playing with plastic swords. Outside the snow briefly came down faster but then slowed, large flakes floated past the windows.

Exiting the dining room they headed up the broad wooden staircase to the second floor. They entered a wide hallway with a floor made of dark wood, covered by a slim carpet that dampened the noise of their footsteps. There were several closed doors on both sides of the hallway.

Finn took Ailie's hand and led her to a room at the left end of the hall, with the number three on the door. "I think it's this one that she meant."

By now, having toured the charming inn, Ailie was bubbly with anticipation. She thought about how her morning started off at home, as usual, but now she was enjoying a weekend away on an impromptu adventure. And with *him*. She was looking forward to meeting everyone at the dinner and spending the night with Finn. She could tell the excitement was mutual as Finn laughed and joked as he tried the door for the bedroom, but found it stuck, having expanded from the heat in the hallway.

Except for the sound of the vacuum cleaner in the next room, it was quiet upstairs. Ailie giggled and tickled Finn's ribs as he finally managed to pry the door open. The door was barely ajar, when he hastily nudged their bags inside with one foot, and he laughed and turned around to kiss her. What started off as a gentle meeting of the lips quickly intensified as the two of them pushed the door open, wrapped in each other's arms. Finn reached behind with one arm and managed to shut the door with a quick push. In a matter of seconds they were in front of the bed.

He kissed her lips and neck, while she unbuttoned and unzipped his pants, tucking her hand into the back of his jeans. "God, I want you," she whispered, sliding her hand to the front.

He quickly pulled off his shirt and started to unbutton hers, fumbling with one of the buttons. She gently, but hurriedly, pushed his hand away, adding hastily, "I can't remember, but this might be one of my favorite travel shirts. If so, it's Burberry. It's not like the shirt was ridiculously expensive, but…" She yanked at the buttons, but her progress was slow, the buttons too small.

"One of my buddies is a textile expert," he replied, just as quickly. "This stitching's too loose." He indicated the shoulder and promptly looked at the inside of the collar. "It's not Burberry."

"Okay, then just rip it," Ailie demanded, frustratingly pulling at her shirt.

"Really?" he asked, surprised. "But it's not a bad shirt…"

"Rip it!" she insisted. "Get it off!"

He tore her shirt open, and then cupped her face with his hands as they resumed kissing, her fingers gliding back down, below his stomach.

The two of them fell onto the bed, into a thick, down duvet, a soft, warm nest—lips and hands exploring as their breaths came quick and sharp. He kissed the soft, supple skin exposed at the top of her breast, while he held the lower half that was still covered by the bra. She gasped with pleasure as he pulled aside the bra, revealing her nipple. Then he moved his hand to her inner thigh.

Susan walked in carrying a stack of towels. "I wasn't sure if you'd need these…"

A moment of chaos ensued. Susan screamed wildly; she immediately covered her eyes and face with her hands and arms and attempted to walk backwards toward the door. Ailie shrieked from embarrassment, rolling from one side and then to the other, nearly tumbling off the bed. She pulled at her bra and shirt, but her clothes felt too small and her fingers weren't moving fast enough. At the same time Finn tried to jump off of Ailie, but Ailie's quick movements caused him to stumble and land on his stomach. He sighed, audibly, a mixture of disappointment and disgust—and perhaps a little pain, Ailie guessed, wincing as she looked at him.

They, all three, began yelling at the same time.
"Why didn't you lock the door?!"
"Why didn't you knock, mom?!"
"Shit! I'm sorry Mrs…"
"You're supposed to lock the door when you do things like that!"
"Who runs a hotel where they don't knock?!"
"Susan, I'm so sorry! Please, excuse me."

Susan made it to the doorway, with one hand over her eyes, and exited promptly, slamming the door behind her. Then she shouted from behind the door. "I did knock! Maybe a little too lightly since you didn't hear me…for obvious reasons! Your room is almost done. Don't do anything else in there because it's your Uncle Ben and Auntie Irma's favorite room. I don't want to have to change the sheets."

"You're killing me, mom," Finn replied, in a quieter tone.

Ailie sat up. "Oh my god, I'm so...mortified." She fretted with her shirt. Mildly shocked, she giggled one second and spoke rapidly the next, her cheeks scarlet. "I just...wow... I'm not sure I can... She's going to think that I'm..." She smiled at Finn, who was smiling back at her, trying to contain his laughter. She laughed and then placed her hands on her cheeks in disbelief. "I'm so embarrassed. This has never happened to me. I don't think I can be more embarrassed. I *just met* your mother. Like an hour ago? I was trying to be *shy!*" Finn began to laugh as Ailie rambled, "What is she going to think? How's this going to make me *look*? I mean...my hand was...was holding your... and your tongue was on my...and your hand was *right there*, on my..." She gasped and plunged her head in the nearest pillow. Then she turned again to look at Finn who was still laughing. Ailie grinned, her face still flush. "Now...when she sees me again, she's going to have this image...of her son...trying to...to mount me." She squeezed her eyes shut, cringing, but also suppressing laughter—the embarrassment was too much. Ailie buried her head in the pillow once more.

Finn laughed as he brushed Ailie's hair aside, so he could see her face. "That was...that was pretty bad. But I wouldn't worry. Please don't worry. She's raised three very curious boys and she runs an inn. It's possible she's seen worse...maybe. I have no idea. And...I'm pretty sure I wouldn't use the word 'mounting' to describe what we were doing." Ailie picked up a small pillow and threw it at Finn. He ducked the pillow. "Okay, okay. You're obviously worried about how you looked—and you looked very sexy when I was trying to mount you."

"You're not helping!" she replied, hiding her smile in the pillow.

He spoke more softly now. "Don't worry, she gets over everything real fast. As soon as one issue is resolved she's got something new she goes on about." He caressed her wrist. "I'll go down and talk to her. I promise. And she won't have any...images to think about, she'll be so busy with the dinner." Finn traced the outline of her lips with his index finger.

"Don't start again because then you'll *really* get us into trouble," Ailie replied, giggling, standing up slowly. "Okay...I think I'll just...take a quick shower, to cool off, and then hopefully people will start to arrive…and then I'll feel like the pressure's off. I can…blend with the crowd…" She gave Finn a kiss and walked toward the bathroom, but not before kneeling at her bag to pull out another white blouse. "Hey! I did bring my Burberry!" Delighted, she waved it at Finn as she entered the bathroom. "Yay, I can wear this for dinner."

"I'll be okay!" Finn shouted, propping himself up on one elbow. "I'll be fine…I'll just…cool off out here…by myself…"

Ailie popped her head about the corner again, grinning. "I'm serious. If you do anything to mess up those sheets while I'm in here…"

"Don't worry…I'm…going to relax for a minute…" he conceded. "And then I'll go talk to my mom." He heard her turn the shower on and he laid his head back down on the bed.

***

Ailie felt better after a quick shower. She didn't wash her hair, but the water felt good on her skin and cleared her senses. With her confidence renewed, she dressed and headed to the stairs to find Finn.

As Ailie descended the steps, she heard voices coming from the kitchen. Turning the corner from the stairway, she proceeded down the hallway toward the kitchen, recognizing the voices of Finn and Susan. But as she approached the doorway, she heard mother and son raising their voices at one another, so she quickly retreated as it sounded like a serious discussion was taking place.

Ailie tiptoed back to the bottom of the stairs, and entertained the idea of searching for a magazine to read; this was an inn after all, where guests might look for something to read.

But then she overheard Susan stating her name. This, of course, piqued her curiosity, so she attempted to listen, but couldn't hear very well from the bottom of the stairs. Climbing the steps cautiously, she stopped near the center step where she could distinctly hear what they were saying.

"I just don't want you to repeat the same mistake again, like you did with Lorelei," said Susan. "Don't get me wrong, Finn, we love Fiona. She's a precious gift from that time in your life. But you weren't compatible with Lorelei, there wasn't a real connection, and you found that out as soon as Fiona was born. And how long did it take for you to get partial custody after you left? I'll tell you how long – it felt like forever. I was so worried I'd never see my granddaughter again. I don't want to see you make the same mistake. But I feel like I'm seeing the same thing happening all over again."

"Mom, I can tell you're upset," said Finn, in a frustrated tone. "But let me reassure you, this is nothing like what happened with Lorelei."

"It's exactly the same as what happened with Lorelei," protested Susan. "You show up here with this girl, Ailie. She's pregnant. You're not married. You haven't once mentioned her to us. Did he say anything about it to you, Gerald?"

"No, I haven't heard about this either," replied an older gentleman. Ailie guessed that Gerald was Finn's father. "When did you meet her?" Gerald asked. "And where?"

"I didn't mention her because we just met, dad. It's all been happening very fast." Finn paused. "We met like a month…I don't know, two months ago."

Susan spoke, "Wait a second. How far along is she?"

"She's due in May. May 7th I think…last time we talked about it."

Susan spoke again, "So… wait… is she pregnant with someone else's child?"

"Kind of…" replied Finn, his voice trailing off.

"Oh my god, I had a feeling. I had a feeling. I knew it!" Susan despaired. "Two seconds ago you're telling me this woman might be different. Why did I think you found someone…"

"Susan. Susan," interrupted Gerald, gently. "You haven't listened to the whole story yet. Let the boy talk. Give him a chance to speak. Go on, son. Go on."

Finn replied, "Um….Well…where to begin…Ah…Levi, I mean, Garret, is the father of her child. I mean the father of her children."

"What?" Susan shouted. Ailie heard the sound of a chair pushed across the floor. She heard footsteps, pacing.

"Don't upset your mother like that, son." Gerald spoke quickly, but patiently. "This is not a time for jokes."

"Mom, please, sit back down," said Finn.

"I can't sit down! My son thinks this is all a joke. Now you're telling me that my baby, Garret, is coming back from the dead and impregnating women! How can I sit down at a time like this?"

Ailie heard the side door of the kitchen swing open. "What's going on in here?" Michael asked, in a leisurely tone.

"This is not a good time, Michael," replied Susan.

"I just came to get some toast…"

Finn spoke again, "Mom, I think you're being overly dramatic here. Please. I can't talk to you when you get angry like that. And I hate it when you pace."

"Please, sit down, Susan," said Gerald. "It really can be irritating when you walk back and forth like that."

"It helps me think."

"Okay, go on, son," said Gerald. "Now you'd better speak slowly and clearly."

Finn cleared his throat. "I know you probably won't believe this, but bear with me. Garret set aside some sperm before he died."

"Set aside sperm? My baby? What?"

"It was a donation. He made a donation at a sperm bank. Just before he died. Ailie… bought that sperm and…well, you've heard of in vitro fertilization? Well, she… used his sperm."

Gerald, Susan, and Michael spoke in unison.
"From ten years ago?"
"They can do that?"
"Wow, my son gave the gift of life."

"And now Ailie is pregnant," continued Finn. "She is having twins. Two girls."

"Oh my god, the poor woman. Twins is hard enough with two parents, but she was going to do this alone?" Susan spoke with sentiment and concern. "You remember, Gerald, what it was like in those first few months when the twins were born."

"We just wanted to sleep," agreed Gerald. "Good God, it was awful. Truly awful."

Everyone was quiet for a minute.

Susan spoke again, her voice strained. "So… now you're in love with this woman? You're going to marry her?"

Finn didn't reply right away. "Marry? Mom…I just told you we just met. We've barely…"

"What do you mean you've just barely?" Susan interrupted, her voice rising again.

"Well, we're still getting to know each other," Finn's voice also rising.

"You certainly seemed to know each other pretty well when I walked in on you, upstairs, shtuping."

"Oh, that's terrible," said Michael. "Why didn't you lock the door, Finch?"

"First of all, no one's shtuped anyone," responded Finn.

"Not yet," Michael quipped.

"And since when do you use the word 'shtuping,' mom?" asked Finn.

"What? It's a word. They use it all the time at book club."

"What kind of books are you reading at book club?" asked Michael.

Gerald answered, "Lots of recent divorcees in the club. Don't ask."

"I don't know," pondered Susan, aloud. "I'm still having a hard time believing that Garret would've done something like that. But if he did, I can't believe you'd do something like this to Garret."

"Do *what?*" Finn voiced impatience.

"This is your brother we're talking about," replied Susan. "The mother of his *children* shows up at your door, and you decide you're just going to have fun? Think about the rest of us for a change. If these really are Garret's babies, then I don't want to risk losing that connection. I don't want her to just disappear as soon as you guys break up."

Ailie heard nothing for several seconds. Finally, Susan spoke again, slowly, in a softer tone. "I don't feel good about you continuing this relationship if you're not serious about her. Think about it, Garret passed away, but he left behind something wonderful—a part of him is going to live on with those babies. I mean, all of this is so unexpected…but if it's true, I can't think of a more beautiful gift…and after so many years. And I know, you keep saying you just met her…"

"Which is why I don't have all the answers for you right now, mom," Finn interjected in a firm tone.

"Hang on. Listen. Please...sit back down. Finn...When you love someone, you just *know*. Your father and I knew each other only a couple of weeks before he proposed to me. We knew. We knew right away we'd spend the rest of our lives together. It wasn't this thing where you feel each other out for a few weeks or months and then go your separate ways... If you really care for her—and I certainly hope you do—then you need to figure out where this is going."

The front door to the inn opened, and a few people walked in, chatting jovially as they removed their coats. None of them noticed Ailie on the steps yet. She strained to listen to the conversation further, but she could no longer hear what they were saying in the kitchen; the noise and discussion in the entryway dominated.

Ailie heard quick footsteps coming down the hall. She took hold of the banister and stood up, carefully descending the steps. She was still on the staircase when Susan rushed passed her, greeting guests with open arms. "Hello! Bud, Jan, David, Mary! It's so good to see you! We're so glad you could make it!" Susan embraced everyone with quick kisses on the cheek.

Within minutes more guests arrived, all at once it seemed. Several conversations took place at the same time, building an ongoing cacophony of chatter.

Ailie observed the scene in front of her as people entered through the door, greeting each other, in festive spirits. Suddenly she felt someone take her hand. It was Finn. He stood quietly beside her, looking in the same direction.

A few of the guests walked over and Finn introduced Ailie. Soon she lost track of names and faces as he introduced her to neighbors, friends from high school, the parents of friends from high school, and a few relatives who lived close by. The various rooms of the downstairs became packed with people talking, drinking, and mingling, and children running around, giddy with excitement.

Everyone was gathered in the dining room about an hour later, catching up with friends and filling their plates at the buffet. Fresh logs burned in the fireplace and a rotation of holiday tunes and various types of jazz played in the background. A couple of little children danced near the center of the room and others ran around the tables, their parents telling them to sit back down. Caterers moved between guests, refilling glasses and removing empty plates.

Ailie sat next to Finn, politely conversing with those around them. She was unsure how she should introduce herself or explain her relationship with Finnian, so she generalized as much as she could. She noticed that Finn also gave very broad answers to questions that pertained to their relationship, and he skirted some topics altogether.

As discussions went on, Ailie felt very confused and mildly emotional. At the beginning of the night, she was elated to partake in the family's longstanding tradition of a pre-Thanksgiving dinner and flattered that Finn introduced her to his family. But, after overhearing that conversation in the kitchen, she wasn't sure what to make of her relationship with Finn. She barely had time to process these thoughts though; she was busy keeping up appearances, chit-chatting with so many new people. Ailie managed to duck outside for some fresh air a few times; she needed the chance to collect herself. Every time she returned to the room and sat back down, Finn reached for her hand and held it under the table.

Two hours passed and Ailie had her fill of listening to discussions about hip and knee operations, life in Florida, life in Arizona, who had died, who was still alive, new babies, old cars, and a debate about the signage used for last year's 4th of July parade—a woman named Donna had painted the signs in brighter colors so that out-of-towners wouldn't miss them, and an older woman called Auntie Sarah insisted they should stick with pastels and muted colors that blend more with the town's surroundings. Ailie was ready for a substantial break, so she politely excused herself from the table and left. Finnian followed. "You okay?" he asked, concerned.

"Well, it's a lot for one night. I'm tired. I just need to lie down."

He smiled, anxiously. "Okay, I'm sorry. Um…I didn't really plan this through very well. It was all last minute. I know I keep saying that, but…" He tried to think of what to say next.

"You know what?" Ailie replied, gently. "This night has been… incredible… overwhelming, insightful…so many things. It was so…out of the ordinary. I can't imagine wanting to be anywhere else right now. This is beautiful. All of it. I'm touched. But I think I'm done for tonight. My brain is…overrun."

"I'll go with you," he responded. "That is, if you don't mind the company?"

"Sure," she said, smiling.

They walked up the stairs to the grand hallway, when he stopped her. "Are you really very tired?" he asked.

"I'm okay. Why?"

Finn took her by the hand and gently pulled her in the opposite direction of their room, to what looked like a locked door. He tried the door and it opened. "This is my parents' room. I just wanted to show you some pictures." Two bedside lamps dimly lit the interior, so he turned on a floor lamp near the far wall. Once the light was on, Ailie saw family photos covered nearly the entire wall. Frames of all sizes, shapes and colors created a mosaic of photographs. Old mixed in with new, black and whites mingled with colored images, and the dull yellows and greens of the seventies contrasted with the exceptionally bright, stunning photos from today.

"Here's a picture of Fiona," he said, pointing to a little girl, sitting in a stroller, holding a balloon. "I think she was four." Ailie sat down on the bed as he pointed to another one. "And that's me and Levi, or Garret." Ailie scanned the wall and took note of all the photos that had the twins in them—riding bikes, at Christmas, by the lake, playing soccer, first days of school, sometimes with their older brother, other times with the whole family.

Finn reached for a photo that hung closer to the nightstand and pulled it off the hook. He brought it over to Ailie and sat down next to her.

The image was of Levi and Finn, donning wide grins, one arm each around the other's shoulders, standing in front of an airplane. "This was the last photo Levi and I took together. It was the last time I saw him."

With the cuff of her sleeve Ailie wiped aside a thin layer of dust, and stared at the faces of the two men. They looked to be in their twenties. Their broad smiles showed confidence, the kind of confidence that feels almost fearless when you're a young adult, just starting to make your way in life.

Finn lay back on the bed and looked up at the ceiling for a few minutes before he spoke. "When we went to college my mom made sure we went to different schools. I always took after Levi, and he always looked out for me. So she figured it would be a good way for me to find myself, so to speak, or become more independent. At least that's what she said, and then later on I found out that Levi wanted the same thing. He wanted his own life, his own friends. He was ready for it. I guess we were both ready for it." Ailie set the photo down on the table and lay down beside him, propping her head up with one arm and laying the other one on his chest.

"Something I didn't tell you that night that you came over to my house, Ailie, was that Levi wasn't really himself in the last week or two of his life. He was a partier, but in his last weeks he became…I don't know, erratic…and sometimes he didn't come to work. But that wasn't really new. He'd done it before. He got bored easily. But that last week or two, he seemed…different. He wasn't himself. Maybe it went on for more than two weeks. It's tough to remember now." Finn cleared his throat. "We didn't talk. He didn't answer his phone… that last week. The coroner said he had a bunch of drugs in his system when he died, and there were some more in his pockets."

Ailie put her arm around Finn's chest, and they embraced as they lay on the bed. She wondered what Levi must've been experiencing in his last days.

The muffled sounds of music and lively banter continued in other parts of the house, but in the quiet sanctity of the bedroom Ailie rested her head in the crook of Finn's arm. She looked at the wall again and silently considered the photos. Her eyes moved slowly from photograph to photograph, from face to face, imagining the emotions evoked by each expression—delight, determination, indifference, intensity, sadness, fortitude, fascination, hope. Every image was such a brief moment caught on film. But for that split second in time, the ones that loved you the most were there with you, to pay witness to your life. Some of these people were gone now, leaving only images whispering like ghosts, to prove that they once existed, that they once celebrated with you. As she thought about the number of years represented on the wall, Ailie reflected on how few photos she took with her mother and grandmother in all the years that she lived in New York.

Finn noticed that Ailie was quiet, so he propped himself up on one arm and looked down at her. He brushed a tear from her cheek and then kissed it. But she gently put her hand up in protest. "You know what I…I should tell you something," she said quietly.

"What happened?" he asked, concerned. "What's wrong?"

She closed her eyes, rubbing her forehead with her fingers, unsure of how she should proceed. "I overheard you. I heard you guys talking in the kitchen. About me. About us."

"Oh…okay." He lay down on his back again, beside her. "I'm sorry you heard that. My mom just...she's a bit dramatic sometimes. I apologize."

"I'm sorry." Ailie covered her face with her hands. "This probably isn't a good time to talk about this. You've just finished telling me about Levi, and I… I'm feeling a little emotional. We can talk about it later."

"No, tell me," he pleaded, softly.

"Well I just… I mean, I know you've brought me here to this beautiful place and… introduced me to so many people that…that mean something to you… But, after hearing that conversation, I just…you know I left you that voice message—that we've barely talked about—and I…I said a lot of things in that message. I feel so much for you. And I think about us, and I think about the future, and…so I wondered…what do *I* mean to *you?* Or…what do you think of me?" Ailie's eyes began to water.

"I…I'm in love with you." He propped himself on one elbow again so he could see her eyes. "I'm completely and totally and madly in love with you. I want to be with you. I want *this*. Whatever crazy adventure this is. I want *us.*"

Ailie wiped her eyes. "What?" She sat up, her voice straining. "How? *When*…did you…?"

"Since the day that I saw you at the museum," he responded.

"What?" she asked again, in a quieter voice.

"You walked past me…You were walking to the museum and I saw you. You were radiant. You looked so happy, so carefree. And a little frazzled, too—very adorably frazzled. I was captivated. And when I saw you go into the museum I went in too. You paid and went in and then I paid and went in."

He stopped talking, but Ailie just stared at him, expectantly. He brushed the hair from her cheek. "I loved the way you smiled as you walked through the museum, from room to room. Your hair the way it fell around your shoulders. The way you secretly nibbled on food when you're not supposed to eat anything in those rooms. The way you gazed at those fertility statues…for hours it seemed. I thought for a second you were going to to pet one of them. It's probably why you're having twins."

"You were following me the whole time?" Ailie tried to recall if she'd done anything truly embarrassing while at the museum that day.

"Well, not in a creepy way…"

"No, no, I'm actually quite flattered, really."

"I…I was so drawn to you. I wanted to say something, but I was nervous."

"And then I looked at you at the fountain," she replied. "And then you stopped... to look at that painting...with the gilded frame."

"Yeah, I wasn't sure what to do after you saw me. And then I saw that painting, by Alphonse Mucha. My brother loved him...because he painted women."

"But then you left, so quickly," she replied.

"Well...yeah...but I was already a half hour late to meet my mom. So I wanted to say something, but when I looked at you, and then you didn't say anything. I froze. I felt like an ass. And then I had to go. But...but I swear I saw you later...at the train station. You were far away, so I wasn't sure. I was about to walk over, but then you... ran."

Ailie's eyes widened as she digested everything he just told her. "Wow..." she whispered, wiping her eyes again.

"So when you showed up at the store in Santa Monica, I was floored. I was so happy. I couldn't take my eyes off you. And then... suddenly we were surrounded by people, and then I had to leave to make that phone call. I panicked. But then you came over and talked to me. I was thrilled. And at one point I wanted to see if you remembered me, so I asked if we'd ever met, and you didn't answer the question..."

He stopped for a minute to reflect. "So when you left my house that night...after telling me about Levi...I had so much to think about." He laughed, gently. "I mean, really, that story was *not* what I was expecting...But...but no matter how much I thought about everything...no matter what details I remembered... all I knew was that I just wanted to see you again..."

Before Finn could say anything else, Ailie kissed him. They kissed for several minutes but stopped when Finn reminded her that they were in his parents' bedroom.

He took her by the hand, and they tiptoed out of the room. Once they were back in the hallway he led her down to the other end. There he opened another door to a grand room with a king-sized bed. "What? This is a huge room! This is for us?" Ailie asked, her hand searching for the light switch.

"Wait, don't turn on the light," Finn said. "Come over here and look at this." He motioned for her to follow. They both sat down on the bed and lay back, looking at the ceiling again. But this time they were staring at the night sky through an enormous, turreted skylight. The snow had stopped and the sky was clear. Except for the occasional passing cloud the entire Milky Way was breathtakingly painted above them.

"This is so cool! I feel like I can see everything!" Ailie squealed.

"Yeah." Finn grinned. "It was our favorite room when we were kids. It used to be my grandparents' room, and back then it was more like a small studio. My grandma hated the long winters. She'd always complain about the darkness. So one year my grandpa built this for her…so she could see the sun in winter."

"Wow, I love it," she replied, marveling at the number of stars.

As they lay there on the bed he turned to her and kissed her, gently at first, on her neck and then her ear, and her cheek until he found her lips. He was careful not to lean on her stomach as she wrapped her arms around him. Standing up, she hastily removed her blouse and giggled as she struggled with her pants.

"You look beautiful," he whispered, lifting her onto his lap. She unbuttoned his jeans, moving her fingers along his skin as she pushed down his zipper. She moaned with pleasure as he pulled her hips closer, softly kissing her breasts.

As they kissed and undressed a sliver of the full moon appeared in the skylight above them. Ailie noticed the sudden change of light in the bedroom and stopped to look at Finn. "What is it?" he asked.

"Hang on," she whispered.

"Seriously?" he asked, with a smile, voicing the slightest hint of exasperation. "You've got maple syrup in your bag, don't you?" he asked, cheekily.

"No!" She giggled. She was a few feet away from him and ran back. "I *love* that you know me so well," she said, kissing him, softly. "I just want to look at you, in this light."

She stood up and walked to the nearest corner of the room and looked back at him. He lay on the bed, propped up on one elbow. He looked at her, patiently, wondering what she was up to. As she watched him he smiled at her again. In the light of the moon, with its dark shadows and light blues, greys, and pale whites, for one second, maybe more, she was reminded of the black and white photo that was taken so many years ago, the image that she carried with her for ten years. She thought of his playful smile and the eyes that looked at something, or someone, beyond the camera.

"You know, it's actually kind of cold in here," Finn said, standing up to turn on the fireplace.

What if, we'd never met, thought Ailie, watching Finnian.

She quickly jumped back on the bed and the two lovers ducked under the down comforter to find warmth.

Outside, the full moon illuminated the night sky, like a mistress in her bright silver cloak on the lookout for her mate. Thick layers of soft snow clung to tree branches, rooftops, and the occasional light post. A very peaceful evening, cut only by the gentle whir of engines in the distance from a small airplane, silhouetted in the moonlight.

The End

About the author

Born in Sweden, to Hungarian refugees, Rita Szollos moved to the United States as a small child and spent most of her life on the east coast. Today she resides in the San Francisco Bay Area with her Kiwi husband, daughter, and nephew, and their brood of small pets. She's not crazy about long walks on the beach, but she loves to drink coffee, hike, camp, listen to oral histories, explore ghost towns, and read read read – everything from history books to classic novels and mommy blogs.

She is currently working on her second novel.

You can follow Rita online at ~
Facebook: https://www.facebook.com/RitaSzollosAuthor/
Instagram: @ritaszollos
and Twitter: @histrypubgrl

Feedback
Did you enjoy this story? If you'd like to contribute to its success or offer feedback, I'd love to hear from you!

Please share your review on Amazon or Goodreads:
http://www.amazon.com/What-If-romantic-comedy-photograph-ebook/dp/B013FADUF4/
https://www.goodreads.com/book/show/26047569-what-if

Or send me an email: loveinflipflops@gmail.com